B19 27!

CW00377151

The Killing of
Emma Gross

This book is dedicated to everyone who supported me in writing it. In particular, thanks to Mum, Mel Bach and Julian Ridgway, my most patient and painstaking first readers.

Thanks also to Al Guthrie, ex-agent, first publisher and all-round good egg. Not sure I could have done this without you.

The Killing of Emma Gross

Damien Seaman

Five Leaves Publications

www.fiveleaves.co.uk

The Killing of Emma Gross
by Damien Seaman

Published in 2013 by
Five Leaves Publications,
PO Box 8786, Nottingham NG1 9AW
www.fiveleaves.co.uk

First published,
in a slightly different version,
as an ebook by Blasted Heath in 2011

ISBN: 978-1907869815

Five Leaves acknowledges
financial support from
Arts Council England

Cover design: JT Lindroos
Design and typesetting by Four Sheets Design and Print
Printed by Imprint Digital in Exeter

Author's note

Fact and fiction are jealous siblings. They might play nice from time to time, but really they don't like each other much and delight in ruining each other's clothes. Try shaping real events into a story of pace and verve sometime and you'll see what I mean.

Of course, a lot of folks read historical fiction in order to learn something while being entertained. For all I know you might be one of those folks. So I'm not going to lie to you: although this novel is based on the notorious Peter Kürten murders of 1929-1930, I have jumbled up the real events and even cut some of them altogether in the name of artistic licence.

To cover myself – and for those who want to know what really happened – I have included a timeline at the back of this book. To my knowledge, it's the most detailed and accurate account of the case published in English since 1938. And in case you were wondering, at the time of writing yes, that does include Wikipedia.

Düsseldorf
Friday, 1st March 1929
0.22 a.m.

Detective Inspector Michael Ritter pulled the clasp knife from his pocket and opened the blade with fingers made clumsy by the rubber crime scene gloves he wore. Emma Gross was lying naked on the divan, her hair fanned out in a blond net over the blue upholstery and dark wood.

Sweat rolled into Ritter's eyes and gathered there. He blinked away the worst of it and left the rest, the discomfort and the saline sting as good a way of keeping sharp as any.

Emma's eyes were closed, at least there was that. She didn't need to see him stab her.

'I'm sorry,' he whispered, for all the good it would do.

He scanned the lock on the door, the curtains pulled shut against the window. Yes, damn it, the door was locked and the curtains were closed. He had to get on with this before it was too late.

He raised his knife and took aim for the area below the woman's left breast, ignoring the squeak of floorboards underfoot. Then he stabbed her.

Her whole body shook, a gurgling sigh struggling from her lips as her head lolled forward. He kept stabbing, not daring to stop until he'd lost track of the number of blows.

After that he did stop, pulling away and giving himself some time for his agitated breathing to return to normal. There wasn't much blood except what was on the knife – the divan and the floor remained spotless. She'd bled less than he'd expected. There was something sad about that somehow, not that he could explain why.

7

The woman's clothes were in a loose pile on the bed across the room. He didn't need to touch them: they were fine as they were.

He turned back to the body and moved closer, forcing himself to look. She may have been a streetwalker but she had the right to a little respect. Didn't everyone, at the end?

Anyway, he had to get this right. He counted the stab wounds in the woman's torso and got to a half-dozen bunched around the heart, eight or ten more further down in the lungs and stomach. He'd strayed lower than he'd meant to in his urgency – in his panic, if he was being honest, and it would come to something when he couldn't be honest with himself.

The grouping was fine, though. What wasn't fine was the size of the wounds. They weren't broad enough to fit the pattern and he'd have to fix that if he wanted the criminal investigations department to link them to the MO of the Düsseldorf 'Ripper' and call him in to take the case.

He re-inserted the knife into each wound, jiggling the blade from side to side to tear the puckering skin wider.

That done, it was time to wipe the place down. He pulled out a handkerchief and noticed he'd got blood on it, probably from the gloves he hadn't taken off yet. He opened the handkerchief and refolded it to hide the blood away, then he passed it over all the usual surfaces that the white-coated boys would dust for fingerprints.

He folded the clasp knife and put it back in his pocket with the handkerchief. He took a last look around the room and then at sweet Emma's body on the divan where the cleaning staff would find it in the morning.

He opened the door, listening out for movement in the hallway beyond. There was none. Muted sounds of *schtupping* from one or two of the rooms, but that was to be expected in a place like this where Emma and other *beinls* took their 'suitors'. The hallway itself was clear.

He turned off the light and left the room, pulling the door to with a click. He left the key inside, the door

8

unlocked, and took off his gloves as he padded down the back stairs to the fire exit and out into the street in the direction of his house and the wife who was waiting there for him.

Düsseldorf
Saturday,
24th May 1930
2.22 p.m.

1.

High pitched, like a yapping lap dog, a woman started reading aloud. I recognised the story from the late morning edition.

Can there be any doubt that this girl has been taken by the infamous Ripper? Does this mass-murderer have supernatural powers to have eluded the efforts of Düsseldorf and Berlin Kripo *for so long? How, in this age of the production line automobile and the Graf Zeppelin, of telephones and transatlantic telegram, of wireless radio and cinemas in every conurbation, can such a fiend exist? This is not the slums of Whitechapel forty years ago. Nor is it the wilds of Transylvania. One is tempted to say this must be some travelling rogue of Roma blood, or some other maniac at the fringes of civilised society. Indeed, so great are the crimes, and the fear inspired by them, it is almost as though Vlad Tepes himself has risen from his sarcophagus to terrorise our town. This Ripper, this Vampire, must be caught.*

It sounded no less hysterical the second time around, in both senses of the word. My coffee tasted of ash. I let the cup clatter down on the table and I laughed, throat raw with cigar smoke and lack of sleep. Raw like the pulse in my left eye, the grit floating across my vision every time I went back to staring at the Church of St. Rochus across the traffic-filled square.

I glanced at my watch instead. Five minutes to go. If Peter Kürten turned up at the church as promised, that is. If he turned out to be the Ripper – as he claimed – and not just a common rapist with delusions. And barring any intervention from the good Inspector Ritter, officious *arschloch* that he was. All I needed was for him to turn up and ruin this arrest. Granted, it was his case and not mine, but this was my lead. Besides which, a girl's life was at stake. We didn't have time for personal squabbles over this one.

There was no way Ritter could've heard about this meeting though. Well, not unless Sergeant Schütz had raided my desk back at the precinct house after Kürten's wife had gone. Goddamned klepto-careerist *muschi* at the best of times, that Schützie. It would be just like him to go digging around and then try to brown-nose his way into Ritter's affections with my interview notes. I shouldn't have left them in that drawer. It was going to bother me, the threat of Ritter blundering in.

'Excuse me?' The lap dog spoke, this time with the hint of a warning growl. Oh yes, that was right. I'd laughed at her, hadn't I. Or at least at the story she'd been reading.

I turned my head in the direction of her voice. She turned out to be a woman with a creased brow sitting behind me at a dark polished table just like mine, except that her table wasn't as far out on the pavement. She held her newspaper close to her body, black earrings swaying in time to the movement of her head. The earrings were jet, onyx, something like that, heirloom quality. They went with the fur-trimmed hat, the forty or so years she wore in the lines on her face. Next to her sat a white-haired older woman dressed in a fur-lined brown coat. What I was looking like I didn't want to guess, though there'd be some purple flesh under my brown eyes and a dark day's stubble on my chin.

I drowned my smoking cigar stub in the coffee I couldn't finish. My gut bubbled and stomach acid lashed the back of my throat.

'Responsible journalism, eh?' I said. 'Where'd they get that vampire rubbish from?'

The woman who'd spoken to me blushed and set her mouth in a thin line.

'It says he drinks his victims' blood,' she said, stabbing a finger at the page.

I wanted to laugh again. 'Well, then it must be true.' I turned back to the church tower dominating the square and tried to ignore the gigantic Christ on the cross suspended from the stonework. What was it about Catholics that drew them to the suffering? The church sprawled out behind the tower in a succession of domes in the old Roman style, despite the building being just thirty years old. Behind me, the women mumbled to each other, something I didn't catch.

Another check on the time. Two minutes to go and still Kürten hadn't turned up. Leastwise, he wasn't waiting outside the church door and I hadn't seen him go in. He could have changed his mind, or never intended to give himself up at all. A hot needle of pain jabbed at my bowels and I rubbed at the belly scar from where the regimental surgeons had pulled shrapnel out of my intestines back in March of '18. They'd had to take some of my insides out too and sometimes – like now – I felt the loss.

A yawn shook through me and I groaned through clenched teeth, stretching the tension out of tender shoulders and trying to take my mind off the gut burn. The paper rustled behind me:

We can only take solace in the wisdom of Chief Inspector Gennat of Berlin Kripo, who is, after all, one of Europe's foremost experts on the mind of the mass murderer. We remember his words in November when he joined the case and described the London Ripper as a mere beginner compared with his Düsseldorf disciple, and when he added that no such case has been known hitherto in the whole of criminology. This is a sobering message. Yet if we accept it as true then we can take DCI Gennat's other comments as such also, that he and his men are even now searching for what he called "the one mistake every criminal makes in the course of his career, and which in the end is bound to lead to his capture". We hope and pray that this Vampire makes his mistake sooner rather than later, before the blood of innocent little Gertrude Albermann is spilled too.

'Albermann?' I asked the woman, scraping my chair legs on the pavement to get her to look up from her reading.

She hesitated before clearing her throat: 'The name of the missing girl.' She cast her eyes down at the paper, that blush of hers gathering in the hollows of her cheeks.

I covered my head with the sweat-stained homburg I'd been resting on my knee. 'You think this vampire drank her blood too?'

She covered her mouth with a gloved hand. Her white-haired companion hissed something about manners. Ah, bad manners, a true crime against society. Never mind the abduction and possible murder of a five-year-old girl. No, never mind small matters like that.

I smiled and touched my hat brim, got to my feet. I dropped a pile of coins next to my cup and struck out across the square.

Of course I'd known the name of the Albermann child: I'd read the same story two hours earlier. I was about to meet the man who might have abducted her.

***

I scanned the street in front of the church door three times to be sure, but no one was there who matched the description I'd been given. I took a deep breath and pushed my way inside.

Sunlight filled the church, diffused and softened through two rows of tinted windows. Sweet spices hung on the still air. The door banged shut and a man hunching in the nearest chair turned and tutted. I tracked his gaze to the top of my head and removed my hat.

A choir of voices floated above the rumble of organ accompaniment. I scanned the service times listed in the vestibule. There were no services scheduled until after five p.m. Must've been choir practice. I recognised the tune, but not its title or the composer. The music smothered the sounds of street traffic from outside, but only the way that smog smothers an industrial town. The car engines and horse hooves were still there underneath, nagging at my senses.

I walked between varnished pews and marble columns to the pulpit. Halfway up the walls, marble and gilt gave way to black brick that went the rest of the way to the domed ceiling. I circled the nave, passing open chapels and a cluster of curtained confessional booths. No sign of him among the loners or small groups huddled in prayer. Maybe Kürten and his wife knew nothing about the missing child and they'd just been playing me for a fool.

As I was about to come full circle to the tower where I'd come in, I glanced into the last chapel. Through the widely-spaced bars, a man knelt at an iron frame of small votive candles arranged before a solid marble altar. He touched a match to a candle wick, blew out the flame and dropped the smoking match onto a mound of at least a dozen others. His hair shone like oiled gold where the light caught it. He matched the victim's description of Kürten, from the neat parting combed into the hair to the bland symmetry of his facial features and the pencil-line moustache. I entered the chapel and stood behind him.

'Are those for all the people you say you've killed?' I said, pointing at the spent matches.

He turned to me. His eyes were supposed to be blue, but there they reflected the wine-bottle green of the chapel windows. He smiled and gestured at the stock of unlit candles. 'I fear there are not enough here for all of them,' he said.

He got to his feet and brushed dust from the creases in his dark suit. Behind him, a splash of red drew my eye: a fire bucket filled with sand huddled next to the altar.

'You got my wife's message, then,' he said. 'I was beginning to wonder.'

I'd got the message all right. The woman who'd delivered it had been a shivering mess of smudged eye make-up and traces of mucus gumming her upper lip by the time she'd unburdened herself in my office. And she hadn't been a looker to start with.

I stepped forward, ID in hand. 'Peter Kürten, I'm arresting you on suspicion of the rape of Maria Butlies on the evening of Wednesday 14th May.'

'For a rape?' He giggled.

Despite Frau Kürten's statement, I had a hard time believing this was the Ripper. The damn woman had only been repeating what her husband had told her, after all, when he'd confessed to her. She might have felt duty bound to believe him but I didn't.

He raised an eyebrow. 'You're alone?'

I didn't respond.

'No pistol?' he said. 'No handcuffs? You can't think me much of a threat.'

'Do you intend to be?' I said. In truth, I was annoyed that I'd left my equipment satchel at my apartment. Along with my diverse powders, plates and test tubes, the satchel held some vital evidence: Maria Butlies' statement, a letter she'd written to a friend describing her rape, and a pair of blood-caked scissors I'd picked up while searching Kürten's home.

'Mind if I see that?' Kürten held his hand out for my ID. I came closer but kept hold of the document as he read it. 'Thomas Klein?' The words came out as a breathless whisper. His sea-green eyes moistened. He clasped his

15

hands together and glanced past the altar to the glitter-ing mosaic of some bearded saint on the wall behind it.

'Oh this is too good! You are a cousin? Her brother, per-haps? Christine was my first, you know.'

I wanted to ask who Christine was but I knew better than to interrupt.

He grabbed my shoulder. There was a scar on his right cheek. None of the Ripper's surviving victims had men-tioned that, but it was so small I'd noticed it only now, up close. It probably wasn't the first thing a girl recalled about being raped or stabbed. The scar didn't put him out of the running.

'Her blood... it... gurgled, and dripped on the mattress. Spattered my hand.'

He showed me the hand, splaying the fingers for me.

'My God, she must have been only – what? – ten years old at the time. She bit my hand when I throttled her, the little minx.' He smiled at the memory and closed his eyes. He moved his hand from my shoulder and aped the act of throttling, his cheeks darkening. A lock of thick hair came loose from its pomade and dangled over his creased forehead, nostrils flaring above his thin moustache. 'So when she stopped struggling I penetrated her. With my fingers, you understand?'

His eyes snapped open and searched mine. I found myself nodding, and I hated myself for it, for giving him that measure of recognition. His voice had thickened, the words fighting their way from his throat as his breathing came fast and loose.

'When she passed out I took my pocket knife and cut her throat. Like this. And then... the blood.'

His forefinger traced an arc of arterial blood spray as he closed his eyes again. Sweat beaded his top lip. His panting slowed. He straightened and when he grinned there was blood on his teeth, though whether he'd bitten his lip or his tongue, or whether my mind had conjured some fancy under the influence of his tale and too little sleep, I couldn't say.

'No more than three minutes, the whole business.' He took a handkerchief to his fingers as though trying to clean them. He smoothed back his hair and cleared his throat. 'Then I left the room and made off.'

I cleared my throat too, not trusting myself to speak clearly without doing so. 'And what about Gertrude Albermann?' I said.

He replaced his handkerchief in the breast pocket of his pinstriped jacket. 'You'll see.'

It seemed like he wanted to confess. If I took him through the motions he might tell me about the Albermann girl. 'When did all this happen?' I drew a notebook and pen from my pocket.

'Summer. 1913. I was doing a lot of theft at that time. It was a Sunday evening, a feast day, about ten or eleven p.m. when I broke in. It was an inn on the Wolfstrasse, but then you know that. Nothing worth taking. No possessions, that is.'

'And the girl's name?'

'Christine, you fool, like I told you.'

'Christine who?'

He punched my arm. 'Stop playing with me, detective. Christine Klein, as you well know.'

'Is Gertrude still alive?'

'Who?'

'The Albermann child. If you are the Ripper then you're the one who took her, aren't you. Aren't you?'

'Oh I'm the Ripper all right, Thomas, I can assure you of that.'

I stepped in close and made fists of my hands. 'Then tell me where she is.'

Someone sneezed. I spun round. A plump man in a white gown dithered at the threshold, his small eyes rolling a lot of white my way. Had he overheard Kürten's confession? The choir had stopped singing and the organ had stopped bellowing. Whispers echoed in the nave in place of the music. And cutting through them, something like shouting outside the church. The cough and splutter of road traffic had ebbed away.

'Yes?' I had to stop myself shouting at the man.

'Is one of you gentlemen Detective Thomas Klein?' he asked through thick lips that turned down at each end of his mouth.

'That's me,' I said.

'There are some policemen outside in the square,' the man said. 'A lot of them. And they're asking for you.'

'Ritter,' I said. It came out on the crest of a sigh. *Gott in Himmel*, not now. If anyone in this city had supernatural powers, it was him. Kürten inclined his head as though he understood the importance of the name.

'A friend of yours?' he said.

My turn to smile. I had to, otherwise I would have cried out in frustration. I seized Kürten's arm and said, 'Tell me where Gertrude Albermann is, now.'

'So fearsome, Thomas.' He was grinning. 'I'm glad you're the one to bring me in. And I hope you realise the awesome significance of this moment. You, Thomas Klein, finally bringing the Düsseldorf Ripper to heel. They'll write songs about you. Make moving pictures. Write novels. The Sancho Panza to my Don Quixote of death!'

'The Van Helsing to your Count Dracula more like,' I told him. 'Come on.'

I didn't like that this arrest was going to be Ritter's, but the sooner we got Kürten to headquarters the sooner we could get Albermann's whereabouts out of him.

We entered the nave, where over a dozen white-robed choristers had gathered between us and the exit. Several of them were just boys who were talking in the loud voices boys use when they know something dangerous might be about to happen.

'Are you the choir master?' I asked the chubby man who'd come to find me.

His chin merged with the trunk of his neck as he nodded. I pulled Kürten through the crowd to the door, forced him down on his haunches in the vestibule and shouted at the nearest choristers to clear a space away from the door. Some worshippers had got caught up in the crowd too.

I lay on my front and pushed open the door a few centimetres. Blue-coated *Schutzpolizei* ringed the square. They'd cut off the traffic flow at each exit point and within their cordon the square was empty. Each blue coat I saw carried a bullet hose machine pistol, and most had them trained on the church door.

'Is that you, Thomas?' called a voice I recognised. Ritter had turned up after all, murder commission in tow no doubt, though I couldn't see any plainclothesmen from where I lay. 'Come on out!' he shouted.

I let the door swing shut and stood up. Kürten made to copy me but I shooed him down with a palm. This was a dangerous moment. In his eagerness to steal my credit, Ritter might not notice the civilians in the way. I had to get them clear.

'Choir master?' I shouted. The chubby man approached, his face full of panic. 'Do you have a spare gown?'

'Gown?' He frowned.

'Those things you're wearing, whatever they're called. Do you have a spare one?'

'In the back somewhere.'

'Get it.' He didn't move so I shouted: 'Now!'

He waddled off. I faced the rest of them and held up my hands for silence. The whispers died down.

'Okay ladies and gentlemen, I'm a policeman. This man here,' I pointed at Kürten, 'is a wanted felon.' Wide eyes focused on Kürten. He waved at them.

'Is it the Ripper?' a male voice shouted. I didn't see who'd shouted but I ignored it anyway.

'The choir master is going to lead you outside. Everyone put your hands on your heads and walk calmly, all right?'

'It must be the Ripper,' the voice said. 'Why else would they send so many armed men?'

The choir master returned with the spare gown. I took the garment from him and tore it in two, handing him the larger piece and keeping the smaller for myself. I pushed the church door open again and waved the white cloth out of the opening.

'Ritter?' I shouted. 'It's Klein here.'

'Always a pleasure, Thomas,' Ritter shouted back.

'Never mind that, Ritter. There are several innocent people in here. The choir master is going to lead them out into the square, and then I'll bring him out.'

'Yeah, bring who out?' the voice muttered behind me.

I turned back. 'Hands on your heads!' I growled. The younger choristers beamed as they complied. Some of the older ones did it more slowly. A couple of the worshippers didn't do it at all. I patted the choir master on the back and said, 'Now lead them out. Slowly. Wave the gown. Don't make any sudden moves, and do as they say.'

I held the door open and the choir master led the group into the square while Ritter shouted directions. The stragglers in the church vestibule glared at Kürten on the way out. I kept my eyes on them, just waiting for some upstanding citizen to lash out the way that upstanding citizens are wont to do. They disappointed me, though.

Several long minutes later, I was alone with Kürten. I lifted him back to his feet. He passed a hand through his hair and checked the knot in his neck tie.

'You look fine,' I said. I wanted to slap him.

'Do you think there are any press photographers out there?'

'You looking to create a police brutality situation here? 'Cause that's the way we're headed.'

I dragged him along and kicked open the door, waving the scrap of white gown with my free hand. The clouds had parted while I'd been inside and the sun shone in my eyes.

A burst of submachine gun fire drove bullets into the stonework around the church door. I pulled Kürten to the ground with me. Something dug into my face, tore my cheek. Ritter shouted at the *Schupo* to hold fire and stiff leather soles double-timed it across the square.

They hauled me upright and cuffed my hands behind my back.

Ritter squared up to me, buck-toothed grin more pronounced than ever. His blue eyes squinted in the sun and he'd picked up some grey in his black hair since I'd seen him last. It also looked like he was trying to grow a moustache – to cover those teeth? – though the limp fur blooming in patches over his top lip didn't seem to want to play along. His grin worried me and so did what he was carrying in his left hand. My satchel.

'Bucky,' I said – his nickname back when we'd been partners.

'Thomas,' he replied with studied formality.

'Was that wise, shooting at Kürten?' I said.

'What makes you think they were aiming for him?' Ritter said. He smashed his fist into my nose and the cartilage gave out.

2.

They drove us to Mühlenstrasse HQ, took my belt, shoes, wallet and watch and threw me in a holding cell. The door clanged shut, shaking clumps of mould from the brick walls. I kicked a brown-stained bucket into the middle of the room. It swayed from side to side as I slumped on the hard wooden bunk lining one wall, rumpling the thin blanket beneath me.

This beef between Ritter and me, it was personal. Probably I shouldn't have slept with his wife, but she'd been the one who came on to me, after all. My mistake: Ritter had kept me off the murder commission despite my record and made sure I was kept in exile in a suburban police precinct at the *arsch*-end of nowhere. Meanwhile his Ripper investigation had achieved nothing in over a year. So yes, I'd wanted the arrest. I'd wanted the glory. I'd wanted to rub Ritter's nose in his failure and prove to everyone else how full of shit he was. Was that so bad?

Well, perhaps it was. Give it some time and Ritter would send for me and then I would find out what form his revenge was going to take this time. But I couldn't forget that there was a lost five-year-old girl out there, maybe dead. Or maybe worse, still alive but dying for lack of food or water or medical attention. We needed to find her, and soon.

I hoped that while Ritter was leaving me to stew he was sweating Kürten for all the information he could. I wasn't going to get anywhere by worrying though, and I needed sleep, so I took off my jacket and rolled it up. I placed this makeshift pillow at the furthest end of the bunk from the door and I lay on my side.

Warm sunlight blared in through a high, barred window. My mind buzzed with the events of the day. My nose throbbed and my nostrils had filled with dried blood, making it hard to breathe. I tried sniffing hard a couple of times, but that dislodged the crusts that had formed and caused fresh blood to flow. Settling on my back made the blood drip down my throat so I went back to lying on my side and breathing through my mouth.

Later, a banging noise dragged me awake. I raised my head from my rolled-up jacket. It was still light outside, but only just. The sky through the bars was a deep blue. The wound in my cheek throbbed now, worse than my nose, and my head was pounding too. My mouth was dry and a sticky white residue clung to my lips.

A metallic rasp came from the corridor outside my cell.

'Hello?' I called out. Nobody answered.

The hatch in the thick cell door was open so I got up and staggered towards it. I gazed through the hatch. Darkness gazed back. Were those whispering voices I could hear out there? I put my eye as close to the hatch as I dared, trying to make out any movement beyond.

Just then, the light in my cell died and cool liquid splashed my face. I pressed my lips together before any of it got in my mouth: I hoped it was water but I wasn't up for taking any risks. I stumbled and fell, cracking my hip against the side of the bunk. I found the blanket and used it to wipe my face. Laughter leaked through from the corridor. I wanted to go back and bang on that door, all night if need be, shout and scream and call them names. But that was what they wanted.

I settled back against the bunk. I counted silently and my breathing deepened. The pain in my head lost some of its intensity and some time after that sleep found me again.

Banging, outside the cell door. The metallic rasp from my troubled dreams back to pull me awake. This was classic stuff to deprive me of sleep ahead of my upcoming interrogation. I opened my eyes as the cell light came on.

I was ready for it this time; I'd fallen asleep with the blanket twisted around my head. I blinked until I could bear more of the light, then I cast off the blanket.

The door opened. Two *Schupo*men pulled me out of the cell and carried me up several flights of stairs. I lost count of how many floors we went up, but I recognised the second floor offices from when I'd worked at HQ, back when Ritter and I had been partners. The *Schupo* led me down a hallway painted in two-tone institutional grey. They locked me into an interview room which had the unremarkable look of interview rooms everywhere, consisting as it did of two cheap wooden chairs arranged either side of a chipped wooden card table.

I took the chair facing the door. It creaked under me, so I moved and took the one opposite. That creaked too, and the table wobbled when I leaned my elbows on it. Damn it, had they shortened one of the legs on purpose? A breeze pushed its way through the open window and I shivered. This window was four times the size of the one in my cell downstairs, but the bars outside were just as thick.

Ha, listen to me. My cell. They'd got me thinking I belonged there already. The thought made me laugh aloud. The ragged quality of the laughter made me laugh all the more until there were tears of pain dripping off my chin. I caught some of the tears on my tongue but the salty tang only increased my thirst. My stomach muscles ached like I'd just done a hundred sit-ups: tension, pure and simple, tightening me up. Even though I was familiar with this interrogation technique, it was starting to work. I'd have to watch that: Ritter could go the whole hog and try for a charge of withholding evidence. He probably had enough on me for that.

The door opened and I resisted turning round to look. The door shut again. I thought whoever it was had left, as I didn't hear any footsteps. But then a man in plain clothes came into my line of sight and sat in the chair at the opposite side of the table. He'd left his jacket in another room, waistcoat hanging loose over a solid belly, shirtsleeves rolled to the elbow exposing a red and green tattoo on his left forearm. He had unruly blond hair and a red patch along the left side of his jaw that looked to be a shaving rash. I didn't recognise him and he didn't introduce himself.

He took a cigarette from a silver case and lit it. Then he offered the case to me.

'Why am I here?' I said.

No response.

'Look, there's a five-year-old girl out there, missing, or dead. We don't have time to play Ritter's games.'

He just waved the case under my nose, the clown. Clearly, I would have to wait for the ringmaster.

'You don't have a cigar?' I said.

He scratched the side of his flat nose and shook his head. I took one of the little white tubes and he lit it for me. I gulped down as much smoke as it took to make my vision dance with purple and white lights. On the exhale the damn thing tasted of nothing.

'Can I have some water?' I croaked. 'Something to eat?'

He looked me up and down and thought things over for a while before he said, 'I'll see what I can do.' I couldn't place the accent.

He paused with his hand on the doorknob. Finally, he said, 'And I do read the papers, you know.'

Having thus informed me that he knew all about Gertrude Albermann, and that he cared just as much as I did, he left the room. I smoked my cigarette. I tried to take my time over it but it was all I had to occupy me and it was gone before I knew it.

This time when the door opened I did turn around. Ritter stood smirking at me, his arms full of items bearing evidence tags.

'Has Kürten said anything about the Albermann girl?' I said.

Ritter came and sat down. The overhead light lengthened the bags under his eyes as it lightened the blue of his irises. It also made his top lip twinkle. I couldn't stop looking at his moustache. He noticed me looking, pulled out a handkerchief and blew his nose. He took his time wiping it. There was a lot of silver in his five o'clock shadow.

The blond detective had followed him in and now stood in the corner by the window. His arms, I noticed, were empty. I hadn't expected him to bring me anything – it made more sense to make that conditional on the answers they wanted me to give – but that didn't do much to dampen my disappointment. My mouth felt drier than ever and I doubted I'd be able to talk for long. The plaster behind the detective was crumbling and spotted with black marks. More mould. Seemed like someone had blown the building's maintenance budget on the horses.

On the table Ritter laid out two plain brown envelopes, my notebook, and Kürten's bloody scissors. I didn't bother to read the labels on the envelopes. I knew what they would say.

'So how long exactly were you intending to hang on to this evidence before you recorded it and handed it in?' Ritter said.

'How long are you intending to torture me before you charge me or let me go?'

Ritter rubbed at the corner of his right eye and flicked the results in the direction of the window. He leaned back in the chair and put his feet up on the table. It wobbled and he put his arms out to steady himself like some tightrope walker. Guess that meant the short leg wasn't deliberate.

'You know that the possible political nature of your crime outweighs all other considerations,' he said.

So that's how he wanted to play this: the political angle. I looked at his moustache again to try and throw him off. He took his feet off the table, sat up straight and blew his nose on the same handkerchief. Again he took his time with the wiping.

'Look, Ritter, we can't spend all night buggering

about while a child is out there somewhere needing our help.'

He stared me into silence. 'You accuse me of buggering about, Tommy-Boy? You? After all this?' He indicated the items on the table with a sweep of his hand.

'Just tell me. Do we know where she is? Whether she's alive? Did he say anything to confirm that he's the Ripper?'

'You finished?'

'She could be dying out there while you sit here getting your stupid goddamned revenge on me!'

'Finished?' He was smiling, the bastard. If Albermann died because of his time wasting, I'd make him pay.

Meanwhile, I was going to have to play along, so I sat back. 'What are you going to charge me with?'

Ritter watched the detective take notes. 'We'll start with obstruction. But that depends on your ongoing links with the Red Front.'

The old blame-the-leftists game. Never mind being a mass murderer or child abductor, if you really wanted a hard time in this town you had to join the Communist Party. Or, as in my case, just be suspected of having done so. I hated the goddamned Commies, but that hadn't stopped Ritter pretending I was one of them.

'I have no links with the Red Front,' I said. 'Never did.'

'Well what about your friend at the *Volksstimme* propaganda sheet?'

'It's a newspaper.'

'A Commie newspaper. Sounds like one of those paradigms, right Vogel?'

'Paradoxes,' the detective – Vogel – said. That made me warm to him a little. Anyone who challenged Ritter was worth the benefit of the doubt.

'Why don't we split the difference and call it a contradiction?' I said, which got a smile from Vogel.

'No one likes a smartarse, Thomas,' Ritter said. 'Specially not a Marxist smartarse.'

'That *Volksstimme* reporter was one of my noses, a casual

informant, as well you know. The rest was trumped up charges invented by you.'

He spoke over me: 'You're accusing me of making false accusations? In front of a brother officer?' He gestured at Vogel. 'What possible reasons could I have for doing such a thing?'

He had me there. I couldn't offer any evidence to expose him without exposing myself and he knew that.

'You do know that high treason is still a crime?' he said, threading his hands together and putting them behind his head.

'Falsifying evidence, too,' I said. 'Look, I'm going to be late for my night shift if you don't let me go.'

'Oh don't worry, I've informed your watch commander as to recent events. He didn't sound particularly surprised.' Terrific. Like the old man needed any more excuses to haul me over the coals when I got back. Ritter indicated the tagged evidence. 'I'll try and piece things together and you go ahead and stop me if I go wrong.'

He pointed at the first envelope. 'According to this letter, on Wednesday the 14th Maria Butlies takes the train in from Cologne to look for work here as a domestic servant. She gets picked up at the station by an unsavoury character who tries to have his way with her in the park. Before he can succeed, another man comes along to rescue her and take her to the women's hostel at St. Gertrude's. Only, irony of ironies, her rescuer takes her to the woods and rapes her instead. Three days later, she writes to a friend she met on the train to describe the incident. In her statement to you she gives no reason for this odd delay.'

He pointed at the second envelope. The label confirmed that this one held the statement Butlies had given me.

'Now,' he said, 'here's the bit where you might have to correct me. She writes to her friend but the letter is delivered to the wrong woman?'

He paused and looked at me. I wasn't getting out of this

without giving him everything I had on my lead.

'That's right,' I said. 'She got the name wrong, apparently. This Frau Brugmann who got the letter thought the rapist might be the Ripper so she handed the letter in at the precinct house.'

Ritter smiled. 'See?' he said. 'This is what cooperating with a police investigation feels like. Not so bad, is it? So, you tracked Butlies down at the hostel. She'd already found her rapist's apartment from her memory of the night he attacked her. Am I right?'

'He took her there for something to eat before taking her out to the woods,' I said.

'Thoughtful man,' Ritter said. 'You went with Butlies to the apartment house.' Ritter held up the scissors and I saw that the lab boys had scraped off much of the blood for testing. 'Sometime after this you discovered which apartment was Kürten's. You gained entry. Somehow.' He lingered over the last word and raised an eyebrow. 'Where you found these.'

He dropped the scissors back on the tabletop.

'Now why in God's name didn't you come to the murder commission at this point? Or at least notify your watch commander?'

I opened my mouth with no idea what words would come.

Ritter cut in before I could think of any:

'You know what this looks like? It looks like you were going to pass this lot onto your Commie friends, is what it looks like.' He turned back to the detective. 'Wouldn't you say, Vogel?'

Vogel looked up at Ritter, then at me, then back. He shrugged. 'Not for me to say, sir.'

'No, good man, I suppose not.' Ritter turned back to me. 'Well?'

'Well what?'

'The question, Thomas, is what the hell you were planning to do with all of this. Solve the Ripper case all by yourself?'

29

I blushed. 'Hey, it wasn't like I could have done any worse than you. I wanted to find Gertrude Albermann before it was too late.'

'And you think I don't?' Ritter bellowed. A few seconds passed while that little flash of anger filled the space between us. 'Come on, Vogel.' Ritter got out of his chair, gathered up the items on the table and went to leave the room.

I couldn't leave it at that. 'Say Vogel, that nose of yours. You used to be a fighter?'

'I boxed for a couple of years in the war.'

And a pretty poor fighter he must've been judging by that drunken monkey shuffle he was passing off as a walk. 'No kidding? Which unit?'

He showed me his tattoo: up close it turned out to be a red number three on a green background, the insignia of the third Jäger battalion from Brandenburg. That explained the accent: Vogel was a farm boy from the fields outside of Berlin.

I judged his weight at around ninety-five kilos. Take some off for being in his prime back in the war, say he was eighty, eighty-five kilos then. That put him at heavy-weight – or light heavy. 'You were, what? Middleweight?' I said, with a smile so he'd know I was joking.

He grinned at me. 'Light-heavy, you cheeky bastard. From the look of it, you must've been super-heavy?'

'Middle.'

Vogel winced theatrically. 'Don't know how to tell you this, but you've let yourself go.'

I patted my gut, fingers lingering over the scar. 'I'm still handy. I was *Sturmbataillon Rohr.*'

Vogel whistled, and with good reason. My battalion had been the first shock trooper unit in the German army – hell, the whole damn world. That hand-to-hand trench fighting? We pioneered that. The brass had even had us going up against British tanks with canvas sacks full of stick grenades. And winning. Those tanks hadn't stood a chance against our training.

'Since my unit was the one that trained you Jäger boys up in shock trooper tactics, how is it that I don't remember you?' I asked Vogel.

'Didn't join the Jägers till '17,' he said. 'You must've been invalided back by then for old age.'

Ritter was hovering in the doorway, ripe for another shot. I nodded at him: 'Bucky didn't see much action in the war, did you Bucky? He was navy.'

Vogel laughed. It was a deeper, more natural sound than Ritter's. Ritter glared at him.

'You were at Kiel weren't you, Bucky? When the revolution kicked off?' He shifted his gaze to me and I held it. 'Which side were you on, I wonder, comrade.'

Ritter pulled Vogel out of the room and slammed the door. The lock clicked into place behind them.

I counted until the door opened again, twenty-some minutes later. Vogel dropped off a carafe of water and a tin cup. So that last salvo of mine had won me something, even if it was the least of the desires on my list.

'Thanks,' I said. 'By the way, how long's Ritter been trying to grow that god-awful moustache?'

We laughed.

'You know, for a treacherous Commie bastard you're not so bad,' Vogel said.

'Did Kürten talk yet? About the girl, I mean.'

He shook his head. 'Drink up. And just hope no one's pissed in it.'

He smiled as he shut the door. Piss or no, I was in no state to be squeamish. I gulped down a couple of cups and then forced myself to stop. I sniffed at the carafe, a useless gesture given the state of my nose. I poured a third cup and sipped it, deciding firstly that Vogel had just been having his little joke, and secondly that comedy was not his forte. Police work either, based on what I'd seen of him so far, how openly contemptuous of Ritter he seemed to be. Not that I was going to complain about that, but it was hardly professional. I kept to one cup every five minutes or so. Five cups later, Ritter and Vogel returned.

Ritter went over my story, wanting the details of how I'd got into Kürten's apartment, my attempts to track Kürten and his wife at their places of work, how it was that Frau Kürten had dropped by to see me. All of this took another half hour at least but I could tell we were winding down and Ritter was getting ready to throw me back into the street. When we'd finished, he slapped his hands on the tabletop.

'Okay, Vogel, that'll do.' Vogel left, but Ritter loitered at the door: 'You can go, Tommy-Boy. But try and derail my investigation again and you'll regret it even more than you do now.'

'If Albermann is dead because of this delay then you're the one who'll regret it. Trust me on that.'

Ritter slammed the door on me, then Vogel came back to sign over my possessions and escort me out. Didn't much fancy hitting the street the way I was, so after signing for my things I pointed down the hallway.

'Bathroom still this way, is it?'

3.

The bathroom was dark when I went in and flicked the light switch. The bulb flickered as it warmed up, exposing the cobwebs clinging to the corners of the room. I passed a row of lavatory stalls on my way to the bank of porcelain sinks beside the *pissoir* trough on the far wall.

I ran cold water from the tap on the first sink I came to. The pipes chugged and spat out brown gobs of water for a few seconds before the flow stabilised and came out clear. I drank but I couldn't get rid of the dry feeling at the back of my throat. I took a look at my ruined face in the mirror while I plugged and filled the sink.

The door creaked open behind me and Vogel appeared in the mirror.

'What, you don't trust me not to steal the towels?' I said.

'You know she's most likely dead already, don't you?'

I didn't need to let on that I'd been thinking the same. I'd failed Gertrude Albermann. I knew my watch commander wouldn't go for it if I asked for a transfer onto the Ripper case. Ritter wouldn't go for it either. But I had to do something.

In my reflection, brown scabs ringed my nostrils and bruises haloed both eyes. I splashed my face and winced as the sink water blushed pink.

'The Albermann girl, I mean,' Vogel said.

I turned around. 'Every minute we've lost here has made it that much more likely, yes.'

'What makes you think you care so much more than the rest of us?'

Good question. It wasn't something I wanted to talk about.

'Listen to me Klein,' Vogel said, 'there's nothing you can do to help. If you try, you'll just get yourself deeper in the shit, and that won't do that little girl any good either.'

Was he trying to help me, one ex-army boxer to another? Or was it a simple warning not to get in the way? Either way he was right. I couldn't think of anything I could try that wouldn't make things worse or end up delaying the investigation. But hell, if Albermann *was* dead...

'You think I deserve this kind of abuse?' I dabbed the cut in my cheek. Was something still in there? I turned back to the mirror for a closer look.

'Depends what you did. I never met a man yet who wasn't guilty of something.'

'Including you?'

The thing was that I did deserve that kind of abuse. Sleeping with Gisela Ritter had been a bad move, true. But there was more to it than that. I poked at the inside of my cheek with my tongue. Then I poked a little at the outside with a finger until the blood welled thick and ruby red. That was a lump in there, all right. I squeezed at it until I had to cry out with the pain and something plopped into the water. It was a piece of church masonry. I tried to wash the blood from my cheek but it kept on coming.

I went into a lavatory stall and noticed Vogel had left the room and shut the door. I grabbed a handful of toilet paper, went back to my sink and dampened a wad to stick to my cheek. I patted moisture from my forehead and chin with what remained of the paper, avoiding my injuries.

When I was done, Vogel was waiting in the hallway. He led me out to the street in silence, nodding hello to the plump brunette in the cotton summer dress by the door who was smoking a cigarette and humming a tune I recognised all too well.

'The Eroica Symphony?' I said.

The woman turned to me. Okay, so her hair was shorter – and darker, of course – than I remembered, and

34

she'd put on some weight. But I should have recognised her sooner considering I'd just been trying so hard not to think about her. Besides, that extra weight had only added to her curves, and I'd always been a fan of those. Clearly it was going to take more than wishes to keep the past at arm's length.

'Waiting for anyone in particular, Gisela?' I said. 'I believe I'm free for the rest of the night.'

She exhaled cigarette smoke. 'It's after midnight, Thomas.'

Hmmn, frosty. But she wasn't fooling me. 'I'm just getting started.'

'Yeah, you look like it.'

'What did you do to your hair?'

'This is my natural colour.'

'I liked you as a blonde.'

'My husband suggested changing it.' She looked me up and down. If the wounds on my face concerned her, she didn't show it beyond raising a pencilled brow above those chocolate brown eyes of hers. 'I prefer it now.'

'Funny, you didn't used to do everything your husband said.' I had to get that one in, but she managed to ignore it.

'You two know each other?' Vogel said, looking at me. Maybe that was a little click behind his eyes too: him working out what the problem was between Michael Ritter and me.

Gisela fiddled with a string of wooden rosary beads.

I clamped a cigar between my lips. 'Got a light, Gisela?'

'Here.' Vogel passed me a box of matches. Gisela turned away and smoked off the last of her cigarette.

I lit my cigar. 'Happy birthday, by the way,' I told her.

'My birthday was last week,' she said, grinding her cigarette into the cobbles. Under the pale street lights, the lines in her forehead went deeper than I remembered.

'Yeah well, you've got those nice emerald earrings I gave you last year.' She stayed silent as her full lips hovered somewhere between a smile and a sneer. She looked down at my belly. I didn't know how long I'd been rubbing at that scar, but I decided to try distracting her with more earrings talk. Besides which, those little bastards hadn't come cheap. 'Say, where are they anyway? You don't wear them any more?'

'I pawned them. And it was the year before last. I didn't see you last year.'

Blood had soaked through the tissue on my cheek. It dribbled to my chin and I wiped it on my sleeve.

'So,' she said, 'I know you're dying for me to ask what happened to your face.'

'Your husband happened,' I said. 'Right, Vogel?'

Vogel wouldn't meet my gaze. I gave him back his matchbox.

Gisela covered her cleavage with folded arms. I hadn't even been staring at it all that much. 'Didn't happen to get in the way of his Ripper investigation, did you?' she said.

I smiled through a cloud of cigar smoke, shaking my head and trying to block out thoughts of Albermann. 'He always did tell you too much about the office. Did he tell you I arrested the Ripper in your goddamned church? Or that his goons shot up the stonework around the front door? Or that a little girl might be dead because of him?'

Gisela looked right at me, eyes coal black and diamond hard.

I leaned in and whispered, 'I don't excuse what we did. But Michael doesn't have to make this so vicious.'

She stood on tiptoe and pulled my ear down to her lips with the hand that held the rosary beads. 'Maybe you should just turn the other cheek,' she said. 'God's judgement is the only kind that matters, and He is watching us. He saw everything we ever did. All of it.'

Not this Catholic abdication-of-responsibility crap again. If Gisela could've nailed herself to a cross she would have. A nailing, she needed. Just not to a cross.

I forced a smile. 'Well I hope he liked the show we gave him, the dirty bastard.'

She slapped my injured cheek, beads catching my flesh and bringing tears to my eyes. That would be another bruise come morning.

Red patches bloomed on her pale skin all the way from forehead to shoulders. She'd always blushed in patches like that. When we'd made love it had been the same. A thousand filthy memories of us filled my mind and this time I couldn't hold them back. This time I didn't really want to.

I seized her wrist as she pulled back for another slap. My dick was getting hard: this was more like the girl I knew.

Vogel stepped between us, a warning for me in his eyes.

I held up my hands in a gesture of surrender. 'All right, all right, I've had enough beatings for one night. Detective.' I smiled at him, then at Gisela. 'Frau Ritter. Thanks for the chat.'

I left, the sting of Gisela's slap still warm on my cheek and my stomach aching worse than ever as I headed home.

4.

My own snores shook me awake, air dry-whistling through my nose. Then my bed rocked, and I started thinking something else had awoken me, like someone trying to open my door without realising I'd wedged the bed up against it.

A dark pot-bellied man loomed against the far wall, picked out by the sunlight coming through the open curtains. I blinked a couple of times and the man resolved himself into the shadow of my corner stove. I'd got home close on three a.m. to find the lock broken and my room ransacked by Ritter's mob. Funny though how the mess hadn't dragged me down as much as the realisation that my room was little bigger than the holding cell at Mühlenstrasse.

Plus the fact that somehow, in some way I couldn't understand, I'd felt more at home in that cell than I did in my actual home.

The door crashed against the bed. I sat up, rubbing sleep from my eyes.

'Hold on, for Christ's sake,' I said.

'Klein, wake up.' I recognised Vogel's honeyed tones.

'I'm awake, damn it!'

The door across the landing creaked open. I checked my watch. Just gone eight a.m. Good Christ, was I never going to get enough sleep?

'What's all this?' That was the voice of my neighbour – and landlady – Effi Schneider. She didn't sound happy.

Vogel stopped pushing at my door and said, 'I'm sorry madam, but we need to take Detective Klein to headquarters.'

'On a Sunday?' Effie said.

I sat as still as I could and held my breath. What did Vogel and Ritter want with me now? I wanted to tell the inspector to go to hell, to submit his request in writing to my precinct house and have to wait days for the response. On the other hand, maybe he wanted me to help find the Albermann kid after all. Or, worse, they'd found her. No, scratch that last one: if they'd found her they wouldn't need me. Not unless Ritter was looking for a scapegoat.

'And I suppose you're the cretins who smashed the place up yesterday?' Effi went on. 'Honestly, you think this is a good use of tax payers' money while there's four million unemployed and people queuing round the block for the soup kitchens?'

'Madam, I really couldn't say. I've been sent down here from Berlin, and I didn't have much say in the matter, I can tell you.'

'Berlin, eh?' Effi made a sound somewhere at the back of her throat. 'Explains a lot.'

I wrapped a cotton sheet around my midriff and I got up. I scraped the bed back and opened the door. 'You found her?'

Vogel put a finger to his lips. There was something different about him today, but I couldn't work out what it was. There was another plainclothesman beside him, a squat man with thin hair draped across a dry scalp. Beyond these two, Effi stood at the threshold of her rooms. Hot curlers steamed in glossy dark hair which came down over her ears. A black velvet jacket strained to contain her and she was wearing a thin silver chain around her neck. Three dark-haired young girls peered out from behind her skirts.

'So what, it turns out I can help after all?'

'I thought they'd caught the Ripper?' Effi said.

'Well, we have...' Vogel said.

'Heard on the wireless yesterday evening. There's talk they interrupted the opera and the cinema to announce it and everything.'

'Well, yes... We need to take him down to headquarters

for a word with the chief.' He made a point of looking around and down the stairwell, then he stage-whispered: 'DCI Gennat, you know...'

My heart was pounding all the way to the hole in my cheek. Ernst Gennat, *der volle Ernst:* Germany's most famous detective, head of the country's only dedicated murder squad. He'd been brought in to head up the Ripper investigation from Berlin at the insistence of the Prussian interior ministry. Had Ritter dropped me in it with the top brass, or was Gennat looking to grill me for his own reasons? Either way, I was in for a long day and I didn't much fancy it, though I didn't have any choice now. Refusing to see Gennat would be career suicide beyond any of the bad decisions I'd made in the past. I'd have to find out what he wanted and then do my best to appease him.

Effi nodded at me. 'Well, he's not going anywhere in his birthday suit. Coffee?'

Vogel checked his watch. 'I'd like that, madam, but we must be going.'

'Nonsense!' Effi crossed the landing in a couple of steps and wrapped her arm around Vogel's shoulders. 'Give the man time to get some clothes on, eh?' She winked and managed to slap my *arsch*. She steered the two detectives into her kitchen just as my sheet fell around my ankles.

I retreated into my room and wedged the door shut with a chair. My clothes were still strewn across the floor and on top of my battered leather trunk, clean and dirty mingled together where Ritter's men had thrown them the day before. I picked out the cleanest looking under-clothes I could find. A film of sweat covered my body at the thought of meeting Gennat.

I dug around in the mess for some suit trousers, found a pair that went with my double-breasted jacket. I'd bought them when my waist had been a size larger, before this damned Depression had left us all hungrier and leaner. I fastened my belt on the last notch.

I tried to ignore the roughness of the woollen trousers

against my legs while I retrieved the jacket and waistcoat that went with them. I checked myself out in the cracked mirror on the back of the door. Even after buttoning the jacket I looked like a tramp who'd stolen his clothes off a corpse.

I crossed the landing and pushed open Effi's door. Effi and the two policemen broke off from forced laughter at my entrance. The three of them were sitting at her circular dining table in the centre of the room, drinking coffee from her best blue-and-white glazed china cups arranged around a pot of the same manufacture.

The girls were standing at the threshold of the second room dropping fruit cake crumbs on the floor. The smallest came over and thrust her nibbled wedge of cake at me, her cheeks pouched like those of a rodent. I waved her away. On her way back, she knocked the family's tin bath from its resting place against the peeling wallpaper and gave a squeal, running into the next room before her mother could shout at her.

'Look Effi, I'm sorry about this disturbance. And the mess from yesterday.'

She talked over me: 'Never you mind, Herr Thomas. I'll just add the damages and the cost of the new lock onto your rent at the end of the week.'

Vogel rose from his seat and scratched the side of his nose. Now I realised what was different. He was wearing a jacket and his shirt sleeves went all the way down to his wrists. He had even oiled his hair, though on him the effect was unfortunate, as though he'd dunked his head in a grease puddle.

'You ready to go?' he asked, buttoning his jacket.

'Does he look ready?' Effi said. I rubbed the stubble on my chin. I should have shaved, but I didn't relish the thought of negotiating a razor around all those cuts and bruises. Effi passed me a cup of coffee and a bottle of aspirin. On the cup, blue tulips bloomed. I uncapped the bottle and shook three aspirins into my mouth, washing them down with coffee.

41

'All right, let's go,' I told Vogel. With a little luck Gennat would be done with me before my shift was due to start. Then I could either help find the girl, or I could try and put the Ripper case behind me and move on.

The squat guy with the bad scalp drove us back to Mühlenstrasse in a drab closed-top sedan from the *Schupo* auto pool. Vogel had taken the passenger seat and removed his jacket before getting in, draping the garment across his legs. We didn't talk. I played with my homburg in my lap and watched the city pass by through the window. Vogel even whistled a tune for part of the way. *Watch on the Rhine*, I think it was, though I didn't ask.

I sat back, the sting of Gisela's slap still with me from the night before. It had been a shock to see her. The good Frau Ritter. I chuckled. Vogel stopped his whistling to turn and look at me. Well, let him look. The image of Gisela as the dutiful wife, it irritated like a chicken bone stuck in the gullet.

I pictured a meadow in summer, Gisela and me eating a roasted chicken. The bread had gone dry and the Riesling had warmed in the sun, but none of it mattered. We'd eaten until our lips shone with chicken fat and Gisela joked about Ritter having to make do with the leftovers. Then we'd made love in the sun until my back burned bright red and her tinted hair went a shade lighter still.

Funny how people changed. That Gisela – my Gisela – was gone forever, replaced by a mousy matron clutching at her rosary as though that could save her from her sins.

But then, how much of that change was my fault?

Vogel's redundant, 'We're here,' announced our arrival at headquarters.

We pulled up to the entrance. The front of the building stretched along most of the block, three stories of large, evenly-spaced windows set in pale stone. This neoclassical façade had been one of Schinkel's efforts, or so people liked to think. I wasn't so sure. Why come all the way to Düsseldorf from Berlin in the days when that would take a week in a jittery horse-driven mail coach? My money was on one of the great man's less favoured disciples.

The squat guy drove away and left Vogel and me to enter the place. We passed through the high double doors into the first courtyard. Again without a word, Vogel led me across the cobbles through a smaller door and up the stairs beyond. When we got to the second floor he turned left and we entered a familiar institutional world of two-tone grey brick and overheated hallways. The stuffiness made me shiver after the cool air outside. Each face I saw belonged to a man I didn't know even though I'd worked on this floor for over six years. Maybe they were all from Berlin.

Raised voices echoed down the hallway from the end corner office. One of the voices was Ritter's. I grinned at the thought of him being angry and then I thought of him turning that same anger on me and my fists clenched.

Ritter, yelling: 'He's not trustworthy enough. You've seen the file!'

Through the open door of the corner office I got my first glimpse of Gennat's pudgy red face. He wore a small pair of reading spectacles and his moustache bristled as he sucked on a cigar. No doubt this was where Ritter had got the inspiration for his ill-conceived experiment in facial hair.

Gennat spoke through a smoke cloud: 'We don't have any choice in the matter.' His thick accent shone through: a real *icke Berliner*. I hoped I'd be able to understand him okay.

I tried to dredge up what I knew about the man, but that was nothing, pretty much. He had an unrivalled case clearance rate and was popular with the press. So what did that mean? He wasn't above forcing a few confessions, he liked publicity and he enjoyed the sound of his own voice.

He'd had a hand in solving that messy Fritz Haarmann business in Hanover back in 'twenty-five mind, so he knew his stuff when it came to mass-murderers.

Vogel knocked.

'Enter!' Gennat called. He waved us in and beamed at me. Ritter stood with a coffee cup in his hands, his face just as red as the chief inspector's, I was glad to note.

43

Ritter clocked me looking at his moustache, raised his cup to his lips and looked out of the window.

Beneath the window was a small pine table bearing a scorched metal coffee pot and a sugar bowl alongside a typewriter and a stack of files.

'This the fellow?' Gennat asked Vogel. Vogel nodded and Gennat came over and shook my hand. His palm was damp and warm. A glimmer of shock lit his face, presumably at the sight of my wounds.

'Now then,' he said, 'Kl... er, Thomas, is it?' He didn't wait for me to answer. 'I'm not one for politics when public safety is at stake. I hope we can agree on that?' He was using the word 'politics' the way political people do, as a slur on the politics of others. I hoped he was just trying to fool me and not himself.

Gennat's glasses had slipped to the end of his nose. The lenses magnified his soft brown eyes. I pumped his hand again and murmured a yes.

'You want someone to fix up your face?' Gennat removed his spectacles, leaving indentations above his ears. 'Bandages and so forth.'

All of this dancing around the maypole was chafing at my patience. 'May I ask what all this is about?'

'He wants to know what it's all about,' Gennat repeated, as though mid-way through a press conference. I glanced around to check for hidden press men, but the audience comprised just me, Vogel and Ritter. 'Fine quality in a detective, sir. Fine quality.'

He replaced his spectacles and gestured to an empty chair. The room was crammed with rows of chairs facing a map of greater Düsseldorf tacked to a cork board on the far wall. A dozen or more red pins adorned the map, half of them clustered in the south-eastern suburbs. A series of pencil-drawn circles rippled outwards at half-kilometre intervals from an epicentre in Mettmannerstrasse: Peter Kürten's apartment building.

I picked up the chair Gennat had indicated. I turned it round to face him and I sat.

'Well,' I said, 'it's just that the city does pay me to clock in at eight p.m. I fear you may be forcing me to deprive it of my services if you keep me around too long.'

Gennat sat on the edge of a paper-strewn desk, toppling a black phone in the process. He slammed the ear piece back in the cradle, lifted the phone with both hands and deposited it on the other side of the desk.

I got a glimpse of an open personnel file with my photograph on it. They'd been discussing me, then. I didn't like that. But if that was true then why was the idea of it making my heart pump faster?

Gennat hitched his charcoal grey trousers at the knees, took a puff of his cigar and blew smoke rings through small lips. The smoke stank of wet autumn leaves. I hoped he wasn't going to offer me one of those cigars, because I'd have had to say no and that would have got our burgeoning professional relationship off to a terrible start.

When Gennat spoke, it was clear he'd decided to ignore my concerns regarding my night shift duties. 'What it's about, Thomas, is we've been sweating your Herr Kürten for the last,' he checked the wall clock and mumbled under his breath for a second, 'seventeen hours, give or take. Or at least, we've been trying to, haven't we Ritter?'

Ritter turned from the window and declined to answer. He stood stiff-backed, making a point of not sitting while I was in the room. How I wanted to laugh in his stupid fluffy face.

'That is to say, Ritter has tried.' Gennat's voice was a rumble from the sternum that soothed as much as it unsettled. 'Vogel has tried. Hell, even I've tried.'

Gennat got to his feet and threw his arms wide, another theatrical gesture for the gallery. He'd be declaiming Goethe at this rate, God help us. 'He won't talk, it's that simple. Won't talk to me, won't talk to Vogel, won't talk to your precious Inspector Ritter.'

He pointed at Ritter who still said nothing. Instead, Ritter ran his tongue over his teeth in a way that made his top lip bulge and emphasised his overbite. The circles under his eyes went deeper than the day before. Could it be that he'd got less sleep than me? Had Gisela even managed to drag him home last night after I'd left her? Was he feeling jealous at our getting reacquainted? I did hope so.

Gennat slapped a hand on my shoulder and brought me back to the matter at hand.

'Kürten won't talk to anyone, Thomas, you understand me?' he said.

It was a message I'd have had a hard time missing. I opened my mouth to say so and he added:

'Anyone except you.'

5.

Thirty minutes later, Ritter escorted me down the hall. Half an hour with Kürten's file wasn't long enough. After Gennat had got a girl in to bandage up my cheek I'd had twenty minutes to read the thing, and if there was a more convincing argument for sterilising the criminal classes I'd yet to see it.

1897 saw Kürten's first conviction for theft at age fourteen. He'd stolen from the foundry where he'd worked as an apprentice sand moulder with his father. He'd then spent eighteen of the following thirty years behind bars, and his rap sheet heaved with arson and rape.

'Just get him talking,' Gennat said when he gave me the file, 'and Ritter can take care of the rest.'

Damned if I was going to leave it at that. We could spend all day talking and only just scratch the surface. And spending all day talking to Kürten was not a pleasant prospect. Those scant fifteen minutes we'd spent together in the Church of St. Rochus would have done me. Albermann had to be the priority. As far as I knew she was still out there somewhere and we still didn't know where.

Ritter halted beside a door and said, 'Look familiar?' He opened up and ushered me inside.

It was the same interview room where Ritter had interrogated me. Nice touch, that. But then, there were only two in the building. There was a difference today, though. Today four chairs circled the table. Kürten sat in the one facing the door, picking at his fingernails. His suit jacket was buttoned tight and his shirt collar had rubbed his neck red raw. In the chair to his left sat a stenographer with a pad. The stenographer wore a grey suit and the dark circles round his eyes supplied his face with its only colour.

Kürten smiled at me. There was a gap in his upper right jaw where one of his molars should have been, a detail I noticed now only because that had been in his file too.

'Thomas!' he said. He got out of his chair and extended a hand. I hefted the file to show him why I couldn't shake it. He pulled the hand away and ran it through his hair, which had begun to lose its shape. He pulled out the chair next to him and bid me sit down before returning to his seat.

'Are they treating you all right, old chap?' he said.

The women I'd offended at the pavement café the day before came to mind. I wondered how they'd react if they knew that their fiendish vampire had such good manners. And if I'd wondered at how a man such as this might have convinced so many women and children to go off with him, here was the answer. Manners went a long way, especially with certain kinds of romance-novel reading domestics and ageing spinsters: the lonely, the unloved. When our morbidly polite society was full of such people all crying out for a little charm then a little charm was all it took.

'I'm your warm-up act.' I sat in the chair Kürten had prepped for me and pointed over my shoulder at Ritter.

Kürten glared at him. Ritter ignored the last empty chair and loomed across the table. 'Where were you Friday evening, say between five p.m. and nine p.m.? You know, the time when you were abducting Gertrude Albermann? Around then.'

So much for my plan. Kürten half-shrugged, looked at me and rolled his eyes. The eyes were cornflower blue in the morning light. Prussian army blue. The blue of Queen Louise's mythical flight from Napoleon, of the lamented – or was that lamentable? – Kaiser Bill and his withered left arm. The blue of withered machismo.

Ritter squatted beside Kürten's chair. His lips brushed the prisoner's ear.

He bellowed: 'We have a witness who can place you with the girl! So where is she?'

'Who? The witness? I have no idea.' Kürten tittered, pleased with his joke. He kept those twinkling little cornflowers on me. 'Why is this man shouting? Why is he talking to me, even?' He addressed the stenographer. 'I believe I was quite specific. No one but Detective Klein.'

Ritter reached across the table and grabbed Kürten's tie. He pulled Kürten out of his chair and across the table, the points of the prisoner's shoes scraping the table top.

'Where is Gertrude Albermann?' Ritter said.

Kürten's eyes went flat. His mouth twisted in a look of – what? Anger? Disgust? It wasn't fear. Though I despised him for what he might be – a killer of women and children – I admired his composure, his balls in opposing Ritter. The thought came to me out of nowhere and I tried to feel shocked about it. I tried really hard.

'Tell me where she is!' Ritter shouted.

Kürten stuck out his front teeth and gnashed at the air. Ritter threw Kürten at the nearest empty chair.

'Play games all you want,' Ritter said, heading for the door. 'But you'd better give us something soon so we know you are the Ripper.' He shot me a look, pulled his handkerchief and covered his lips with it. 'And not just another deluded fool.'

He slammed the door shut behind him. Meanwhile, the stenographer hadn't so much as raised an eyebrow at all the commotion.

'Did you get all of that okay?' I asked him.

'Yes sir, thank you.'

'Good, cause I don't know how I'm going to follow that bravura performance.'

'Sir? Did you want me to get that down as well?'

'Never mind.'

Ritter's questioning confirmed that no one had stumbled across Albermann's body yet, so she could still be alive. Probably his claim about a witness was so much horse shit, otherwise they'd have thrown a lot more at

Kürten before bringing me in. Kürten's response told me that the direct approach wasn't going to work. Maybe Gennat had been right when he'd emphasised the need to get him talking first.

'You feel it now,' Kürten said, still squatting on the floor. He looked at the door as though Ritter were still there, or listening on the other side. Which, for all I knew, he was. 'You feel that?' Kürten cried. 'You feel the fear? You feel it now?'

He got to his feet. He pinched the seams of his trousers and tried to flick out the creases. He gave me a small, embarrassed kind of smile, picked up the chair he'd knocked over and sat so that now he faced the window.

I reached for the steno pad and tore off the top couple of sheets. I dropped Kürten's file on the table and jiggled at it to see which leg was the shorter. I folded the paper three times and jammed it under the errant leg, then I leaned on the table. Still some give there, but it was a definite improvement.

The file said Kürten was born in 1883 but he didn't look forty-six years old, not to me. And from what I'd read none of the surviving victims had thought him any older than his mid-thirties. Murder kept you young, it seemed. If he was the Ripper, I reminded myself. That's what we still had to prove, he and I, if we were going to find that missing five-year-old.

'The fear?' I said.

'They treated me like a dog,' Kürten said.

'Who did?'

He didn't hear me. 'No, worse than a dog. With their fettering and their solitary and their work details.' He tapped a forefinger on the table, as though rehearsing his day in court. 'Well, you beat a dog often enough, eventually you get bitten.' He turned to the door. He yelled, 'Bitten! You feel it? You feel it now?'

This wasn't going anywhere. I rubbed my left eye, forgetting it was bruised. Pain flooded that side of my face and I had to blink back tears.

'You wanted to see me?' I said.

'I wanted to see you?' His face blanked. Then he smiled. 'Ah, Thomas. My friend. After all we've shared. Your eyes look terrible. You want to try a bit of meat on that. Raw meat, you know. Does wonders for a bad eye.'

'Why did you ask for me?'

'These people don't get it. But they haven't endured loss, not like us. They don't know what it's all about.'

Like us? My thoughts flashed on Lilli. How could he know about that? Then I realised he meant Christine Klein – had probably assumed we were related somehow.

'How did it feel when your father raped your sister?' I wanted to snap him out of his thoughts, direct his rambling. Wanted to snap out of my thoughts of Lilli, too. Keep the focus, keep to the job. Keep on going. The file said Kürten senior had served seven sentences in his time for assault and the like. Also eighteen months for incest with Kürten's eldest sister in 1897.

He frowned at me. I repeated the question. He shrugged.

'Rape is a strong word, wouldn't you say?' he said.

'What would you call it?'

'What is one supposed to feel about it, anyway?' He waved his hands through the air.

'You were there, weren't you? When it happened? And all of what? Twelve? Thirteen years old? How did it feel to watch him do that to your sister?'

He blew air through loosened lips, like a horse. 'She was a whore.' He dismissed the sister with another wave at nothing in particular. 'Even tried to sleep with me once. More than once.'

'I need to ask you –'

He spoke over me. 'What, detective? What do you need to ask me? What they tell you to? Those fools out there who hadn't even the insight to put you on the case?'

I stared at him and played out the moves I could make next. I lit myself a cigar and offered one to Kürten who shook his head. I was tempted to offer one to the

51

stenographer, but that was just the sadist in me. Poor bugger looked ill enough already.

'How did you know that?' I said.

'How long have I been in here?' Kürten asked.

I pulled my watch from my waistcoat.

'No, don't answer that,' he said. 'It was rhetorical. I've been in this little box a long time now. Many hours. You're the man who brought me in, yet in all that time you haven't been back once. Why? More than this, if I think back to yesterday afternoon, and you coming to bring me in with no back-up...'

'What do you think all the blue coats outside were about?' I said.

'They weren't yours. You were surprised when they turned up. And they opened fire even though you were there, in the way. Why?' He held a finger in the air to forestall any more questions. Staying seated, he reached across for the dressing on my cheek. I lurched to my feet before he could land a finger on me.

'There is only one answer that makes sense.' Kürten stood and pointed at me. 'And now here you are, at my behest. Where you should be.'

I felt like a *muschi*, a goddamned rookie. I'd allowed this man to derail my line of questioning and he'd driven me out of my chair with some words and a prying finger. I covered myself with a few puffs on the cigar, filling the space between us with smoke. The stenographer sat poised over his pad, pencil in hand ready to go on.

'Sit down,' I said, pointing to Kürten's chair.

Kürten laughed and did as I asked. I retook my seat, pulling it back from the table so he couldn't try his little trick again.

'You were raised a Catholic, Peter?'

'My dear Thomas, that's my file you have in your hand there?' He looked at the paperwork I was holding.

I nodded back at him.

'Well then you know perfectly well that I wasn't raised at all.'

'So why a Catholic church?' I said.

'I'm sorry?'

'Why give yourself up in a Catholic church?'

'I thought it best to meet at a church so big even Düsseldorf *Kripo* could find it.'

I stood and crossed to the window, patting the brick-work and turning back so the light silhouetted me. In the corner, the mould was gone, replaced with a damp patch as though someone had tried sponging the wall since the day before.

'Wasn't anything to do with your need to confess?'

'What need to confess?'

I tapped the wall again. 'You know what this place used to be before it became police headquarters?'

He shrugged.

'A Jesuit monastery,' I said. 'You could say that confession, guilt, it kind of runs through the bricks and mortar. Suitable, wouldn't you say?'

'Suitable for what?'

'For a man like you with such a... need to get it all out in the open,' I said. He was shaking his head. His denial riled me and I felt the heat rise in my face. 'You told me about Christine Klein within two minutes of meeting me.'

He looked puzzled. 'Well of course I did.'

'You gave yourself up to us. Willingly.'

He waggled a finger at me. 'That's where you're wrong, Thomas. You turned up at my apartment with a woman I'd raped. What, I was supposed to go on the run? At my age? With a wife to support?' He gave a kind of grunt. 'No, it was only a matter of time before you locked me up. And with my record.' He tailed off and shivered.

'So you thought you'd confess to being the Ripper? Peter, you could face the death sentence!'

'With this bunch in office? You really think so?'

I most certainly did. Granted, Social Democrat law and order policy tended towards pinko-liberal sludge, what with its anti-capital punishment bent. But not even the SPD state government would hesitate to cut public anger off at the knees by cutting the Ripper off at the neck.

'Even so,' I said, 'you'll get longer behind bars this way than for a rape, record or no. How does this support your wife?'

He straightened his tie, moving his chair to face me before leaning back and crossing his legs. 'There's a reward for information leading to my arrest, isn't there?'

'Conviction, yes.'

'So, who gave you the information that led to my arrest?'

Then I got it. Although his logic was so warped, I still wasn't sure. 'You mean, you got her to come to us so she could get the reward money?'

He winked at me.

'You really think they'll pay her anything?'

'Why not? She's as good as any other informant.'

He seemed to mean it, that was the weirdest part. All those women he'd killed, and he wanted his wife to profit from his downfall. Did that fit? Or was this guy still just a rapist looking to make the most of a bad situation? I felt my excitement slipping away. Maybe this wouldn't be the day I embarrassed Ritter.

'You know, Inspector Ritter had a point,' I said. 'How do we know you are who you say you are?'

'Why would I lie?'

'Financial motive, Peter. The reward money. You just admitted it.'

'How many people would have the audacity to claim to be me?'

'In person? Four hundred and thirteen at the last count.' I didn't know the exact figure, but the one I'd just given him wasn't far from the truth. 'More by letter. The anonymous ones.'

His mouth hung open for a second. I knew some of what he felt. It didn't say much about our city that so many of its inhabitants were willing to admit to mass murder. Or rather, it said an awful lot, none of it good.

Kürten closed his mouth and sat up straighter, folding

his hands in his lap. I came back to the table and sat across from him.

'Oh yes,' I continued. 'You'd be surprised. You want to know the real reason they haven't brought me in to see you until now?'

I blew cigar smoke in his face and his nostrils flared. A brief look of annoyance crossed his face. I tried not to smile at that as I leaned closer.

'It's because they think you're just another crazy. Just another unhinged cretin looking for a few thrills by claiming to be the Ripper.'

'No!' he breathed.

'I mean, look at you. That suit, the haircut. You're a quiet, respectable man, not a killer at all.'

'My file. What about my arrest file?'

'We both know that's not you. You've been abused, Peter, punished for things that weren't your fault.'

He gazed out of the window. God alone knew what patterns he was seeing in the brick wall out there.

I thought of a detail from the file, his longest prison term. 'Seven years for deserting the army, Peter? Seven years? Does that seem fair to you?'

He didn't answer. I hoped I hadn't laid the sympathy on too thick.

He turned away from the window.

'So you've got to see it how we see it, Peter. How do we know? How can we be sure?'

'Take me to Papendell.'

'What's at Papendell?'

'Just take me there,' he snapped, turning back to the window. 'And bring a shovel.'

6.

Kürten insisted on riding to Papendell with no one but me. That meant I had to drive one of the *Schupo* pool autos. It was an open-topped coupé, and thank God it was a newer model with no starter handle, as I stalled it twice on the way out of town. We drove east. Kürten directed. Ritter and his detectives followed along in a sedan. Two closed limousines packed with *Schupo* trailed them.

We passed Flingern Nord. We passed Grafenberg. All the while I thought of what we were likely to find in Papendell and tried not to think of Gertrude Albermann. The suburbs gave out to row upon row of allotments, then meadows and parkland. We took the road south-east to Ekrath, then took a sharp turn north onto a narrow road signposted for Papendell. A road-side café came up on the left and Kürten told me to stop.

I indicated with my arm so Ritter and his goons wouldn't motor into the back of me. We pulled over just beyond the café. The engine coughed itself out. I turned to Kürten as I applied the handbrake and he pointed to the meadows across the road.

I cuffed Kürten's wrists together: Gennat's one stipulation. Then I picked up the shovel on the back seat. I went to put on my hat but the sweat smell on the band was so strong I left it.

Clouds huddled over us as we got out of the car. The breeze was soft against my face and I closed my eyes for a moment to enjoy a brief flush of normality. When I opened them, there was Kürten, also hatless, waiting for me. Behind him, Ritter's sedan and the two beetle-black limousines. The blue coats disembarked. Ritter issued some orders to Vogel, back in shirtsleeves. Vogel relayed the order and four *Schupo*men peeled off to secure the café.

I caught Ritter's eye. 'Remember,' I said, 'no closer than fifty metres.' We'd agreed that with Kürten in exchange for his bringing us out here.

Ritter said nothing. Fine by me. I'd said it more for Kürten's benefit anyway.

We crossed the road and entered the flower-dotted meadow. Long, damp grass clung to my legs. Behind us came the distant clanking of semi-automatic weaponry. Kürten seemed to be leading me down the road to a cluster of low brick buildings encircled by a wall.

'I met her at about five o'clock,' Kürten said, out of nowhere. 'On the Ackerstrasse. I talked to her, asked her if she would come with me.'

'How'd you get her here?' That wasn't what I wanted to ask most. I wanted to ask who he was talking about, only I knew already and I wanted to put off hearing it from him for as long as I could.

'Walked, of course.'

'All this way?'

How'd he kept a five-year-old quiet on a long walk like that? It must have taken us half an hour to drive here. What was that on foot? Two hours?

'She came willingly,' he said. 'She didn't cry, didn't complain. I strangled her when we got here.'

'Where?' I said.

Kürten pointed to the wall up ahead. He had to do it two-handed, thanks to the cuffs. A painted sign on the wall read 'Haniel & Lueg GmbH'. So, a business premises of some kind. A factory, judging by the brick smokestacks.

We stepped over weeds and loose bits of builder's rubble until we were close enough to touch the crumbling wall plaster and see the smoke.

'Where were you pointing?'

'Down there in the shadows.' He pointed again, and

then I saw what he was pointing at. Any doubts I'd ever had about his being the Ripper, well, they evaporated pretty damn quickly.

The body lay atop a pile of bricks, hard up against the factory wall. A thick patch of nettles covered it and weeds clung to the wall. A soft spring breeze blew across the open meadows between the factory and the woods and tugged at the girl's green coat as though willing her to get up and live again. One of her buckled shoes had come loose but it was the smallness of her that got to me. My legs gave and I fell to my knees, the shovel I'd been carrying hanging heavy in my hand.

The man at my side drew back, his baby blues full of indignation rather than fear. No, not fear, never fear, not for this one.

'Tell them to stay back!' he commanded.

I turned. The *Schupo* cordon behind us closed in, bullet hoses held chest high. Of course, from where they'd been standing they couldn't see what I could. I used the shovel to push myself up and waved at the *Schupo* to keep their distance. It was enough. They shrank back to the edge of the meadow. It was just me and the Ripper, the Ripper and me, for this part of the proceedings. Kürten's hair had dried and paled and knotted in the breeze. It was the only real hint of untidiness in his appearance since his arrest. Ever the dapper man about town. He was talking, presumably to me, though I caught only some of his words.

'She was so trusting. Put her arms round my neck when I carried her. Told me all about her family. I wish... sometimes, I wish...'

The girl – Gertrude, her name was Gertrude damn it, and I wasn't going to depersonalise her in death – lay on her front. Although the coat covered her, her bottom was poking into the air and her legs were parted. Five years old, and this man – this excuse of a man justifying himself to me – hadn't just killed her, he'd raped her first.

My heart gave a tug. I thought of my own darling Lilli, snuggling safe and loved in a warm cot, face shining with the happiness she'd never had the chance to know. Prickling salt water stung my eyes.

My knuckles were white where I gripped the shovel's handle. I imagined sinking its blade into Kürten's face, cracking open his skull and releasing the evil that dwelt within. Maybe then the pain would go away.

The Ripper smiled at me. 'You want to kill me,' he said. It wasn't a question.

I said nothing. What could I say? The wind cooled the tear tracks on my cheeks and ruffled the bandage on my face.

Finally, I cleared my throat. 'She's not buried,' I said, lifting the shovel. 'Why did you tell me to bring this?'

'You'll see.' The Ripper's smile deepened as he crooked a finger and beckoned me to follow him still further into hell.

'Wait!' I called.

He stopped and turned back, a puzzled look on his face. I made it to my feet and handed him the shovel.

'Not yet,' I told him.

I didn't want to contaminate the body but I was first officer on the scene. Duty decreed I file a report on this.

'Do you still have your handkerchief?' I asked Kürten.

He fumbled at his breast pocket but he couldn't get a grip on the material because the handcuffs got in the way. I rose and pulled out the white cotton square for him as he gave a shrug and a smile. I examined the material for contaminants such as blood or phlegm and found none, then I returned to the body. I wrapped the handkerchief around my hand and pulled the coat aside as far as I could without moving the limbs.

The coat caught on something. I pulled harder and it came loose; it had been stuck to the girl's back with dried blood. The blood patch spread from her left side to her lower back. That told me Kürten had moved her to her current position some time after death.

'It was raining that night,' Kürten said.

Under the green coat, the girl's white knickers were exposed and torn and her buttocks were bared.

'You molested her?' I said over my shoulder.

Kürten cleared his throat. No words came. I looked back at him. He stood with his feet apart and both hands stretched out in front of his face, eyes wide, mouth stretched into a grin.

'I stabbed her with my scissors and I strangled her,' he said. 'With this hand,' his left-hand fingers flexed, 'I kept hold of her throat, while with this one,' his right hand wriggled, 'I felt the... the...'

He coughed. He cleared his throat again.

I blocked him out, leaning over the girl's head and pushing aside some of her hair. Flies buzzed around us. No maggots had hatched on her yet, so she hadn't been there long.

The hair on her crown had dried in the breeze, though around her face it was still damp. The flies settled back on her and I tried to wave them away.

Two stab wounds to the left temple. A brown crust the rain hadn't washed off still clung from temple to chin.

Her face was red with congestion, which sometimes came from the way a body lay after death. But for that to work in this case she'd have been lying on her front when she bled out. The blood patches I could see told me she'd bled out on her back and been moved to her current position afterwards. *This* congestion had been the result of throttling.

I couldn't get a look at the girl's throat to check for bruises without moving her, and I couldn't do that until someone had sketched her position or called out a photographer. I stood up. The rest I could leave to Ritter and the autopsy.

I crossed to Kürten and took the shovel from him.

'Where next?' I said.

He led, I followed. He stopped at the edge of the woods that bordered the meadow. *Schupo*men surrounded us, some lurking in the meadow, some in the trees. Ritter

60

hadn't kept pace. He and Vogel and the other plain-clothesmen were hung up with Albermann's corpse.

Kürten scratched his head.

'Somewhere round here,' he was saying to himself. Then, to me, he added, 'We're looking for a rock, a large flat one. It's poking up through the earth somewhere... around here.'

He took a few paces into the woods. The *Schupo* guys in the trees took the same number of paces back. Kürten emerged from the tree line, counting his steps like a child playing at *Treasure Island*.

'How many people are buried out here?' I said.

He laughed.

'Who are we going to find?' I said. 'Another child?'

'I'm not a monster, Thomas,' he hissed, looking around. 'I'm a man with normal appetites, that's all. Normal appetites denied too long.' He jabbed a finger down at the ground, took a couple of breaths and then ran a hand through his hair. That is, he tried to, but the cuffs didn't make it an easy operation. He mussed up as much as he smoothed down.

'So?' I said. 'Who is it? Who have you buried out here, Peter?'

'My dear chap, I really don't know. She didn't tell me her name and I didn't ask.' He unbuttoned his jacket. 'Tell me, do you still have any of those cigars?'

I ignored him and dug into the loam. The grass roots knotted the wet soil into lumps and made it hard to break through.

The breeze picked up. It had an edge to it and the clouds seemed to have fattened and darkened and crept closer. If we were going to find something I wanted it to be before the weather broke.

Kürten wiped his nose on his shirt cuffs and watched me dig. Voices drifted to me on the wind and I looked back in the direction of the factory. Ritter and Vogel had come up to the *Schupo* cordon and were talking to the squad sergeant.

How much of this was on Ritter? Would Gertrude still be alive if he hadn't got in the way?

'You don't like him, do you?' Kürten said, nodding at Ritter.

I shovelled more earth out of the hole. This far down, it was more tightly packed.

'Come on,' Kürten said, 'you can tell me. I'm a good listener.'

'Yeah, I'll bet.' I tried to ignore the fact that I felt closer to this bastard than to any of my so-called colleagues. After all, it was thanks to him I was back at head-quarters. I had to keep telling myself *he'd* killed the girl, not Ritter. Ritter had just made it easier for him. He hadn't done the deed.

'Aren't you going to ask me why I did it?' Kürten said.

'Did what?'

'All these... things I did. The murders. The rapes. You know...'

With that, I paused, stabbing the shovel into the earth and leaning on it. My arms shook, my shock trooper days feeling a long way off. Didn't I want to ask why? Didn't I want to know? I thought about it, then realised that, whatever this man said to me, I would never know. Not really.

'There's no answer you can give me that I would under-stand,' I said.

I hefted the shovel again, sending a hot wave of pain down my spine. The blade struck something hard and slid off.

Good Christ, had I hit bone? Searing stomach acid rose to the back of my throat. I choked it down.

I shook creases out of the handkerchief I was holding and smoothed it between my palms. I got down on my knees and pushed soil away from the misshapen lump. I dug beneath it with my hand and pulled upwards. The bone came loose and I fell backwards.

The bone turned out not to be a bone at all, but a large flat rock.

'We're close now,' Kürten hissed.

The nearest *Schupo* crept forward. A shout from Vogel brought them up, but they didn't retreat. Kürten didn't notice their approach, or affected not to. The hole in the ground transfixed him.

I went at the ground with the shovel once more. The adrenaline from the digging was beginning to ease the back pain. I dug out two more spadefuls before the shovel hit another rock.

'*Gott in Himmel*, Peter,' I said, 'there's a lot of rocks in this meadow. No wonder they don't plough it.'

With bare fingers I gripped the rock and pulled. This one felt like it was covered in soft plant roots or decomposing grass. It plopped out of the loam, my fingers tangled in the roots.

It was light for a rock. The surface texture on the other side was smooth, slippery, like it was coated in wax. A chunk of the wax flapped loosely around a narrow base as I brushed the earth away and turned the rock around.

Two sunken eyelids met my gaze. Something black and shiny crawled out from under the left one. I dropped the head in the hole, scrabbled out and retched in the long grass, Kürten laughing all the while.

This time when the blue coats rushed towards us I didn't try to stop them.

7.

Someone was hanging around outside my apartment building when I got back from Mühlenstrasse at seven.

He was wearing a shapeless brown overcoat and a workman's cap against the chill evening. He was smoking a pipe, clasping the end between teeth that reflected the street light through his dark beard. He saw me and waved.

'Hello Tom,' he said, shoving himself off the lamp post he'd been leaning on. The voice did it.

'What can I do for you, Du Pont?' I asked.

'More a case of what I can do for you, I'd have thought.'

I wasn't too interested in Du Pont's favours. It was one of said favours that had got me into trouble over my non-existent Red Front contacts all those months ago, and right after the Prussian interior ministry had issued a blanket ban on all Red Front activities. All the excuse Ritter had ever needed to start spreading rumours.

'Still talking in riddles,' I said. 'Whatever it is, can't you find someone else to deal with it? I've been burned enough handling your information.'

Du Pont squinted at me. 'What happened to your face?'

I unlocked the front door, crossed to the mailboxes on the blue-and-white tiled wall. Du Pont followed me into the foyer. I unlocked my mailbox. It was empty.

'Popular as ever I see,' Du Pont said. He held the front door open and tapped out his pipe. Then he put the pipe in his hip pocket and let the door swing shut.

I ignored him and tramped up the wooden stairs opposite the mailboxes. The stairs creaked under my weight. Du Pont followed me up, the two of us creating a chorus of off-tempo creaks and echoes.

'Hey,' Du Pont said, 'don't think I'm not grateful for what you did for me. There's not everybody would stick their neck out for an informant the way you did. You know, a bombing –'

'What the hell do you want, Du Pont?'

We'd reached the top of the stairwell. At the end of the landing, beyond Effi Schneider's closed door, was my room.

'That's what I been trying to tell you, Tom,' Du Pont said. 'I'm looking to pay you back for protecting me the way you did.' He was a chubby man underneath his heavy proletarian clothes and he was out of breath from climbing the stairs.

I walked along the landing to my room, hoping Effi might be in so I could ditch this guy. Effi's apartment remained quiet as we walked by.

'You know, if you dropped all the faux proletarian duds you might be able to make it up and down stairs that bit easier,' I told Du Pont.

'Your concern touches me,' he said, removing his cap.

I put my key in the lock and the door swung open without my needing to unlock it. Ah yes, I'd forgotten about that. Seemed like Effi had too. The door crashed into the bedstead. I turned on the light and the bulb threw restless shadows around the room. I couldn't face tidying the mess, but if I didn't do it now then when would I?

'Ritter still taking it out on you?' Du Pont said. He tugged my arm. I shrugged him off. 'Let me take you out for a beer, Tom. You need it. I mean, look at you. Look at all this.'

I started picking out dirty clothes, throwing them onto the bed.

'As you can see,' I said, 'I've a few chores to do. I don't have time for your nonsense. I'm tired as it is. I've had a hell of a day.'

'Yes, up at Papendell, right?' Du Pont said.
I paused with my arms full of clothes.
'What did you say?'
Du Pont grinned. 'You heard me.'
'How did you know about that?'
'Let me buy you a beer and I'll tell you.'

8.

The bar was dark and warm, a welcome relief from the cool breeze sweeping the streets. Hints of cooking fat and stale beer permeated my swollen sinuses. We found a table in a corner away from the draught at the door. Someone came to take our order and Du Pont asked for a couple of Pilsners.

We made small talk until the beer arrived. That is, Du Pont made small talk. My mind kept wandering until I was seeing torn panties and blood-caked little faces everywhere. And Ritter, leaning back in the interview room needling me over withholding evidence when all he'd had to do was let me at Kürten from the start and then at least we could have found the girl earlier. At least that.

'So come on Tom,' Du Pont said, 'what did happen to your ugly mug? Is it anything to do with this St. Rochus church arrest yesterday?'

'Christ, Du Pont, is there anything you don't know?' No way was he getting anything out of me today, not after what had happened.

'You know, I often ask myself the same question. Great reporter that I am, I feel sad for everyone else that I'm so far ahead of the game.'

Du Pont was doing a good job of being the right guy to take my anger out on.

'Not forgetting, of course, that without you I probably wouldn't even be around any more,' he said.

The beers arrived and Du Pont drank half of his down. I couldn't face mine. I felt sick, had done ever since Vogel had driven me back to Mühlenstrasse from the Papendell meadows.

'How did you know I was in Papendell?' I said.

Du Pont put down his glass and wiped his lips with the back of his hand.

'Elementary, my dear Watson. First, the mud on your shoes is characteristic of the light loamy earth we get up there in the meadows this time of year.'

He paused to take another drink. I waited. He took longer over his drink than was strictly necessary and after a few seconds it occurred to me he was waiting for me to respond. I sipped my beer instead. He wanted something, so let him work for it.

'There's also this,' Du Pont said. He reached into an inside pocket of his coat – which he was still wearing despite the heat, though he'd unbuttoned it at least – and pulled out an opened envelope. He passed it to me.

The envelope was addressed to the editor at the *Volksstimme* and postmarked *Düsseldorf, 24.5.30.* I reached in and took out a folded piece of thick, waxed paper and smoothed it flat. It was covered in scribbles and sketches.

I turned it around and looked at it from several angles before I worked out it wasn't so much a series of sketches as a single sketch, a map. At the top was a wavy line drawn in pencil. Above the line the word *woods* appeared six times. Below the line was the word *field* scribbled twice. Between the second *field* and the wavy line above it was an *x*. Below that the word *meadow* was written three times above a thin double-line which seemed to represent the Papendell road and bisected the map from bottom left to top right. At the bottom left end of the pencil road were the words *Murder at Papendell*. Bottom right of the paper was another squiggly line surrounded with more cramped writing. I had to tip the paper to catch more lamp light so I could make out what was written there. The first part said, *In the place marked with a cross a corpse lies buried.* Under the squiggle it read, *The body of the missing Gertrude Albermann lies beside the wall of Haniel and Lueg.*

When I looked up, Du Pont was grinning.

'You realise you've just got me to smear my prints all over this evidence?' I said.

He waved away my protest. 'You know how many people have handled that at the office? Or perhaps what bothers you is the idea that the police lab might find *your* prints on there?'

He took the letter back and rubbed at it with a tissue he'd pulled from his pocket. I was too tired to think of stopping him. Besides which, he was right. If I insisted he left it for lab testing and the lab boys found one or more of my prints, I'd have the devil of a time explaining that one to Gennat.

'You know I can't talk to you about the case,' I said. I could see now where all this had been leading.

'I don't need to talk to you about this.' He put the folded sketch map back in the envelope and waved it at me. 'This is self-explanatory. Consider my showing you more of an advance warning.'

'But you can't publish the letter?'

'How could we not?'

'You'll cause out-and-out panic. Or anger. We haven't filed charges yet. The public might doubt whether we got the right man.'

'Tom, the anger is already there, due to *Kripo*'s piss-poor handling of the Ripper case thus far.'

'How does printing an inflammatory letter help the public good? And anyway why haven't you published it already? You must have received it yesterday.'

'We didn't get around to opening it until yesterday's final edition had gone out.' He paused. 'Do you know that under Comrades Lenin and Stalin the Soviets have come close to eradicating murder altogether?'

'Oh please.' I took a mouthful of beer. I couldn't feel any sicker, so bugger it.

'No, it's true. Under Communism, with more equitable distribution of wealth, there is no need to murder. Avarice and greed are things of the past. There you see mankind shed of the dehumanising effects of capitalism.'

I belched. My stomach ached, and the belch hadn't helped any. That beer wasn't sitting right. Nor was Du Pont, of course. Perhaps he was the problem.

'I see you haven't disputed the letter's contents,' he said.

'I thought you weren't going to pump me for information about that?'

He held up his hands. 'All right, all right. That's true. Let's not get all riled up over nothing. I want to talk to you about something else. The pattern of the Ripper's crimes.'

'What are you talking about?'

'It's the Albermann child's death that's the key, you see.'

'The key to what?' I was close to getting up and leaving.

'The key to a grave injustice.' He spoke over my groans of protest. 'No, Tom, not just the department's general systemic incompetence. I'm talking about a deliberate perversion of justice, for nothing more than convenience. And with dire consequences. Little Gertrude's murder for one.'

I stood up and riffled through my pocket for some cash. I didn't want this man paying for my drinks if all he was going to do was slander the department and implicate me along with it, or use the girl to try and get a story.

'It's Ritter,' Du Pont said.

I ceased riffling. 'What's Ritter?'

'This injustice I'm talking about. Ritter is the one responsible.'

I sat back down and waved away the waiter who'd come over to see what I wanted. Du Pont had something.

'Yeah,' he said, 'I thought that would get your interest. You heard of Johann Stausberg?'

I nodded. Not a case I'd had anything to do with, but his arrest and subsequent trial had hogged the headlines for weeks during the previous spring.

Du Pont went on with his lecture anyway. 'On the 9th February last year they found the body of that eight-year-old girl Rosa Ohliger. You remember that?'

'Hard to forget.'

'Right. Strangled then stabbed to death. Body burned with kerosene, right?'

I sipped more beer. Du Pont pulled out a tobacco pouch and filled his pipe as he talked.

'Then on the 13th February they found the corpse of Rudolph Scheer. Grabbed round the neck and stabbed to death. Both in the Flingern district, both attacked at night, both stabbed numerous times and both strangled.'

Du Pont gestured with his pipe to ask if the smoke would bother me. I shook my head and pulled out a cigar, thinking a smoke might help settle my stomach. Du Pont lit his pipe and then struck a second match for me.

'Okay, the third one was a prostitute killed at the end of February, yes?' I said through a cloud of my own cigar smoke. 'And Johann Stausberg was the guy the department put away for all three killings. That's where you're going with this? But Stausberg wasn't arrested until months later.'

Du Pont nodded. 'April, to be exact. He tried to strangle two young women with a rope. They survived to testify. Witnesses were involved. Open and shut. Then Ritter intervened and decided the strangling method was similar enough for him to try and close out the Ohliger and Gross murders, for which he'd been lead investigator.'

'Stausberg confessed to Rudolph Scheer's murder as well as Ohliger and Gross, if I recall.'

Du Pont snorted. 'Scheer wasn't even Ritter's case. That was just an added extra. As you no doubt also recall, Stausberg, besides being an epileptic with a temper and memory loss problems, is, and was, a half wit. I don't imagine it's very difficult for an experienced interrogator to get someone like that to confess to anything.'

So what? Ritter pushed a confession to clear his in tray? Nothing to get excited about yet. 'No comment,' I said.

71

Du Pont had more though, I knew he did.

Sure enough, he grabbed my arm. 'Then try this. Four months after Stausberg was arrested and put away in Grafenberg, two young girls, foster sisters, were killed in Flehe. You want to guess how?'

'Strangled and stabbed?'

'Right. And the afternoon of the very same Sunday on which the two girls are found, what should happen?'

Guessing games weren't my thing, but he'd got me by the nose now. 'Another murder?'

'Rape and attempted murder. Gertrude Schulte, a domestic servant, twenty-six. It was her afternoon off. She accepted the offer of a stranger to escort her to the outdoor market at Neuss. He was a pleasant enough looking chap, this man, name of Fritz Baumgart, only when they got to a meadow within hailing distance of the market place, this Baumgart forced Schulte to the ground and tried to get her panties off. When she resisted, he stabbed her. Thirteen times. She survived to give a description of her attacker. You know what Baumgart looked like?'

'I've a feeling I'm about to find out.'

'I've a feeling you already know. Neat oiled hair, a pencil-line moustache and a smart suit. Blue eyes and a tooth missing, here.' Du Pont bared his small, even teeth and pointed to his right upper jaw. 'Sound like anyone we know?'

'Kürten.' I flicked ash into the glass ashtray between us on the table. If Du Pont was right, then Ritter's forced confession had led to the prosecution of the wrong man and allowed Kürten to carry on killing. 'What's your point?'

'You know what my point is. I can see you've made the connection.'

'There's no proof linking Kürten to the murders this Stausberg is supposed to've done. Not in what you've told me, anyway.'

'Just tell me one thing,' Du Pont said, 'and I'll leave you

alone. How did the Albermann child die? Was she strangled and then stabbed?'

I blew cigar smoke at the ceiling.

'Before I say anything,' I said, 'are you going to hand that letter to the department after you publish tomorrow?'

Du Pont rolled his eyes. 'Come on, just tell me. Was she killed the same way?'

Finally, I said, 'You know I can't tell you anything about an ongoing investigation.' But I was smiling as I said it.

He smiled back and slapped my shoulder. 'That's all I needed.'

He left me alone in the bar and it was ten minutes before I realised what he'd done. Gennat hadn't released Kürten's name to the press yet, and Du Pont had got it out of me without my even noticing. Or maybe, and I was clutching here, maybe he'd got the name already from one of his other sources, and had just needed me to confirm it. Whichever way it was, I was in for a night of heavy indigestion.

9.

KILLER REVEALS SITE OF LATEST MURDERS, TAUNTS POLICE INCOMPETENCE

was the scoop that took up pages one, two and three of the Monday morning edition of *Volksstimme*, complete with a fuzzy reproduction of Kürten's sketch map and a lot of padding. My guest appearance came on page five:

HERO COP NAMES KILLER, BELIEVES JOHANN STAUSBERG INNOCENT OF MURDER

When even a hero is scared to speak out on wrongdoing within the police department, the people know something is rotten in Düsseldorf Kripo.

When that hero is Detective Thomas Klein, who, over the weekend, arrested the man police are naming as the mass-murdering Düsseldorf Ripper, the people know our legal system is corrupt indeed. And when colleagues can christen such a man 'Doubting Thomas' for his courage in voicing the truth behind closed doors, well, it makes you want to hang your head in shame.

But what truth could be so incendiary as to make a hero look over his shoulder?

Over a beer in a neighbourhood bar, Klein glanced furtively around before revealing the identity of the man he arrested on Saturday as forty-seven-year-old married man and Mettmannerstrasse resident Peter Kürten.

This Kürten is the man who mailed us his letter taunting the police and public over his abduction and killing of

74

five-year-old Gertude Albermann last Friday night.

Yet, unbelievably, the death of poor Gertude has brought to light an even more sinister secret.

'It's her death that established the pattern,' Klein told me, his eyes haunted with the prospect of being overheard and reported to his superiors.

'She was killed by a combination of strangling and stabbing, just as in the cases of Rosa Ohliger, Rudolph Scheer and Emma Gross back in February of last year. The method of killing is the same, but there's also the fact that Rosa Ohliger was eight. Even the most hardened killer will still balk at the prospect of murdering a child, so we have to consider the possibility that these cases are not separate, as we previously thought.'

The people of Düsseldorf are fortunate to have this brave champion of truth and enemy of capitalist corruption to speak for them. Unfortunately, few others in the police department share these traits with Detective 'Doubting Thomas' Klein.

For, as Klein went on to tell me, 'The problem is, many of those involved in the Ripper case now were involved in the previous murders, and they're not going to be keen to admit what a mess they made of things last year.'

Indeed, the people might even ask if the man arrested on Saturday was really the Ripper, as claimed.

For readers and other comrades with long memories will recall the similar fanfare that attended the arrest of poor Johann Stausberg. Police arrested this gentle giant and charged him with the aforementioned murders of Ohliger, Scheer, and Gross in April last year.

It was only by the narrowest of margins that Stausberg was judged mentally incapable of standing trial under paragraph fifty-one of the German criminal code, and sentenced instead to a term of enforced treatment at Grafenberg Mental Asylum...

Gennat tore the newspaper from my hand. Half the pages fluttered to the floor. Vogel stooped to pick them up as Gennat kicked over a couple of chairs.

'Why is there no space in this room!' he thundered.

No one answered him.

Ritter turned around from tacking a photograph of a set of house keys to the cork board. Blow ups of the unknown vic filled the space to one side of the city wall map, pics of Albermann the other. Two new red pins on the map marked the Papendell crime scenes.

A man I didn't know sat in the chair behind Gennat's desk. The man unbuttoned his double-breasted jacket and put on a pair of horn-rimmed glasses. He was middle-aged with a paunch and Brilliantined sandy hair surrounding a patch of shiny scalp at his crown. He'd been sitting there when I'd arrived.

Gennat reared back at me, nostrils flaring. I needed to get my retaliation in first.

'He told me he wanted to show me the letter, that was all.'

'What were you doing even talking to him in the first place?' Gennat shouted.

'I told you we couldn't trust him,' Ritter said, nodding at me before turning back to his photographs. 'Once a Commie bastard...' I wanted to take his little red pins and nail him to the cork board. If there was any truth to Du Pont's accusations, I wanted to do a lot worse, because it meant Ritter was responsible for Albermann's death after all.

Gennat loosened his tie and crossed to the window, leaning on the table beneath the window with its typewriter and coffee cups. He slammed his palm down and the whole table rattled. One of the cups fell to the floor. The handle smashed off and skittered away.

'Damn it man!' He whirled round to face me again. I stood at attention, pulling my shoulders back as far as they'd go. 'You gave him Kürten's name! Give me one good reason why I shouldn't have you drummed out of the department for this.'

Because you're a goddamned Berliner and don't have the authority? 'Because you need me to talk to Kürten again.'

'Do I? And why would I let you do that? What's to stop you leaking what he says to the entire bloody press corps?'

I took a gamble based on Gennat's public persona, guessing it was an inflated version of the kind of man he wanted to be: 'You want the case cleared up as soon as possible, all the questions answered. Because that's the kind of investigation you like to run.'

'You'll need more than flattery to get out of this mess,' Gennat growled.

'Look,' the paunchy stranger said, 'you know what these newspaper reporters can be like. Always looking to find fault. It's how they operate. Especially the Marxists.'

'Your point is?' Gennat said.

'My point is how easy it is to be fooled by these people.' Who the hell was this guy? My fairy Godfather?

Gennat pointed at me. 'He should never have spoken to the man in the first place.' He faced me. 'Did you really go for a beer with him, like it says?'

The thing about lying, of course, is to lie as little as possible. Easier to remember which lies you've told then.

'Yes,' I said. I hung my head and sighed.

'Oh, now he's hanging his head and sighing,' Gennat said to the stranger. 'He'll be saying how bloody sorry he is next.'

I swallowed down the apology I'd been about to make.

'I have a suggestion,' the stranger said. 'You'll have to call a press conference with the public prosecutor tomorrow anyway. The press are bound to ask about this.'

'Yes?'

'So put Thomas up there to tell them the truth himself. Which is that he never spoke to this man, never revealed the name, whatever you want him to deny. Won't that be penance enough?'

It certainly would. The thought alone was enough to shake my sphincter loose. My fairy Godfather was morphing into the Big Bad Wolf right before my eyes. I opened my mouth to say something.

Gennat spoke over me: 'Vogel, draft a wire to Dr

Scheikert. Get him down here, now. And I want approval before it's sent.'

I decided to remain standing. As it was, no one had invited me to sit. Despite that, the stranger was smiling at me. Did he know me? He drained the cup in his hand and put it on the desk, then leaned back and crossed his legs, took out a cigarette case and started toying with it.

Ritter said, 'We don't need someone to come all the way from Berlin.'

Gennat plucked an envelope from his desk. I thought at first it was the one Du Pont had shown me the night before, but this one was a different shape. Gennat brandished the envelope at Ritter. 'And how do you explain this?'

'We've received over a hundred letters since the beginning of the month. Never mind how many we've had over the last year...'

Gennat placed chubby fingers behind his ear. 'What was that, Ritter? Incompetence, you say?'

Ritter rolled his eyes. Gennat crossed the room in a couple of strides, his bulk sending stacked chairs squeaking across the floor boards until he and Ritter were nose to nose.

'And what do you think the papers would do if they found out our man had written to us months ago with the location of the mystery body? And not only had we done nothing to act on this information, we didn't even know we had it!'

'I'm not the one leaking to the press,' Ritter said. 'Chalk that one up to Doubting Thomas over there.' His lips twisted into a sneer.

Gennat removed his spectacles and rubbed the bridge of his nose. He smoothed the thin brown bristles on his upper lip.

'We don't know for sure whether Kürten wrote that letter.' Ritter pointed to the envelope still in Gennat's hand.

'That is precisely the point of requesting a handwriting expert, you imbecile!'

Ritter purpled. 'We have experts here who can do the job.'

Gennat stomped back to the paper-strewn desk where he deposited the letter. He clicked his fingers at me and pointed to the window. A look of pain crossed his face. I didn't know why he wanted it open, but I rushed to oblige. I flipped the catch and pushed at the window. The sudden breeze from outside rattled the blinds and teased loose papers off the table. We all watched them fall.

Gennat let loose a massive belch and then breathed deeply of the fresh morning air. Then, as though to prove the belch was a figment of everyone else's imagination, he went right on with the conversation: 'Scheikert's the best in the country and we don't have time to waste.'

Vogel came back into the room and handed Gennat the wire he'd drafted.

Gennat read it through in one continuous sigh as I tried to avoid looking at Ritter. The window blinds kept up their tap-tap-tapping, which didn't help my nerves any.

Gennat handed the wire back and said, 'Soon as you can please, Vogel.'

Vogel went. Gennat looked at each of us in turn. He settled on the Brilliantined stranger, who stopped fidgeting with his cigarette case. Instead he opened it and selected a cigarette, pocketing the case as he lit up.

'You've only done the Albermann autopsy?' Gennat asked.

The stranger exhaled with a nod. 'We're doing the second one this afternoon. If there are any further similarities I can take you through them.'

'All right, Berg,' Gennat said to the stranger. 'You say the scissors could be the murder weapon?'

Ritter grunted.

'Something to say, inspector?' Gennat glared through his spectacles again.

'The link with the earlier killings is purely circumstantial, Karl,' Ritter said to Berg. 'I grant you we have enough to link the scissors to the Albermann stab wounds, but to the others? That's a fourteen, fifteen-month gap. Bit naïve to want to put all this down to a single killer, isn't it?'

Wait a moment. Earlier killings? Did this mean Du Pont had been right?

'Which killings are we talking about, sir?' I said to Gennat.

Gennat ignored me, or else he hadn't heard. Berg was shaking his head at Ritter. He said, 'Stausberg's statements contained some serious gaps, Michael. I thought so at the time.'

'Funny, Karl,' Ritter said, raising his voice, 'you didn't choose to say so then!'

Berg shrugged and took another drag. 'Granted.'

'Anyway,' Gennat pointed at me, 'that's where Thomas comes in.'

'Sir?' I tried. Still no one responded. It was like I wasn't there. The mention of Stausberg was making my palms sweat. This was all a bit much at eight-thirty on any morning, never mind the morning after finding the body of a five-year-old in the long grass.

'Ritter, give Thomas the relevant files. And fetch that other damned letter from the lab when they're done with it. The one those *Volksstimme* bastards couriered over this morning.'

Ritter started to complain.

'Just do it!' Gennat ordered. 'Now!'

Ritter left the room.

Gennat turned to me. 'Your goddamned pal Du Pont has stumbled onto something, Klein. Kürten's modus operandi matches the three murders *Kripo* pinned on Johann Stausberg last year. Before you got here Berg was telling us that Stausberg's confessions contained some... questionable vaguenesses that didn't fit the forensics.'

He arched an eyebrow at Berg.

Vogel bustled into the room.

'Wire sent already?' Gennat asked.

Vogel shook his head. 'Herr Albermann's downstairs, sir, says he wants to talk to someone in charge.'

'Oh God, not that poor girl's father,' Gennat said.

Berg cleared his throat. 'Would you like me to speak to him?'

'I don't think the man came here for a lecture on stomach contents, Berg.' Gennat said.

'What do you want me to do with him?' Vogel asked.

Angry voices approached from down the hall. Then a door slammed somewhere out of sight.

One of the voices was Ritter's: 'And I'm telling you, Herr Albermann, that shouting is not going to get you anywhere.'

'That's easy for you to say,' the unseen man shouted, 'it wasn't your little girl he murdered.' The voice wavered. 'She'd still be alive today if you bastards hadn't gone and arrested the wrong man last year! You're the ones who left him free, free to roam, free to do those unspeakable things to my baby!'

'Vogel,' Gennat hissed, breaking the spell that had held us motionless, 'go and calm that down, will you?'

Vogel left and Gennat turned to me as the sounds of argument faded.

'You're going to read those reports and familiarise yourself with them.' Gennat came and put a warm hand on my shoulder, pulling me back to our discussion. 'Then you're going to see if Kürten will confess to the murders. I want you to ask about the letter to the *Volksstimme* too, find out whether or not he was the one who posted it. How long do you need to digest the material?'

'So you don't want to throw me off the department any more?'

'Don't push it, Klein. I can still put my complaint in once you're finished with him. Meanwhile you do exactly as I say. Now, how long?'

Full case files, including autopsies, incident reports,

witness statements and all the rest? I didn't want to rush it. There again, Gennat's face was still full of thunder. I reckoned he'd have a pretty clear idea of how long he expected me to take.

'About forty-five minutes?' I said.

'Don't be such a damned fool, Thomas,' Gennat said. 'No one can digest all that in forty-five minutes.' He looked at the wall clock, then checked his watch; he didn't even trust Düsseldorf to get its time right.

'Herr Kürten has an ID parade to attend. You can have an hour and a half. And once you've talked to the man about these Stausberg killings, you are going to sit quietly with the stenographer and you are going to check every statement Kürten makes against the evidence we have. We cannot afford any more mistakes on these Stausberg murders. If Kürten did them, we file charges. If he didn't, then Stausberg did, and that's what we stick to.'

'Sir, about this press conference tomorrow,' I said.

'Forget about the press conference tomorrow. Focus on Kürten today, then focus on getting the paperwork in order tonight. I want everything tied up before we see the PP in the morning, okay?'

Well what did that mean? Was I going to have to stand up in front of the press or wasn't I?

A knock at the door. Dry Scalp was there. Beside him stood a young woman with unfashionably long hair and blue eyes that slanted like a Chinaman's. She recognised me and waved.

'Fräulein Butlies, sir,' Dry Scalp said.

'Hello Maria,' I said.

Gennat looked from Butlies to me. Understanding lit his face and he smiled. 'But of course you two will have met. Silly of me to forget. Ready for the identity parade, my dear?'

'How are you?' I asked her.

She looked at Gennat. When he gave her a nod she turned back to me with a beaming smile and said, 'I have some work lined up next month. In a department store, even.' Her smile flitted away. Still, she had more colour in her face than she had the first time I'd interviewed her over Kürten's rape.

'That's great,' I said. 'Really. I hope it works out for you, Maria.' I took her hand. The fingers were cold. This was the woman who'd led me to Kürten. A department store sales job didn't seem like sufficient reward, especially now her rape was likely to be relegated to a footnote in light of Kürten's greater crimes. Perhaps at some point we could siphon off some of that reward money Kürten was so intent on his wife getting her hands on.

Gennat herded Butlies down the corridor, telling her there was nothing to worry about.

Berg stood and smoothed the wrinkles out of his trousers. 'First time dealing with the wrath of *der volle Ernst*?'

'Tell me, what are these similarities you were talking about? Between the Albermann murder and the Stausberg killings?'

He sighed. He'd disposed of his cigarette somewhere and now he removed his eyeglasses, folded them and tapped them against his teeth.

'You'll see it in my autopsy reports. Basically the stab wounds are so similar they could've been made with the same blade. The scissors you found in Kürten's rooms are a match for Albermann's stab wounds. The dimensions are the same as for the wounds in the Ohliger and Scheer murders. It's enough to try for a confession at least, I would've thought.'

'Could you confirm the cause of death?' I said. 'The Albermann case I mean.'

'The stabbing,' he said, looking out of the window. 'Internal haemorrhage.' He put his glasses in his breast jacket pocket. 'She was likely out cold by then though, which is as much consolation as we can ask for in a case like this.' He shook his head.

'And the time?' I said.

'Oh, well that's interesting.' He took out his case and lit another cigarette while talking, not bothering to look at what he was doing. 'The reports said she was last seen at a quarter to seven in the evening, right?'

'Right.'

'For lunch she'd eaten sauerkraut between twelve and one. For tea at four she ate a butter *brot* with applekraut and at around six she had some sweets and apples and such. In her stomach we found three hundred grammes of chyme, give or take.' His hands mimed the stomach contents, conjuring them from the air. 'Sauerkraut is not easily digested, as I'm sure you know, while bread is digested like so.' He clicked his fingers.

I cleared my throat. He focused on me and smiled, showing bright, even teeth. 'Well, there I go again. To cut a long story short, there was sauerkraut still in the stomach, but no bread. It takes three hours to digest a bread roll. If she ate her butter *brot* at four, then death occurred at least three hours later, but no more than six, after which the sauerkraut would have been gone too.'

'Seven p.m. on the night she went missing,' I said. 'But no later than ten?' So she'd been dead sixteen hours before I'd even met Kürten, if not more. All the delays in the world would have made no difference. But Ritter charging the wrong man with murder? Letting the real killer go free? Damn right that would have made a difference. I had to know whether Du Pont's claims were true, and Gennat was giving me the chance to find out.

Berg had another puff of his cigarette. Then he put on his hat and put out a hand. 'Well, I must be going,' he said. 'But before I forget. You found Albermann lying on her front with legs akimbo. You thought Kürten raped her, I shouldn't wonder. Well, I'm happy to say he didn't.'

'He didn't?'

'No, when I read your report and Michael's I assumed the same as you. But the microscopy shows no traces of semen, and my examination showed no signs of... forced entry. If you take my meaning?'

Ritter stormed into the room and dropped files on the desk.

'Karl, a word,' he said, and they entered the hallway. I sat behind the desk. Ritter and Berg stood whispering for at least a minute as I tried to browse the reports. Files on Johann Stausberg, Rosa Ohliger, Rudolph Scheer and Emma Gross. Ninety minutes to digest all that?

I couldn't decipher any of the whispers. Ritter sounded angry though. I kept my eyes on the paperwork. The whispers petered out and Ritter came back.

'I understand you'll be going through the transcripts with the stenographer afterwards,' he said.

'Yes,' I said.

'Good. I'm sure I can find somewhere suitable for you to do that.'

He was trying not to show it but he was scared. It was there in his tone and his bluster and his need to keep scoring points off me. He had every right to be scared. I was out to get him, and Kürten was about to help me do it.

10.

I entered the interview room and checked the time.
'Nine-fifty-two a.m., right?'
The stenographer nodded and started writing on his pad. Kürten's letter to *Volksstimme* was in my hand. I threw it down on the table.

'What the hell is this?' I said. Soften him up with it, then move on to the previous killings and see how he reacted. That was the plan.

Kürten looked at the letter and back up at me. 'I'd forgotten all about that.'

'No you didn't. I turned up at your Mettmannerstrasse apartment on Friday morning with Maria Butlies. You fled, went to see your wife and confessed to her. You say, so she could turn you in and claim the reward. At that point, lunchtime Friday, you'd decided to hand yourself over. It was just a matter of when and where.'

Kürten steepled his fingers in front of his smiling lips and cocked his head to show how very amusing this all was.

'A few hours after agreeing the details of your surrender with your wife, you abducted and killed Gertrude Albermann. You picked Albermann up at five p.m., killed her shortly after seven. *Volksstimme* received this letter in the mail on Saturday. There is only one delivery on Saturdays, in the morning, and the last collection on Fridays is at six p.m.'

'So what?'

'So you posted the letter before you killed Albermann but after you picked her up. Correct?'

Kürten's grin exposed his now-infamous incisors. Vampiric indeed. There were specks of food between his teeth. I didn't suppose that vampires were comfortable around tooth picks: too much like mini wooden stakes.

'How did you work that out?' he said.

'The letter mentions the girl by name. Either you'd planned to kill her for some time or you wrote and mailed the letter after you'd picked her up. I don't see you as the long-term planning kind.'

'I'm impressed, Thomas. No doubt you've also worked out it's my birthday today?'

'Let's stick to the point, shall we?'

'Well you are sour this morning. What's the matter, did my little practical joke yesterday upset you?' He mimed frantic retching.

'Why did you do it? This was a last hurrah, a last chance to get your jollies, what?'

'So now he wants to know why.' He spread his hands wide, preaching to the room. 'Why do anything?' He leaned forward in his seat. 'Seriously, I was about to be arrested. I needed something to help me say goodbye. You could even say that Albermann's death was your fault.'

I sat back. 'All right, we'll come back to Albermann. Right now I want to ask you about some earlier killings.' I lit a cigar.

'You know what Freud says about cigar smoking?' Kürten said.

'No. What does he say about men who masturbate over the corpses of little girls?'

'What are you talking about?'

'Rosa Ohliger.'

'Who?'

'Rosa Ohliger. The eight-year-old girl you killed on 8th February last year.'

'Who says I masturbated over her?'

'You don't deny murdering her?'

'No, I...' He rubbed the back of his head. His hair was all over the place today, and his stubble was beginning to crowd out his pencil-line moustache. He sighed. 'Rosa. I remember Rosa. I didn't know her name until the papers reported it a couple of days later.'

'She left her friend's house on Albertstrasse that evening. The family there were the last people to see her alive. Tell me what happened, in your own words,' I said. 'Be as specific as you can.'

'It was just after six that night. I picked her up outside St. Vincent's Church. We got talking. She said she wanted to go home.'

Okay, that fit the facts so far. 'Did she tell you where that was?'

'Langerstrasse. I offered to take her, and I led her down the Kettwiger Strasse as far as a hoarding –'

'She didn't notice you were leading her in the wrong direction?'

He smiled. 'It took until we got to the hoarding for her to notice.'

'Then what?'

'I seized her by the throat and put her on her back,' he said. Berg's autopsy report on Ohliger was still fresh in my mind. One sentence leapt to the fore: *Face bloated and livid, characteristic of forcible strangulation.*

'With my right hand I drew my scissors and stabbed the child in her left temple. And in the heart,' Kürten said. Berg again: *One stab wound in left temple... Thirteen stab wounds to the upper torso made through clothing. Cause of death internal haemorrhage resulting from one or more of five distinct stab wounds to the heart.*

'She seemed to be dead. I went back to my apartment and searched myself for blood stains.'

I held up a hand. 'Hold on, Peter. Ohliger was standing when you attacked her?'

'Yes. Then she went limp in my arms.'

'You stabbed her then?'

'Yes.'

'And you left her in the place where you stabbed her?'

'Well, not exactly, no, or the body would've been found straight away. I dragged her back two or three metres to the hedge under the hoarding. I dragged her with both hands, around the neck, like this.' He mimed the action. 'Her feet dragged through the snow and I covered the tracks as best I could.'

That tallied with the crime scene sketch and description Ritter had put in his incident report. One of Ohliger's shoes had slipped off and been trodden into the snow. Ritter's team had found it when searching the scene after the body had been found.

'Okay,' I said. 'You went back to your apartment after stashing the body under the hedge. You were saying you searched yourself for blood stains.'

He nodded. 'I also cleaned the scissors. There was no blood on my clothing so I went out to the movies.'

I drew deeply on my cigar and took my time exhaling.

'What was the feature?'

'I don't have a good memory for these new talkies. They pass me by, most of them. And, to be honest, I was still rather excited by the murder.'

Not too excited to spend two or three hours in a dark movie theatre. 'Which theatre was it?'

'That new one on Graf-Adolf-Strasse.'

'What time?'

'It was the seven-thirty show. I headed home at ten-thirty.'

Okay, something to check on later. It would turn up in the stenographer's notes, but I jotted it in my notebook anyway.

'What did you do then?' I said.

'When I got home I filled a beer bottle with kerosene. We have a kerosene lamp, you see.'

'Which brand?'

'Kerosene?'

'Beer.'

'Oh... it was an *altbier*. Schumacher.'

Another tick against the crime scene evidence. 'Okay, what then?'

Kürten chuckled. 'You know what then, detective.'

89

'I want you to tell me, Peter.' I pointed at him with my burning cigar.

'I went to the murder site with the aim of pouring the kerosene over the body and setting light to it.'

'But?'

'But what?'

'Something stopped you?'

He shrugged. 'Too many people about. I left the bottle propped against a fence and went back home. My wife was due back from work at that time, anyway.'

'So this would have been when?'

'Between eleven and midnight. I got back home by twelve-thirty and my wife got home at her usual time, ten past one.'

'So you didn't burn the body?'

'Of course I did. I went back the next morning.'

'This is now Saturday 9th February, correct?' I dropped cigar ash onto the floor.

'Correct.'

'What time?'

'I got up at six a.m. and told my wife I had to go to the WC. I ran quickly to the scene of the crime, found my bottle, poured the kerosene over the body and set it on fire. There and back didn't take more than five or six minutes.' Kürten tapped his finger on the table. 'I felt no sexual excitement and I did not touch the girl. I did not masturbate on the corpse, nor did I even touch the child sexually.'

'Uh-huh. So how come the lab found traces of your seminal fluid on the inside of her panties?'

'How do you know that was mine?'

We didn't, of course. Beyond an approximate time of ejaculation, and confirming the fluid was human in origin, the lab couldn't tell us anything. I blew smoke in his eyes. 'Peter, who walks past a young girl's corpse in the middle of a snow-bound night and smears cum on her private parts?'

'No,' Kürten said, shaking his head, 'I did it only to

cause excitement and indignation. I set light to her to increase the general indignation.'

'So you did masturbate?'

'No, I mean I did the murder to cause indignation.'

'Indignation?' I said. 'You make it sound so polite. What would you do to get people shitting their pants?'

'You tell me, Thomas,' he said. 'You seemed to find my little stunt yesterday quite effective in that regard.'

I rubbed my hands over my face. Coffee. It was time for coffee. I waved to get the stenographer's attention.

'Time for a break, okay?' I looked at my watch. 'Interview suspended at ten-thirty-five a.m.' I brandished the two letters. 'When I return, we're going back over the Albermann case and you can tell me more about these.'

Kürten smiled and tugged at his dirty collar. He scratched his shirt where it covered his stomach and I had no idea whether he was making fun of me or whether the scratch was genuine. I got up and headed for the door.

11.

The stenographer finished typing up the transcript. He tore it from the typewriter and handed it to me. Last one, thank God.

Q: Okay, we now move to the events of 28th February 1929.

A: You're being very demanding this afternoon, Thomas.

Q: We're almost done. Tell me when you met Emma Gross. And where.

A: All right, all right. She was there on the street corner, waiting for business.

Q: Was this the corner of Ellerstrasse and Vulkanstrasse?

A: Hey, that's right. Were you there too?

Q: What time was this?

A: I left my apartment at just after seven p.m. and headed for the central station.

Q: Why the station?

A: Where else do *beinls* hang out?

Q: You went looking for sex?

A: I went looking for a victim.

Q: Could you look at this photograph please.

A: Yes, that's her.

Q: What time did you meet her?

A: I don't remember exactly.

Q: Try.

A: Well it takes ten minutes to walk to the station from my street. Say quarter past seven. It was half past when we got to the hotel, I know that. There was a clock behind the checking-in desk, beside the pigeon holes.

Q: This is the Hotel Adler?

A: (nods)

Q: Please answer the question.

A: Yes, it was the Hotel Adler.

Q: Whose idea was it to go there?

A: I don't remember. It's the nearest hotel with rooms you can pay for by the hour, as far as I know.

Q: How many hours did you pay for?

A: I don't know. She paid. I suppose all that was included in the price.

Q: And how much had you agreed to pay for her services?

A: We hadn't got that far, yet. I think the idea was that we negotiate once we were in the room.

Q: What happened next?

A: She paid at the desk and took a key. She led me up to the top floor, the third. I don't remember which room, though, before you ask. She opened the door. I grasped her throat from behind before she got the chance to turn on the room light. I kicked the door closed. She didn't have time to cry out. I dragged her to the divan by the throat. She went limp and I drew my scissors and stabbed her in the side of the head and in the chest.

Q: Which hand did you hold the scissors in?

A: The right.

Q: You were holding her by the throat at this point?

A: Yes. I kept hold of her with my left.

93

Q: Was there a lot of blood?

A: I stabbed her, Thomas. What do you think?

Q: I'm asking you.

A: Are you upset with me?

Q: Just answer the question, please.

A: Look, I told you I was sorry about yesterday.

Q: The question.

A: I've forgotten. What was the question?

Q: When you stabbed Emma Gross, was there a lot of blood?

A: I'll say. It got on my hands. I had to wash them afterwards.

Q: Where did you wash your hands?

A: There was a bowl and water.

Q: Where was this?

A: On a dresser, or a night stand. I don't remember exactly.

Q: Did the blood get anywhere else?

A: I checked my clothes but I hadn't got any there.

Q: Any blood elsewhere in the room?

A: My dear Thomas, I had no idea you were so ghoulish.

Q: The question, please.

A: I don't remember. She bled over my hands when I stabbed her, so there must have been some. I don't know where.

Q: What happened next?

A: I left.

Q: Did you try to violate the body in any way?

A: No.

Q: You didn't try to remove her clothing?

A: I didn't touch her clothing.

Q: You didn't remove her overcoat?

A: Well, I might have done. Yes, as a matter of fact I believe I did. I don't really remember.

Q: So you left the hotel soon after?

A: As soon as I'd washed.

Q: And what time was this?

A: I don't know. I'm not sure how long I was in the room before I left.

Q: You didn't see the clock at the desk on your way out?

A: No. I didn't go back to the desk. I left as quickly as I could.

Q: These scissors that you used. Are they the same ones you used in the murders of Rosa Ohliger on Friday 8th February 1929, Rudolph Scheer on Tuesday 12th February 1929, and of Gertrude Albermann on Friday 23rd May 1930?

A: Yes.

Q: You're sure they're the same pair exactly? Not another pair of the same style or manufacture?

A: Yes, I'm sure. They were the same scissors.

Q: Okay, let's go back to when you entered the hotel.

A: What do you want to know?

Q: You say you hadn't negotiated a price yet?

A: That's true.

Q: Then how did she know how much to pay at the desk?

I'd pinned him on his lie with that last question. It was textbook stuff when you saw a gap in the story they gave you to let them run on and come back to it later when they were more likely to've forgotten what they'd said. Then you could nail them on the inconsistencies. He hadn't negotiated a price with a streetwalker and yet she parted with cash at the desk? Not in this town. How much more of this confession was bullshit?

I stretched the tension out of my aching shoulders and drained cold coffee from a chipped cup. We were alone in Records, me leaning on the administrators' desk with my back to the door, the stenographer perched between his typewriter at the end of the desk and a bank of filing cabinets that towered over us and blocked the room's two tiny windows. The only light in there was electric and inadequate and I'd lost track of time. My vision was blurring from having to read in the semi-darkness.

I got up and crossed to a stack of files on a nearby trolley, rooting through for the Emma Gross material. I couldn't find it. I gazed at the nearest shelves heaving with boxes of files and random-looking stacks of paper. Some of them were covered in dust. How many of these files had been touched in the last six months – the last year even? And how many cases, how many nameless victims, had been lost and forgotten about in this room, just because there hadn't been enough media pressure to save them from obscurity, from the endless pressure of the next crime to solve, the next victim to avenge, the next mystery to unravel?

'Hey,' I asked the stenographer, 'do you have the Emma Gross crime scene report there?' I realised I was clicking my fingers at him, realised too that was something I'd picked up from Gennat. He found the file and I stopped clicking my fingers. 'Can you read what it says about the body?'

The stenographer scanned the page. 'Here it is. *Corpse of white female found lying naked, face up on divan. Bruising around neck suggestive of ligature strangulation –*'

'Okay, stop there. Naked?'

'Yep.'

'Thought so. And ligature marks?'

'Yep. Look at the photos.'

I took the crime scene photographs from him and looked at them. Emma Gross, slack-faced and swollen-tongued, surely unrecognisable in death as the young woman she'd been while alive, reclining on the divan, back twisted too sharply for a living person. And naked as the day she was born, if less innocent. Her breasts sagged like empty purses above a chest whose ribs were visible through the skin.

I re-read the transcript in my hand. Two inaccuracies from Kürten. Three if you added the lie about Gross paying at the desk with her own money. That said, these were the only inaccuracies in four-and-a-half hours of cross-examination detailing five murders and Maria Butlies' rape. I gestured at the folder by the stenographer's shiny suit elbow.

'Is that Berg's autopsy report on Gross?'

'Yep.'

I opened the folder. Random phrases leapt out at me.

... *Cause of death asphyxiation from forcible strangulation with a ligature of at least five millimetres in diameter – increased vaginal secretions, facial discolouration and bruising to neck being characteristic symptoms...*

... *Stab wounds inflicted between thirty minutes and two hours post-mortem. Absence of spatter in crime scene description in relevant incident report supports this conclusion...*

'What does it say in the report there about blood spatter?'

The stenographer looked at his watch.

'Yes, okay, I'm tired too,' I said, 'but come on, this is important. Kürten's confession doesn't fit the facts.'

'What, you think he's making it up?'

'That's exactly what I think. I need to tell Gennat.'

'How can you be sure?'

I flicked back through the photos. Pictures of the chest wounds showed them as clotted but neat. Pictures of the

97

room showed no spatter, a pile of feminine clothes on the double bed. No sign of any night stand. There was a dresser but the photos didn't show a bowl or a water jug. Possible inaccuracy number three – or did that make four? My pulse beat loudly in my ears.

There was no telephone down in the basement, so I grabbed the Stausberg file and hightailed it up the stairs to the second floor where Gennat and Ritter were supposed to be briefing the night shift.

When I got there Gennat's corner office was empty, and so was the squad room next to it where they'd moved the map and photographs. I called out, 'Hello,' anyway, feeling a little foolish.

The telephone on Gennat's desk started ringing. I lifted the earpiece from the cradle and leaned down so my lips brushed the mouthpiece. Up close it smelled of stale sweat, or stale saliva, though I didn't want to dwell on that.

'Gennat?' I said.

'Hello? Michael?' said the voice at the other end of the line.

'No, it's Thomas Klein here.' For some reason, I'd put on a posh accent.

'Where's Ritter?' The voice crackled, but I thought I recognised it as Berg's.

'I'm fine, thanks Berg. How are you?'

'Is he there or isn't he?'

'If he was here I'd have passed him to you by now. What do you want?'

'I need to talk to him.'

'Well how's about I take a message?'

There came a sound like Berg was clearing his throat. I didn't know if that was him or interference on the line.

'Messages get lost.'

'Do you want to leave a message or not?'

'Okay, okay. Tell him we need to talk about Johann Stausberg.'

'What? Why?'

98

'Hello?' he said, the voice crackling again.

'Hello?'

'Hello? Can you hear me?'

'Yes I can hear you. Can you hear me?' I said.

'Of course I can hear you,' Berg said.

'Sounded like a bad connection just then. What's all this about Stausberg?'

'Well I really can't say. That's why I need to talk to Michael. I've a message from the director at the asylum that might have some bearing on the case with Kürten.'

'Where are you now?'

'At the morgue. I'm half way through our mystery woman.'

'Stay there. I'm on my way.'

12.

Ten jittery minutes on the city's tramlines with the Stausberg file gave me enough to think Du Pont had been right to blame Ritter but it didn't give me enough to knock the good inspector off his perch.

2.4.29: Stausberg attacks sixteen-year-old Erna Penning. Throws rope around neck. She fights him off. Later IDs him from photo as her attacker.

3.4.29: Stausberg attacks thirty-year-old Frau Flake on her way home from work. Throws rope around neck and drags into the bushes. Couple of witnesses disturb Stausberg, who runs off. Flake lives to testify.

5.4.29: Stausberg brought in: twenty-years-old, blond, broad-shouldered, one metre ninety centimetres tall, hare lip, speech impediment, and a history of epilepsy involving angry outbursts and memory loss. Confesses. Flake witnesses ID him from line-up. Charges of assault filed with public prosecutor.

So far, so competent. But then along came Ritter:

7.4.29: Stausberg transferred to Mühlenstrasse. Ritter takes over and interrogates suspect re: open murders of Ohliger, Scheer and Gross. Stausberg confesses and Ritter files murder charges with PP.

No wonder Ritter'd been so hostile that morning: solid case until he'd got hold of it. All the mistakes had been his. This was getting good.

I read Stausberg's statement on Emma Gross:

I had gone to the station to look for work. A woman was walking in front of me. She was a whore, I could tell by her clothes. That made me angry and I wanted to hurt her. I snatched at her. She said we should go to a hotel she knew nearby. I agreed because then I could attack her in private. We went into the room and I strangled her. It was dark. We hadn't put the light on. She was naked. I gripped her breast and stabbed her first in the head. Then I went on stabbing. I stabbed into the heart.

When the woman was lying on the divan I didn't stab any more. That is quite certain. That is not a lie. Then I listened a bit, to see if she was still breathing. And then I left her lying there. I went home. At home I washed the blood from my coat. My mother asked me where the blood came from. I said from my nose.

The next day my mother read about the murder in the papers. That evening she asked me whether I had done it. I answered, "Yes, I certainly did it". My mother told me to keep my mouth shut.

I checked the date and time on the statement: taken by Michael Ritter at ten-thirty a.m. on the 7th April 1929. I flicked to the statement of Stausberg's mother, again taken by Ritter at headquarters, this time on the 9th April. Every false move bearing Ritter's signature. Better and better. I skipped to the relevant part:

He came home around midnight that night. He woke me up when he entered the apartment. I went to the kitchen. He was washing his coat in the sink. I saw the water in the sink was red with blood. I asked him where the blood had come from. He said he had had a nose bleed. I thought nothing of it until the next day when I saw the reports of the murder in the press. Johann can be such a violent boy. I have seen his terrible temper before. When I came back from work I asked him if he had done the things in the newspapers and he looked at me and said, 'Yes, I did it'. I will never forget the moment he told me that. I panicked. I told him to keep it to himself, not to tell anyone, and to try and forget all about it. But he couldn't do that. He couldn't fight his restless spirit inside and he attacked again. That's when I knew I had to reveal what he'd said.

Well that tore it. His own mother's testimony supported Ritter's case. And yes, Stausberg's confession was vague: no mention of strangling, and more blood than the crime scene photos allowed for. But it was plausible because of his epilepsy and his bad memory. I checked my notes again. The file also confirmed what Du Pont had said about the boy's epilepsy and quick temper. Maybe Ritter hadn't forced a confession at all. Maybe Stausberg really had killed Emma Gross and then decided to lay claim to a couple more murders for good measure.

The only way to know for sure would be to talk to Johann Stausberg myself.

***

I pushed through a set of heavy double doors, wood sheathed in steel. Beneath an oversized anglepoise lamp, Berg had his forearms immersed in the open chest cavity of his autopsy subject. Beside him was a steel trolley for his instruments. Behind him, two white-sheeted bodies lay on steel racks stacked like bunk beds against the tiled wall.

Berg looked up from the corpse on his slab and peered from under his horn-rimmed glasses. He grinned when he recognised me.

'Just in time. Here, put some of these on and give me a hand.' Berg gestured at a glass jar filled with thin rubber gloves. I approached the stainless steel slab, my shoulder brushing the bucket of the grocers' weighing scales that hung from the ceiling. The chill of the room emphasised the hot pounding in my head. I had to get him to reveal what the asylum director had said.

'Where is everybody?' I said.

'Been working since six o'clock this morning so I sent them home.'

'What about you?'

'Talc is on the shelves there,' Berg said. He took hold of a scalpel and dug back into the chest cavity.

I made some space for the Stausberg file on the nearest shelf and took gloves from a jar. I powdered them with talc and pulled them on.

'Here,' Berg said. 'Hold this.' He handed me a sac of rubbery flesh. 'Empty it into that.' He pointed to a steel bowl beneath the curved water tap at the slab's raised end. 'So, did you get anywhere with Kürten?'

I upended the sac over the bowl. A thick substance with the consistency of tar dripped out.

'No, you have to squeeze it.' Berg mimed something like milking a cow. 'Gently though.'

I held the top end with one hand and squeezed down the length of the sac with the other. Air rippled out with a flatulent rasp. Now I was glad of my blunted sense of smell. More liquid came out, along with a damp grey lump.

'Hmmn.' Berg prodded the lump with the blunt end of his scalpel. 'You mind taking a few notes for me on this?'

I didn't mind doing anything that would take me away from squeezing crap out of human organs. 'How much do you remember of the Emma Gross murder?' I said.

'A great deal, given that I re-read my report this morning before going to see Gennat. Has Kürten told you when he killed this one?' He tapped the contents of the steel bowl. 'We're going to struggle with this.'

The corpse's skin bore a pale waxy sheen dotted with brown blotches. The head wasn't attached to the spine of course, thanks to me, and it seemed to loll on the table. Berg had removed the top of the skull and emptied the cavity and I took a sharp breath at the sight.

Berg chuckled. 'Don't worry about it, Thomas. I've seen officers of the law commit worse acts of disrespect than yours.'

'Seems well preserved,' I said, ignoring his little joke. 'Kürten said she'd been in the ground since last summer.'

'It's the loamy earth, mostly. Lack of air, lack of worms. Slowed decomposition no end. Also, you see this wax-like texture to the skin? Adipocere. It's an effect produced by certain bacteria that break down the tissue. Converts all the fatty acids to this.' He chuckled again. I wondered what he was laughing at, then decided it probably wouldn't help to know. 'Helps us by preserving the wounds as though they were made yesterday. Which reminds me: what's the good word on time of death?'

'Seven-thirty p.m. on Sunday 11th of August last year,' I said. 'Give or take ten minutes.'

'Hmmn.' He prodded the bowl contents some more. 'I should have said later than that. Oh well,' he put down his scalpel, 'the limits of science.'

He took the flaccid flesh sac from my unresisting fingers and laid it over the steel bowl. I took off my gloves and pulled out my notebook and pencil. I also let out the breath I hadn't realised I'd been holding.

'Now, as I've mentioned the wounds, let's start with them. Three stabs in the left temple. These penetrated the skull, here and here. The stab nearest the front here also pierced the brain.' He paused. 'Come on Thomas, move in closer or you won't see it all.'

'I can see fine from here thanks, doctor.'

He shook his head, then picked up his scalpel and pointed with it. 'The neck was trickier, given your enthusiasm with the spade. But, as far as I can reconstruct it, this group of seven stabs is pretty superficial. In the breast there are ten wounds. Two penetrated the heart, two the pleurae. You see, there in the lungs?'

I nodded and cleared my throat.

'I cannot, of course, prove throttling in this case, but these stab wounds and those of Albermann are alike. Stabs in the left temple in both cases. In the skull we see the same wedge-shaped forms showing a blade with a broad back. Or,' he looked up and smiled, 'as we know from your search of Kürten's apartment, a large pair of

104

house scissors. These wounds are consistent with the stab patterns I noted in the Ohliger and Scheer cases. Did Kürten say anything about those?'

'He confessed, if that's what you mean. Gave us enough detail not to doubt his word.'

'Oh dear.' He straightened up and scratched his chin with a gloved hand, smearing brown mucus on his jaw. He sniffed. 'So Stausberg was innocent after all.'

'I wouldn't bet on it,' I said.

'What do you mean?'

'The Emma Gross murder. Kürten confessed to it, but he got several details wrong. Just stuff from the papers dressed up the way he thought we wanted it.'

If the asylum director had revealed anything about Stausberg's involvement in the Gross murder, Berg wasn't letting on. He took off his gloves and threw them into a waste bin. 'I need a cigarette. Coming?'

He ushered me out of the room. The warmth of the hallway after the autopsy room made me flush and I yawned. Berg leaned against the wall. He pulled cigarettes from a pocket hidden under his apron, used his lighter to get one going, then offered me the case. I shook my head.

'Please yourself,' he said. 'What about the fingerprint they found at the scene?'

'Fingerprint?'

'Yes,' Berg said, 'the one on the back of the divan. Didn't you compare it with Kürten's?'

What fingerprint? Damn it, that must have been in the part of the crime scene report I hadn't got around to reading. 'I haven't done it yet,' I said.

'Well, you might want to proceed with that first. It didn't match Stausberg.' He shrugged. 'Of course, it's probably nothing. I mean, a hotel room, dozens of people in and out in the course of an average week, could have belonged to anyone. But it's got to be worth ruling out.'

He sniffed his hand, then examined his fingers. I pointed at his jaw. He wiped some of the brown mucus away and stared at his fingers with a furrowed brow before using a pocket handkerchief to clean himself.

'You said on the phone that the asylum director called?' I prompted.

He shook his head. 'I called the director. We've been friends since medical school. After realising Stausberg might have been innocent of a good few of the crimes laid at his door, I was curious to see how he was getting on. With his treatment, you see? Dr Glauser told me Stausberg was beginning to open up in the most extraordinary ways.' He was fidgeting with his cigarette case and lighter, just as he had in Gennat's office that morning.

'What about?'

One of the lights in the ceiling flickered and died. The door at the end of the hallway opened and an overweight woman shuffled in with a mop and bucket. She adjusted something at bosom height and then slopped brown water over the tiled floor. I moved so I was standing facing Berg with my back to the woman. Berg folded his handkerchief.

'What about?' I said again.

Berg's eyes slid to the approaching woman.

'I can't tell you.'

'*Gott in Himmel*, Berg –'

'Because Dr Glauser wouldn't tell me.'

'So how do you know how important it is?'

'You don't know the director as I do. Glauser does not get excited. Not like that. It was extraordinary. The good doctor suggested that a detective interview Stausberg as soon as possible, was quite insistent on it being so soon, in fact. Said it would have a bearing on Stausberg's case. I took that to mean that it might also have some bearing on this Kürten business, but I can't say for sure. Patient-doctor confidentiality precludes the director revealing anything more without Stausberg's consent, but Glauser seems to think Stausberg has got to the point where he might also open up to a policeman given the right circumstances.'

'Can you get me in there?'

'Mmmn?'

'Instead of Ritter. Would you put in a word with the director for me?' If I was going to make this work for me I needed to find out from Stausberg whether Ritter had faked or forced the confession. Get it from the half-wit's mouth, so to speak.

'I don't know, Thomas. Michael handled the Stausberg case originally. Wouldn't it be better for him to deal with this?'

'You know how busy Ritter is with Kürten right now...'

The cleaning woman was humming a tune. She came by and mumbled a good evening in our direction. We mumbled it back at her. She saw Berg tap cigarette ash onto the floor. She mopped it, shaking her head and mumbling something we weren't meant to catch, and didn't. She shuffled a little further down the corridor.

Berg glanced at me. 'Look, I'll think about it, but I can't promise anything, okay?' He flicked more ash on the floor. 'On a lighter note, are you going to be performing at the press conference tomorrow?'

'Gennat didn't confirm it either way.' *No thanks to you*, I wanted to add. 'You going?'

He gestured back to the autopsy room and made a sad face.

'I'll tell you all about it if you let me speak to Dr Glauser,' I said.

Berg laughed. 'You don't give up easily do you? Do you promise I can trust you? I mean, this Red Front issue...'

'A misunderstanding.'

'You sure? After all the trouble with the newspaper this morning?'

I crossed my heart. 'Hope to die,' I said.

'Let's not tempt fate.'

Berg finished his cigarette, looked around and saw there wasn't anywhere he could put the butt without setting the cleaning woman off muttering some more. He pinched it out between thumb and forefinger and tucked it into his cigarette case.

'You going to help me finish up?'

'Why not?' I said, and followed him back in to the autopsy room.

13.

The wind had got up again and I had grit in my eye by the time I rolled up to the front door of Grafenberg Asylum. It was nine a.m., or near enough as made no odds. The cloud cover overhead was so thick the dawn hadn't broken through. A whole day of murk threatened. It was like a metaphor for something. My nagging headache, probably.

I'd spent all night worrying over what to do if Stausberg said he really had killed Gross. It wouldn't stop Ritter being to blame for the Albermann girl's murder, but I could kiss goodbye to any disciplinary action unless he had actually forced Stausberg's confession. Was I really keeping my fingers crossed so's I'd be able to bring down a brother detective? Talk about a stupid question. Now I just had to hope Stausberg was ready to talk after all.

The building itself was all clean lines and red brick, three storeys high – four if you counted the circular windows in the roof space. This wasn't the first madhouse I'd been to in the course of my duty and yet I couldn't shake off my disappointment that it wasn't some creaking Gothic pile. Flocks of songbirds filled the sky, unable to find perches in the wind-blown woods behind the building.

I walked up the small flight of stone steps to the front door. Then I knocked and settled in for a wait. I rubbed at the grit in my eye, agitating the bruising and causing tears to roll down my cheeks. The door opened immediately. It didn't creak open on rusty hinges and the man who opened it turned out not to be a stunted hunchback with a squint.

'Detective Klein?' the man said. His eyes were pale and startling beneath dark brows.

'How did you know that?' I said, extending my ID. I blinked and that grit was still there, lodged at the side of my eye.

He took the ID and looked at the picture, then at me, then back at the picture.

'Hmmn,' he said, stroking his recessed chin, a white space on his ring finger. Was he a widower? Or did the orderlies have to remove all such items for security reasons? 'You seem taller in your photo.'

I must've looked puzzled because he laughed.

'Just joking, detective. How could I get your height from a photo of just your head and shoulders?' And he laughed some more.

'No,' I said, 'quite.' Dear God, perhaps this was an inmate run amok.

He reached for my left shoulder with a thick arm clad in starched white cotton. The sleeves were too short and dark arm hairs matted his wrists and the backs of his hands. He pulled me inside and shut the door. He released me and I blinked at the dark wooden staircase and hardwood flooring in the entrance hall. I jumped when the door locked behind me, turning as the man pulled a set of keys from the lock. The keys were attached to a large ring that hung from a short chain clipped to his belt. His trousers were made of starched white cotton too, and they billowed some way short of his ankles; his shoes of cracked leather and white socks completed the ensemble. I didn't think much of his tailor.

He returned my ID. 'I expect you'd like to see the director?'

I said yes and he led me off to the right, through a series of thick doors, each of which he unlocked with a separate, numbered iron key from the ring on his belt. The third door bore a sign consisting of a white-painted letter P on a black background.

'For the Placid Ward,' the hairy man told me as he held

it open. He was wearing a name badge of some kind, but I couldn't make out the name on it.

Music filled the hallway beyond. Disinfectant fought its way through my swollen sinuses and left a chemical tang at the back of my throat. Dust balls gathered in the joins between the floor and the papered walls. I pushed at the paper with my fingers. It was soft, thick and padded. A little further along, dark red splotches clung to the paper and glistened in the hallway light.

'Hmmn,' my companion said. He rubbed a forefinger through the nearest splotch and licked the end of his finger. 'Strawberry. Looks like they've finished breakfast.' Now that he'd said that, one of the red marks resembled a human hand. I hoped I wasn't about to walk into a food fight.

We rounded a corner. Here the music was louder: a floating waltz-time ditty. Its gentle swell pulled a yawn out of me.

The tall man knocked at the nearest open door. I couldn't see past him to get a look at what was going on inside, but this was where the music was coming from. A short bespectacled nurse came out into the hallway. She was dressed in starched white cotton too. She smiled, exposing yellow teeth between deep red lips as she patted the bun of silver hair at the back of her head. She wore no earrings but the ear I could see had been pierced and allowed to heal over.

'Our visitor?' she said to the hairy man. The woman came and shook my hand. She wasn't wearing a name badge and she caught me looking at her bosom to ascertain that fact. I blushed. Her face wasn't lined, but the skin was dry and chipping off, like old paint. I found myself wondering what Berg and I would find in this woman's stomach should fate lead her to his dissection slab.

'You don't like what you see, detective?' she said.

Shit, I must've been curling my lip. 'Oh God, no, it's not that,' I babbled. 'I see you don't wear a name tag.'

111

'Oh, so that's what you were looking at. I wonder, detective, whether I should be relieved or offended?' Her lips retracted further, showing more of those even, stained teeth. The hairy man let loose with one of his laughs.

'Is Dr Glauser in there?' I glanced at the room the nurse had just left.

'Not at the moment.'

'Where is he?'

'He is standing right in front of you, detective,' the woman said. 'Or rather, she is. I'm sorry, it was *Detective* Klein, wasn't it?'

I wished she'd stop using the word 'detective' so much. She didn't have to make fun of me.

'Oh yes,' the hairy man piped up, 'I've seen his ID and everything. He's shorter in real life.' Again with the laughter.

Dr Glauser touched my arm.

'Karl didn't mention that I was a woman, did he?' she said. The corners of her grey-blue eyes crinkled and softened her features. I noticed the plain gold band on her third finger, the deep red of the fingernails.

I shook my head.

'That's Karl. Never changes. If it doesn't come out of the human gut he doesn't know what to do with it. We're nearly finished in here, then we'll all go to my study, all right? Is something troubling you, by the way?'

'It's nothing.' I'd been rubbing my belly – or, rather, the patch of shirt that covered the scar on my belly – without noticing. 'Comes and goes.' Now that I took my hand away the hot needle began to return, though it was more of a background nagging for the moment.

She nodded as if she understood, her eyes giving nothing away while her smile verged on the smug, a hint of *whatever you say, 'Detective'*. That was how it was with those head doctors, all that Freudian hocus pocus. You couldn't win. A regular doctor says you're ill then you're ill, no argument from me. But a head doctor? They say you're ill and you disagree then you're still ill, but now you're in denial too. What chance does a normal man stand against that kind of *arsch*-about-face logic?

She turned to go back into the room and I got a look at her other ear. This lobe was torn, as though an earring had been pulled out through the skin some time before. I followed her into the room. Men and women dressed in everyday clothes were twirling across the grey carpet. A few couples danced arm-in-arm. Most danced in splendid isolation, bumping and bashing into others or writhing on the spot.

'Occupational therapy,' Glauser whispered. I put my hands in my pockets and kept them there – tried to move as little as I could. Damned if I was going to have her size me up as a potential new inmate.

A long trestle table lined the nearest wall, heaped with plates, slices of different breads and pots and jars of various spreads, along with slices of cheese and cold cooked hams.

Between the trestle table and the door, a small man in a faded suit and high collar hovered above the phonograph. Now I was close to the machine, the music had a rushed quality to it, as though the handle had been overwound. I shuddered.

Beneath the electric chandelier in the centre of the ceiling, I thought I spotted Stausberg dancing, his long arms held stiff at his sides. Straight blond hair covered his forehead and eyes, though it wasn't long enough to cover the hare lip mentioned in his file, or to disguise his girlish peaches-and-cream complexion. There were twenty inmates in the room, all told. None of the other nineteen matched Stausberg's description. None of the others was tall enough or broad enough, either. The wriggling man had to be him.

'What's he doing?' I asked Glauser, pointing at Stausberg.

She wrenched my finger down.

'Don't point, please,' she said. 'Many of the patients find it intimidating.'

113

Patients? Like it was a normal hospital or something. But no, the windows to this room had bars on the outside. These were inmates, all right, whatever the good doctor wanted to think.

'He's letting out his feelings for the day, is what he's doing,' the doctor said. 'We let them express their dreams or their fears, or whatever it might be. It's good exercise, and sometimes it helps with treatment.'

The record on the phonograph spun itself out. The man hunching over the machine removed the needle arm with a scratch and the inmates stopped dancing. That is, most of them did. Some kept on going, dancing no doubt to the tunes in their heads. Stausberg was one of those.

Glauser strode further into the room and clapped her hands.

'Okay,' she said, 'therapy time is over. I will catch up with you all later.'

The inmates didn't seem thrilled at the prospect and I didn't blame them. More men in white coats came to life from positions dotted about the room, going and laying guiding hands on the more intransigent dancers.

Glauser approached Stausberg and said something to him. I was too far away to hear what it was, but he smiled and came along with her. When he saw me his blue eyes widened and he covered his mouth with his free hand. It wasn't enough to cover the wisps of hair on his baby-smooth chin.

'Hello Johann,' I said.

He mumbled something in return, and we all trundled back the way I'd come, back through the three sets of doors and across the entrance hall to the doctor's study, the hairy man locking each door behind us.

The study was small but high-ceilinged, and hot from the blazing fire in the grate. The doctor led Stausberg to one of two low armchairs facing her desk. He curled into it, shrinking as he pressed into its red leather skin.

Stausberg whimpered when Glauser went to shut the door so she left it open. She came back and settled on the arm of Stausberg's chair, gesturing for me to take the other. I pulled out my notebook and pencil and tried to make myself comfortable. I was sweating already, even with the door open.

'Please loosen your collar if you wish,' Glauser said. 'We don't stand on ceremony here.'

I didn't fancy being accused of sexual repression or similar, so I loosened my neck tie and undid my top shirt button. I also opened the top two buttons on my waistcoat for good measure. Clocks ticked in endless succession. I turned. On the mantelpiece above the fire stood six or seven clocks of differing manufacture. Each clock face showed a different time. I wondered how it was they didn't warp with the heat.

I leaned forward, wanted to get done and get out of there.

'Doctor,' I said, 'you telephoned Karl Berg yesterday. When was this?'

Glauser hesitated. 'Around four-thirty in the afternoon.'

I made a note. 'You had interesting news for him,' he said. 'Something exciting.'

She shuffled on her perch. 'That's true. Something from Johann.'

She patted the man-boy's hand and nodded at me.

Stausberg took a deep breath. 'He told me.' He slurred his words as a drunk might, taking time and trouble over the consonants.

'Told you what?' I said. 'That you'd killed Emma Gross? Or what to say to pretend that you did?'

Stausberg crossed his arms and harrumphed up at the doctor. He slid deeper into the armchair.

'Now, Johann, Detective Klein is only trying to help. But you have to tell him. You know I can't.'

Johann took another breath. 'Those women!'

'The women told you?' I said.

He blew a raspberry. His tight hare lip didn't move. For a guy who didn't like people looking, he seemed to be doing his best to draw it to my attention.

'Johann!' Glauser tapped the man-boy's elbow.

He sat up and uncrossed his arms.

'Johann,' I said. His eyes met mine. Great, empty pools, they were. 'Are you talking about Rosa Ohliger and Rudolph Scheer and Emma Gross?' I'd spoken as slowly as I could, the way I'd done once to some French captives during the war. Stausberg nodded. 'I need you to tell me the names,' I said.

'Just those women,' he sighed. He was fidgeting, his face getting redder with every word.

I softened my voice. 'Do you remember Emma Gross?'

'He told me,' Stausberg repeated.

'Told you what?'

'What to say!' he shouted. 'He told me what to say!'

'Do you mean your confessions?'

He was trembling now.

I threw Dr Glauser a look, sweat running in greasy rivulets down my neck. More sweat beaded in my eyebrows and threatened to spill down my face.

'Johann,' I began again, 'do you remember telling the police where you picked up Emma Gross?'

He grunted and shook his head. *Gott in Himmel*, was he capable of remembering anything? Names, times, places?

'Do you remember when she died? Or where?'

'I told you!' he cried.

'Did you kill Emma Gross?'

His head jerked to the left, hair spilling over his face as he lurched out of his chair and fell onto my lap, teeth chattering, body shaking, throat groaning.

'Oh no,' Glauser said. Then, shouting: 'Heinemann!'

'Did you kill her?' I shouted. 'Did you kill Emma Gross?'

I was too late. Stausberg was too far gone in his seizure. My crotch was getting damp from the drool spilling from his contorted lips. The skin on the back of his neck was fever-hot, but that could have been the temperature of the room. His teeth chattered and clacked

116

together. I tried to push my pencil between them to stop him biting my fingers – or anything more vital for that matter – but his mouth wasn't opening wide enough.

Glauser rose from the arm rest as the hairy man rushed into the room and reached for Stausberg's shirt front. Stausberg shouted and squirmed and his eyes rolled back. The shaking racked up several notches, became seismic. He slipped out of the hairy man's arms. The hairy man bent down, took hold of Stausberg under the armpits and dragged him from the room.

Glauser helped me to my feet and then crossed to the door.

'Take him to the baths!' she called. 'And for God's sake be careful! I'll be checking for bruises.'

I sat back down in my armchair, the pulse high in my throat. I had a muscle spasm in my left thigh and I couldn't shake off the urge to jiggle my feet, so I got up and paced. I also hoped the walk in the warm room would dry my crotch that bit quicker. I didn't fancy spending the rest of the morning looking like I'd wet myself.

Stausberg wasn't capable of the murder confessions he'd signed back in April 'twenty-nine, much less the murders themselves. Another point to Du Pont. According to the file, no one but Ritter had interviewed Stausberg over the murders. Who else but Ritter could have told the cretin what to say? Who else could have got fake confessions out of him? And why do it? Public pressure to solve the murders? Laziness? Incompetence? I was plumping for some combination of all three.

Glauser's face had flushed. She went and sat in her desk chair and fanned herself with one hand while she used the other to scratch at her ruined ear lobe.

'Who told him what to say, doctor?' I said.

'I can't...' What she couldn't do was finish her sentence. She switched to a different one. 'I'm sorry, detective. Clearly it was too soon for this. I should have seen it. So stupid of me.'

I leaned on the desk, trying to intimidate her.

'Doctor, do you know who told him what to say in his confessions?' It had to be Ritter. It had to be him. *Just confirm it, damn you.*

She paused. It was a long pause. 'No.'

I slammed the desk, Gennat-style. 'Come on, woman!'

'Detective, I am the director of this asylum. Stausberg is my patient and I am his doctor. I cannot reveal what he tells me in confidence without his express permission.'

'You can. You just won't, is all.'

'All right then, I won't. Betraying his confidence would be detrimental to his therapy.'

'Stausberg's a paragraph fifty-one. He's spending the rest of his life here if he has to. I don't think the extent of his therapy is of great concern to the public.'

Glauser stood and removed a ledger from the top drawer of her desk.

'Could you sign this?' she said, not meeting my eye.

She dipped a fountain pen in a pot of ink set into the desk, and handed me the pen. She opened the ledger on a blank page: columns for names, addresses, times in and out. A visitors' book. I flicked back a few pages too far and the name *Frau Stausberg* caught my eye. I turned the pages one at a time to get to the one I needed to sign, looking for how many more times the name came up. Glauser intervened and turned the pages for me. Then she kept her hand there to stop me flicking back. She was too late though. I'd found what I wanted. I signed my name and glanced at the clocks on the mantelpiece.

'Do you have the correct time?'

'Ten-thirty,' she said, without hesitation.

I wrote it down. My left shirt cuff was frayed where I rested it on the page. 'Look, doctor, please, if there's any-thing...'

'I'm sorry, detective. I...'

'You don't think it would help Johann for the truth to come out? He's here because of confessing under duress to crimes he didn't do. I know he didn't murder Rosa Ohliger or Rudolph Scheer, because we just caught the man who did. And I don't think Johann killed Emma Gross either. Don't you want to help him?'

She shut the ledger and laid it on the desk before escorting me to the front door. I'd taken no more than a couple of paces outside when the door locked behind me. I could hear it even above the wind and the hacking crows and the restless songbirds.

Still, the grit in my eye had gone. And now I had another reason to interview Stausberg's mother. Not only had she corroborated his phoney confession, but the flipped pages in the visitors' book had gone back two or three weeks and her signature had appeared each week. That is, someone called Frau Stausberg had signed in each week, and Stausberg's file said he'd never married. When a boy is ready to confess, to whom does he tell his secrets if not his mother?

14.

I left the tram at Staufenplatz, walked the two minutes to the top of Grafenburger Allee and caught a bus down to Flingern South. There I paced the streets in search of Stausberg mater's address.

Some children were playing on a patch of mud next to the street. The mud contained some leftover spots of grass and a merry-go-round that mewled in rusty protest at the children spinning on it. There were over a dozen of them, boys and girls mixed up together, none of them older than ten or eleven.

School didn't finish till lunchtime, so these kids were playing truant, though they seemed still to be wearing uniforms. The boys wore shorts and braces over dirty linen shirts. The girls wore dark skirts and white blouses with ribbons at their throats and in their hair.

I watched them play as I walked by. Most of the children sat on the merry-go-round while three or four others spun them around and around. A boy with skinny legs and mud on his face toyed with a length of rope fashioned into a lasso. The spinners let go of the merry-go-round and the children on it sent up a chorus of excited squeals. In every face I saw a potential victim for the likes of Kürten. For what were the chances of there being only one man with his perverse desires in a city this size? And what then of the country as a whole? It struck me then how much the laughter of children was like screaming. So hard to tell the difference.

When the merry-go-round slowed enough, the children tumbled from it. The mud-smeared tyke began hurling his lasso. He hooked one of the girls and reeled her in.

She struggled to free herself, but not in earnest; she could have escaped with ease. It seemed to be part of the game. The other children stopped their running and shouting and gathered around the struggling pair. They clapped their hands, beating out a basic rhythm. They began to chant, a nursery rhyme pattern:

Run run run away,
Or big bad Johann will have his wicked way,
Scream scream wriggle and squirm,
Or he'll have you buried down deep with the worms!

Seemed like Stausberg had made quite an impression on these tender minds.

I went over to them.

'Hey Winnetou,' I called. The mud-smeared boy turned to me. Funny how some things never go out of fashion. That book was a best seller back when I'd been this kid's age. I closed the gap and a couple of smaller boys ran around my legs.

'I'm looking for a Frau Stausberg, son. She lives somewhere round here. Can you point me in the right direction?'

The mud on the child's face was arranged in a pattern, two streaks per cheek Red Indian style. When he spoke his voice came out high and haughty.

'I've already got a dad,' he said. 'And he says I shouldn't talk to strangers. You could be the Ripper here to rape and butcher me!' The girls squeaked and ran between the trees.

I took out my ID and waved it at the boy.

'Shouldn't you be out catching the Ripper?' He hooked his thumbs into his braces like a Reichstag deputy.

'We caught him two days ago. Or doesn't your dad read the papers?'

'My dad says the average bull couldn't catch herpes off a ten pfennig whore.'

'Nice way with words, your dad. Tell me, you kiss your grandmother with that mouth?'

'My grandma's dead.' Said with a hint of triumph, like he'd killed her himself.

'Probably for the best,' I said. 'Say, shouldn't you kids be in school?'

'Shouldn't you be in a field somewhere keeping the crows away?'

I deepened my voice and raised it just short of a shout: 'So are you going to tell me where Frau Stausberg lives or not?'

'She's the mum of that cretin, right? The one we were singing about?' More high-pitched laughter. Never let anyone tell you kids are innocent. Either they're lying to you or they're idiots.

'What do you know about Johann?' I said.

'He used to try to play with us, lassoing games and catch and all that. My dad said he was probably trying to touch us and do bad things. He told the cops on him but they didn't do bugger all about it, he said.'

'Did your dad teach you the word cretin?'

The boy laughed. 'No. That was another bull when he came round to speak to the cretin last year.' Then he stuck out his teeth and sucked in his cheeks. Despite myself, I laughed. I'd yet to see a better impression of Ritter.

'You remember this bull's name?'

The boy shook his head. 'He kept licking his rabbit teeth, like this.' And he proceeded to show me Ritter's nervous tooth-licking tic. I laughed again.

'Dark hair, yes?' I said.

The boy shrugged.

'But you can't tell me where Stausberg's mother lives...?'

The boy went back to twirling his lasso. He'd had his fun and now I bored him. I straightened up and turned to leave when I felt a tug at my trouser leg. A small Jewish girl stood there with black eyes and long dark hair. She blushed when I looked at her and she pointed to the next turning.

I tugged at a curl in lieu of my homburg and walked to the next street. The Stausbergs had lived in a lodging house, I remembered that. In the middle of a street of apartment blocks, one building's front door swung on its hinges. Above the door, at least half of the windows facing the street were cracked and brown and grey net curtains twisted in the breeze. I'd have put money on this being the place.

I entered the hallway. The wall bore a bank of post boxes. I pulled the light cord and the bulb popped. No light, and no names on the boxes either. Perhaps the postmen round these parts moonlighted as psychics, or perhaps the boxes were just for show.

There was a faint sound of bubbling from up the hall. I walked through to a kitchen. Two people sat at a scarred wooden table tucked into a corner, unopened letters arranged in a pile between them. Beside this pile was a chopping board covered in cabbage scraps. Against the far wall, an assortment of pans dotted the wooden shelves while a huge copper pot bubbled away atop the stove. I went closer. Half a dozen glass jars stood sterilising in the water and a bowl of pickling cabbage dotted with black seeds sat in the sink next to the stove.

One of the people at the table, a youngish woman with deep bags under her eyes, put down the newspaper she'd been reading.

'Hungry, detective?' she said in a soft voice.

I turned to her with a smile. 'Is it that obvious?'

'The hunger? Or the profession?'

'Either. Both.' The woman wore a dress and an apron in contrasting shades of off-white. Both garments were too big for her. She had her dark hair tied back from a high forehead.

'Well, given the state of you, you had to be a bull or a boxer,' she said.

I pointed at the pot. 'How long's that been bubbling away?'

She went to the stove and turned off the gas. She smiled, the tip of her nose turning up. The newspaper she'd been reading was a copy of the *Volksstimme*. Her companion was a white-haired man who squinted up close at a boys' adventure comic that obscured his face below the eyebrows.

'Listen, I was hoping to speak to Frau Stausberg,' I said. 'About her son.' As though it was ever going to be about anything else.

The woman glanced down at her paper, weighing her options in her mind.

I went closer and handed her my ID. The old man flicked down the edge of his comic. He flicked it back up before I could get a good look at him. I got a flash of white stubble on sunken cheeks, but that was all. The woman handed my ID back and brushed the edges of her newspaper with her fingers. She chewed the inside of her cheek. Hard to tell if she'd recognised my heroic status from the paper or not. She'd have made a mean card player, this *hausfrau*.

I took a breath. 'Look, I'll make it easy for you. I know she lives in this building, so you wouldn't be giving anything away. You'll just be saving me a little time.' The woman's eyes reminded me of the little Jewess who'd pointed me in this direction. Perhaps this woman was the girl's mother.

She sighed. 'Apartment seven, third floor.' That seemed to be all I was going to get. I made for the stairs back in the foyer. Then she shouted after me. 'But she could be in the kitchen.'

I turned back and raised my eyebrows.

The woman got up from the table. She crossed her arms. 'There are kitchens on each floor.' She shrugged, turned away. Looked like that really was it this time.

I took the stairs to the third floor and knocked on door number seven.

The door opened a fraction. I held out my ID and the door opened all the way. A stooping woman in her mid-fifties beckoned me in.

'Is this about my son?' she said.

I took another look: the Stausberg file said she was

forty. She was so thin I could count the tendons in her neck. She wore a wool-lined coat and was smiling the kind of smile that blows away in a stiff breeze.

How hard could I be on her when she looked so frail?

I crossed to the nearest window, which had a long crack in it. I pushed aside the thin brown curtain. Some of the children who'd been playing were now standing across the street. They weren't playing any more, they were watching. Even as I stared at them and they saw me staring they kept on watching.

I turned back inside the room. A draught tugged at the loose sheets on an overstuffed bed in the corner. Facing in from the windows, a couple of easy chairs bore a patchwork of stains and small tears through which the stuffing was fighting its way out. Several tears had been stitched up with the kind of stitching that would give if you sat down too vigorously.

'You getting any trouble from the neighbours, Frau Stausberg?'

'You didn't come here to ask about my neighbours,' she said, with another nervous swallow. 'Or my windows.'

'I need to talk to you about the 28th February and the 1st March last year,' I said.

She hovered next to one of the easy chairs waiting for me to sit first, so I did. She sank down with a groan and the click of brittle knee joints.

'In your statement to police at the time you said Johann came back late and washed his coat in the sink.'

'Yes, the sink in the kitchen, if you'd like to have a look.'

I was about to get up and humour her when I realised she was being sarcastic.

'Look.' The eyes that met mine were soft and watery. 'We know Johann did not kill Rosa Ohliger or Rudolph Scheer.'

She choked and fluid dripped down her cheeks. At first I thought she'd got something in her eyes, but no: she screwed her face up and started gasping. She was weeping.

I wanted to ask if it was possible her son might've lied to her or been confused when he told her he'd killed Emma Gross, but Jesus, how far could I push this woman before she broke?

I spoke softly. 'You understand why I need to check the details with you?'

She took my hands in hers. Hers were so cold I flinched. I hoped she didn't notice.

'You think he's innocent of the Gross girl's murder too?' she said. There was such emotion in her voice I didn't know how to respond. I didn't want to give her too much hope. Didn't want to snuff out what was there, either.

'Look, Frau Stausberg, I don't have the evidence yet, you understand? Did Johann really tell you he'd killed her?'

She tightened her grip and swallowed. 'Have you spoken to my son?'

'Yes.'

She stroked the bruising under my eyes with an icy finger. 'And what did he say?'

'He... that someone told him what to say in his confessions,' I said. 'His memory wasn't clear. He became... upset. That's why I've come to you. Dr Glauser believes Johann's making a lot of progress, opening up about all sorts of things. To do with the case. She said you'd been a big part of that process.'

Okay, so that last bit wasn't the God's honest, but I was trying to make her feel better about talking to me.

Frau Stausberg released me and pulled herself up. Her jawline tensed as she ground her teeth. 'That doctor should mind her own business.' When she turned to face me her eyes were still wet. 'It's so hard for him, my poor dear Johann, with his epilepsy.' She crossed to the door, opened it and wandered out. 'Did you want coffee?' she called back.

'No, Frau Stausberg, please don't trouble yourself.' I got up to follow her.

'No trouble.' She returned with a sealed tin and a coffee

pot. 'Out on the kitchen window ledge,' she said, shaking the tin at me. 'Keeps it fresher.'

'So he told you he'd killed the Gross woman?' I said.

Frau Stausberg dropped the coffee pot lid. She bent at the hip to pick it up and I went over to help ease her upright.

'Would you like me to do that, Frau Stausberg?'

'It's not easy, young man.'

'No, I imagine not –'

'Don't interrupt me, please,' she snapped. 'It's not easy testifying against one's own son. But if it means he can go to a place where he'll be happier, where the people will understand him and his wants...' She gestured past me to the cracked window, her mind's eye seeing further even than that.

'Those damned children out there. Devils, more like. Of course, it's their parents' fault, really.' She swallowed a sob. 'All he wanted to do was join in their games, you see. But they didn't understand. They laughed, and made a game out of *him*, out of running away from him, teasing him.' The lines in her brow deepened and a single tear squeezed its way to her chin. 'They can be cruel, can't they?'

She left the room and I followed her into the kitchen across the way.

The kitchen was empty. Of people, at least. Of bric-à-brac it was chock full. The small circular table was crammed with spirit bottles, none of them empty but none of them full either. A series of open cupboards against the back wall revealed a stash of silverware, china and dusty glass. A clothes line stretched across the room. Amid the hanging bloomers and brassieres were a half-dozen dented cooking pots of some dull grey metal.

Frau Stausberg lit the stove beside the door. She spooned coffee grounds into the top of the pot. I held the top for her while she filled the bottom with water from the tap at the sink. She screwed the two halves together despite my protests that I could do it for her. She placed

127

the coffee pot on the flame, led me to the table and pushed me onto a stool. Light from the tall kitchen window bleached her flesh.

'And now you come here with your questions, your suggestions that my son might be innocent.' A mouse ran along the skirting board on the other side of the room, but Frau Stausberg didn't notice. 'Can you imagine how unbearable it would be to testify against your own flesh and blood? To tell a court of law that he was capable of doing murder?'

I wanted to look away from those eyes but I didn't want to disrespect her either. I shook my head instead.

She raised a shaking hand and said, 'And how much more unbearable if the testimony were untrue?' The coffee pot began to bubble and she got up and headed back to the stove. 'Now, do you take sugar?' She spooned some into a cup without waiting for the no I would have given her. I hated sugar in my coffee.

There was no way of avoiding all the questions I'd gone there to ask. 'During your visits, did Johann tell you who told him what to say in his confessions?'

She put down the sugar spoon with a clatter that cut me short.

'He has told me nothing of any consequence during any of my visits. As he has never said anything of consequence in all of his miserable life. Except for that terrible night two Februaries ago.' She poured coffee and handed me a cup. 'Now drink up, young man. I have to go shopping this afternoon, and I've left it late as it is.'

She didn't want to answer my questions. She probably didn't even want to think about her role in committing her only son to the asylum, and if anyone could understand her unwillingness to dredge up the past it was me. Besides, if I pushed any harder and she made a complaint to headquarters, it wouldn't go well for me. That was how I rationalised my being so eager to leave, anyway. So I just thanked her for the coffee and I drank it, undissolved sugar and all, and then I left her to her guilt.

15.

The dark-haired woman from the downstairs kitchen met me at the foot of the stairs. Her forehead was creased and her eyes darted about, unable to settle. 'Is everything okay?' she said.

I looked back up the way I'd come.

'I don't think so,' I said.

'No, I meant she's not in any trouble, is she?'

'Is there some reason she should be?'

The woman scratched the back of her neck where some hairs had come loose. She moved closer. 'I saw a man. Hanging around, you know?'

'You know who he is?'

She shook her head.

'How long has this man been hanging around?'

'Since you arrived. About five, ten minutes after you.'

I took out my notebook. Seeing that, her shoulders relaxed. She scratched the back of her neck again.

'Tall?' I said. 'Short? Dark hair? Light?'

'Not sure on the height,' she said. 'He was stood across the way there so it's hard to tell.' She pointed at the front door of the apartment building opposite. The door was set into an alcove, further back from the road. 'And he was wearing a hat so I don't know about his hair colour.'

'Eye colour?'

She shook her head.

'Okay,' I said, 'what about the hat. What style?'

'Oh, a fedora. Dark green. Wearing it low, about here.' She touched her brows with her fingers in a kind of loose salute. She plucked her brows. That is, I noticed she was a woman who plucked her eyebrows on a regular basis. Either she wasn't very good at it or she'd done it in a hurry that morning, as there were a couple of beaded scabs in amongst the fine black hairs. The eyes beneath them were the colour of polished rosewood cabinets. She flashed me a smile and I remembered myself.

'Any other remarkable clothing?' I said.

'Well...' She thought about this. 'There is... He's wearing a scarf high up over his chin. I know it's been cold the last few days, but not so's you'd need a scarf, surely?' She chewed on her bottom lip. The lip was plump and deep red without any touch of carmine. 'Or is it just me? Especially not with that big thick wool overcoat he was wearing.'

'What colour is this scarf?'

'It's a kind of dark green, to match his hat,' she said.

'What makes you think he's a threat to Frau Stausberg?'

'My daughter was due for her lunch. I came out front here to see if she was back yet and I saw this man just staring up at her window, standing there like a statue. It was kind of unnerving. Then when I went over to ask him what he was doing, he almost ran off he was so quick getting away. It's a bit too much of a coincidence, is what I was thinking, you here asking questions and then this man coming and staring up at her window like that.'

I tried to ignore the implied criticism. 'So he left when you tried to speak to him. When was this?'

'Not long before you came back down the stairs. Five minutes? I don't know.'

Funny to think if I'd looked out the window a little longer I'd have spotted him.

'I worry about her. Up there on her own.' She scratched the back of her neck.

'May I have your name?'

'Name?' Her eyes widened. I got the feeling she didn't have much time for police officers.

'In case I need to come back for a statement.'

'Oh, it's Frau Wenders.'

130

She walked away before I could ask another question, leaving me feeling a little stupid. I glanced at my notes:

Fedora

Scarf

Wool overcoat

<u>*Dark green???*</u>

Interest in Frau Stausberg?

I toyed with going back upstairs to ask Frau Stausberg if she'd seen this green fedora wearer hanging around, or whether she'd received any threats. Or – I thought of Du Pont – hassle from the press. I could commiserate with her in the latter case, certainly. But I decided against it. I'd bothered her enough and I couldn't face another basting from those washed-out eyes.

When I emerged into the street, the children had gone and, sure enough, there was no sign of any green man. I caught the next omnibus for the train station. It had been about to pull away from the stop and I just made it in time, huffing up to the top deck and reaching for a cigar to help the brainwork along.

I needed to talk to Gennat, that was clear. While Kürten was most likely the Ripper, he hadn't killed Emma Gross. And – his mother's testimony notwithstanding – there was no way Johann Stausberg had done it. So Ritter had charged an innocent man with three murders and left Kürten to kill again. But worse than that, if neither Kürten nor Stausberg had killed Emma Gross, that meant her killer was still out there. My biggest problem was that I had nothing solid enough to counter Frau Stausberg's testimony, so how was I going to get Gennat to take me seriously? Especially after he was done reading the riot act at me for absconding for the whole morning.

The conductor came by and I turned and asked for a single ticket, the cigar still in my hand, unlit. Behind the conductor, a flash of green. I leaned forward to look around the rotund conductor. Sure enough, there was a man in a green fedora and scarf, staring straight ahead and giving no sign he'd noticed my interest in him.

The conductor was speaking, but I hadn't heard him.

'I'm sorry?' I said.

'Two pfennigs,' he repeated, rolling his eyes at me.

I rooted for change and handed it over. The conductor gave me a ticket and moved on. I faced the front of the bus, making sure to put my cigar away. This was too strange. Was this green man following me? That would explain his turning up at Frau Stausberg's place around the same time as me. But that wouldn't explain his hanging around there before now. Of course, he could have followed me from the lodging house, picked up my trail there.

There was one way to be sure.

The next stop approached. There were a good few people in the queue, which was ideal. I got up and walked down the stairs as the bus pulled to the kerb, jumping off before it came to a stop. I walked on for a few metres, then knelt to undo and then retie my shoe laces, giving the green man time to get close. I looked up but couldn't see him reflected among the shoppers in the nearest windows.

I stood up and gazed around. Still no sign of the green man.

Had I imagined it? Clearly brown eyes of a certain type could exert an undue influence on me.

Up ahead was an alley between tall apartment buildings. Perhaps the green man had gone that way. I turned into the alley, my footsteps echoing in the narrow space: blank walls with no windows, no lines of drying clothes, no fire escapes. I walked to the other end and stopped where I had a view of the next street.

I got my cigar, put it between my teeth and struck a match. Only thing was, even though I'd stopped walking, my footsteps kept echoing behind me.

As I lit the cigar, the footsteps got louder.

The door to an apartment building down the street was open. I headed for it and entered the courtyard, clenching

132

that cigar in my teeth so hard that my jaw ached. The footsteps behind me carried on, gaining in speed.

In the courtyard was a padlocked door to some kind of cellar or storage area. The door hung loose on its hinges, and the padlocked latch hung even looser. A good kick would bring it out of the wall, so I kicked it.

Those footsteps got closer.

I kicked the latch again. It popped out of the brickwork and I pulled the door open. I ducked into the cellar, five steps down to the floor.

My pursuer entered the cellar a few seconds behind me, shuffling blindly one concrete step at a time. I pressed my burning cigar to the back of his ankle. He cried out, hopped on one foot and fell off the edge of the steps to the dusty floor.

I put the cigar back in my mouth. I dragged him up to his knees by his suit collar and pulled his loosened jacket down around his arms to restrict his movement. His scarf had disappeared.

'No, Tom, it's me! It's me!'

As always, it was the voice that did it. That and the beard and the workman's cap that tumbled from his head.

'Du Pont,' I hissed, cigar still clenched between my teeth, 'what the hell are you doing here?'

Du Pont shucked off his jacket, leaving it in my hands as he scrabbled further into the shadows in his shirt sleeves. I stood between him and the door. His lip had split in the fall and there was bruising on his cheek.

'I've been following you, Tom, what do you think?'

'What do I think?' I waved his jacket at him. 'I think I should kick you to bits down here for that shitty so-called interview you published.'

'What? Jesus, Marx and Engels, Tom, you're a piece of work.' He tried to get to his feet. His left ankle gave and he fell. 'You make a guy out to be a hero and he beats up on you for the privilege.' He tried to get up again and again he fell down. 'I think you've broken my ankle.'

Panic filled his voice.

I blew cigar smoke at him. The cellar walls were brick, wooden beams running from floor to ceiling at regular intervals with wooden railings to break the space up into stalls. Each stall bore a number drawn in chalk, no doubt corresponding to the apartment numbers in the building above. Most of the stalls were empty, though some still contained small piles of coal.

'So I see you went with my Stausberg-is-innocent theory in the end,' Du Pont said.

'How would you know that?'

'Because I've been following you, you idiot. I saw you go into Grafenberg Asylum. Then I watched you pay a visit to Stausberg's mother. You're onto something, aren't you? I knew it.'

'Why've you been hanging around outside Frau Stausberg's apartment?'

'What?' Du Pont said.

'You heard. You've been hanging around, hassling her for a story.'

'Now why would I do that when I have you to hassle for stories?'

'I ought to kick your teeth in, you know that?' I said.

'I ought to have an ankle left to kick with, you *arschloch*!'

'That's no more than you deserve. Did you know Kürten's name before you spoke to me, or was that the whole reason for showing me the damn letter?'

'Oh shit,' he said.

'Yeah oh shit. You fed me Baumgart's description without knowing his real name, right? Hoping that if it matched I'd just go ahead and give it to you, right? Well, let me tell you...'

I trailed off. Du Pont hadn't moved at all during that rant. He'd just sat and stared past me.

I followed his gaze back to the cellar door. A man squatted on the top step. He was big enough and broad enough to block out the light. He wore a green fedora and had a green scarf wrapped around his neck all the way up over his chin.

He also had a piece of metal in his hand that was shaped very much like a Luger. He was moving the business end of the barrel from one to the other of us in quick succession.

I smiled. Didn't know if this guy had seen any action in the trenches, but I had, and in the gloom and the close quarters I was right back there, shock trooper drill kicking in. Rush them, keep them off balance, never let them draw breath – *Vorwärts!*

I went in close, thrashing Du Pont's coat up and around the hand holding the Luger. I twisted and pulled it to the side. The Luger gave a muffled snarl, compressed hot air singeing the hand I was holding the jacket with, the bullet going wide. I hooked the man with my left fist, but he towered above me. I couldn't reach his nose or his jaw and my knuckles glanced off his chest.

It was enough to push him off balance and make him let go of the Luger. I snatched it away in the remains of Du Pont's powder-burned coat, hurling both of them behind me into the recesses of the cellar.

Disposing of the Luger had taken too long though, and the green man was ready for me as I raised my fists for another blow. He leapt at me, gravity taking the side of his bulk to propel me backwards and downwards. I curled into a ball. My shoulders took the brunt of the fall and I kicked out with my coiled legs. My leather soles hit the green man in the throat. He choked once and dropped to his knees like a stunned bull.

That was all I needed. Du Pont crowded in and I pushed him out of the way to get at the green man with my fists, knocking him onto his back and straddling his chest as I pounded him into a swollen mess. This guy was big and he could handle himself. I had to make sure he wasn't going to get up again.

He stopped moving and I stopped punching, though I kept a fist hovering above him in case he tried anything.

'Shit, Thomas, is he dead?' Du Pont's voice shook with either shock or adrenaline, I didn't much care which.

'Fetch the gun,' I told him.

Du Pont didn't move.

'The Luger,' I told him. He looked from the green man to me. I lowered my fist and then he moved – as I flexed my fingers trying to get the blood to flow back into them – rooting for the Luger in the crumpled material of his ruined coat. He scrambled back to me over some coals and I took the gun and put it in my hip pocket.

Dark blood oozed through the clipped moustache beneath the green man's nostrils. I didn't fancy being there when he came round, but a mystery man with a Luger was a mystery too far for the kind of day I was having. I slapped both cheeks a couple of times. That failed to rouse him, though I hadn't really expected it to. His hat had fallen off, exposing oiled hair that was probably some shade of red, though in that light it was hard to be sure. I pulled away the scarf. A wide, crooked scar ran from below his left ear to his Adam's apple.

'Go through his pockets,' Du Pont said, 'go through his pockets.'

'Shut up, Andre, I'm doing it.'

I went through each pocket in his overcoat and the loose-fitting suit beneath. A wallet and a set of keys in the trousers and some ammunition for the pistol in an inside coat pocket, but that was it. The wallet contained just ten Reichsmark and some lint. No ID. Unusual, and worrying, too. Most citizens carried ID as a matter of course but this guy had a reason not to. A reason strong enough to involve a Luger.

'Who is he?' Du Pont said.

'I don't know. I think he's been following me.'

'Following you? But he can't have. I mean, *I* was following you.'

'He was on the omnibus. You were on there too, right?'

'Right.'

'Well, so was he. Whoever he is, he's been tailing me since Frau Stausberg's place at least.'

'Shit, Thomas. I mean, shit, who is he?'

I shushed he journalist and took the pistol from my pocket. I checked it. Oiled and in good working order. The magazine carried the full load – minus one – and there was a cartridge in the chamber.

What the hell did he want, this unconscious green man?

Until he came to, there was no way of knowing. It was getting close to midday. It was bad enough I'd been absent from Mühlenstrasse all morning: I didn't like to think what Gennat's reaction was going to be if I missed the press conference too.

That said, was I really going to leave my friend Du Pont and a mystery man with a loaded pistol free to roam while I played nice back at headquarters?

'Help me drag him over there,' I said to Du Pont.

I gestured at a set of wooden railings close to the back wall of the cellar. We dragged the man over. It was slow going, with Du Pont moaning about his ankle all the way. When we got to the back wall I pressed the green man's unbroken wrist against a railing.

'Here, hold this,' I told Du Pont. He held the wrist in place and I bound it to the railing with the scarf.

'What are you doing?' Du Pont said.

'Giving you a scoop.'

'Huh?'

The green man wore a thin leather belt. I undid the clasp and pulled it free, handing it to Du Pont.

'If he threatens you when he wakes up, hit him with this until he calms down.'

'What? Are you mad?' Du Pont didn't take the belt.

'Okay then, how about this. You let me get clear and then you leave this guy here and find the first *Schupo* patrolman you can, and you bring him down here and show him this guy.'

Du Pont put up his palms. 'Hey, let's not be hasty.'

137

'Right. That's what I thought.' I pressed the belt into Du Pont's hands and he took it from me. 'Stay here till he wakes up and then find out who the hell he is, and what he's up to, going around shooting at cops and hacks with a Luger.'

Du Pont licked his lips. His eyes followed me as I retreated to the steps. 'And where are you going?'

'I need to get back to headquarters.'

'You're leaving me here?' Du Pont shouted. 'With him?'

The green man moaned and shifted. We both stared at him until he stopped moving. Then Du Pont started up again, this time in a whisper:

'You're leaving me here with him?'

'I'll be back soon.'

I went up the stairs with Du Pont's protests chasing me out of the cellar.

16.

When I got back to Mühlenstrasse, the *Schupo* at the door took one look at my dust-covered clothes and barred my way. I had to show him my ID before he'd stand aside. Even then, the salute he threw me was hesitant in the extreme.

A variety of parked sedans and convertibles crowded the cobbles outside the entrance. I pushed into the court-yard, hoping I could brush off the worst of the dust and slip into the press conference quietly enough to pretend to Gennat I'd been there from the beginning. The hum of voices came from the old Jesuit chapel building – now a training gym for the *Schupo* recruits – that lined the longest side of the yard.

Someone grabbed me by the ear and said, 'And where've you been, comrade?' It was Vogel. He sniffed and spat phlegm onto the cobbles. 'You're a mess. You been applying for a job in the Ruhr valley this morning or something?' He brushed me down with his free hand.

'I don't have time for this.'

'No, you don't have time. Gennat wants you at the con-ference.' Vogel pulled me towards the chapel.

'Come on, Vogel, I can't go in there looking like this.'

Vogel let go of my ear and came round to face me. He ran his eyes up and down my sorry clothing. He broke into a grin and shifted a trilby to the back of his head. Odd, but he'd never struck me as a trilby wearer.

'You are in one sorry state.' He laughed. 'Here, take off your jacket.'

He helped me out of my dusty suit jacket and handed me his. Then he put his hat on my head.

'There,' he said. 'Not great, but much better.'

'The sleeves are too long.' I stretched out my arms to show him.

'At least they're not covered in coal dust.' He grasped one of my outstretched arms and towed me towards the chapel. 'Though I don't reckon he's going to want you to make any kind of public announcement like this.'

'Thanks. This is *your* jacket.'

'Keep it. I hardly ever wear it, anyway.'

We'd crossed the yard. Vogel raised a fist to knock on the chapel door but I held his wrist to stop him.

'What is it?' he said.

I was feeling bad about leaving Du Pont with the green man. Much as I distrusted the journalist, I didn't want to see him dead on my account.

'I need you to do me a favour,' I said.

'I just did you one, in case you hadn't noticed.'

'No, a real favour. Someone tried to shoot me today.'

'What are you talking about?'

'How much clearer do you want me to make it? Some guy's been following me around all morning and half an hour ago he tried to shoot me.'

Vogel narrowed his eyes.

'I knocked him out and locked him in a cellar. I need you to go and pick him up before he comes round and buggers off.'

'Christ, Klein. Aren't you in enough trouble without shit like this?'

'What can I say. It follows me around.'

Vogel was shaking his head, a big smile on his face. Then he knocked on the door. Ritter opened it, straightening up when it registered who he was looking at. I stared at his moustache until he took out a handkerchief and blew his nose.

I turned back to Vogel. 'So you'll help me out?'

Ritter reached to pull me inside the chapel but I shrugged him off.

'You'll help?' I asked Vogel again.

'I must be crazy,' he said. 'But hell, okay. Where did you say that cellar was?'

I whispered the address. Then I let Ritter drag me into the chapel and shut the door behind me.

A score of reporters and photographers sat in folding wooden chairs on the floor where the pews had once been. I recognised a couple of faces. The others must have been from the nationals, some of them, and the news wires too. They'd been following the case in Paris, London and New York as well as Munich, Hamburg and Berlin. A brace of hats in the group marked out the exotic lady reporters. The men, of course, sat with bared heads. I had no intention of following their example.

'Hey, it's Doubting Thomas,' someone shouted. That got a few laughs. A flashbulb went off and I covered my face with Vogel's hat. So much for intentions.

Gennat stood at a lectern facing the reporters. He wore Harris tweeds and smoked one of his cigars. All he needed to complete the look was a monocle. Behind him stood the public prosecutor, a tall man whose softening jawline announced the onset of his run to fat and whose ruddy complexion betrayed high blood pressure. He wore a sober charcoal-grey worsted.

'And so, in answer to your question,' Gennat was saying, 'while we would have been happy to consider any theories brought to us by Mr Wallace, the gentleman made no such approach to the murder commission during my time on the case. Anything you've heard to the contrary is just hearsay, I'm afraid.'

'But it is true you are a fan of Mr Wallace's novels?' asked a reporter with an English accent. Or possibly a Dutch accent. It was hard to tell the difference: neither nationality could handle German consonants without softening them. And what some island monkey crime novelist had to do with a real-life murder inquiry like ours, I could only guess. Goddamned reporters. Was a murder case not interesting enough for them anymore?

'Why certainly,' Gennat replied. 'I like nothing better than to read myself to sleep with one of that esteemed gentleman's most entertaining fantasies.'

A chuckle rippled through the reporters and Ritter dragged me towards the lectern as I jammed the trilby back over my dirty hair. Gennat acknowledged my presence with a nod and turned back to the throng. That was all. Just a nod.

'And now, ladies and gentlemen, as promised, I must hand you to the public prosecutor for a few moments for the meat and drink of the legal case. No interruptions, please.'

The PP stepped forward, placed pince-nez upon his nose and began reading from the statement in his shaking hand.

'Detailed examinations of the accused, Peter Kürten,' the PP paused and looked up, then back down at his statement, 'have been carried out during the whole of Sunday, Monday and this morning, in some cases in the presence of witnesses. The entire results cannot be made public.'

Shouts of protest filled the chapel. Gennat raised his arms for quiet and the PP raised his voice:

'Cannot be made public, as in view of other investigations still to be made, it is necessary to prevent...' another groan rang out '... it is necessary, that it is necessary, ladies and gentlemen, to prevent witnesses making the mistake of confusing their own experiences with those we are about to make public. This generally recognised danger of influence makes it imperative that in the interests of objective truth full publicity cannot yet...' another groan '... I say, I say that it is in the interests of objective truth... of objective truth, that full publicity cannot yet be given. For the same reason it is not possible to publish a picture of Kürten at the present moment.'

Gennat rounded on me.

'Where have you been?' he said. 'You knew we were going for formal confessions this morning, and you knew

142

how much trouble we'd be likely to have without you there, but you buggered off anyway.'

Yes, and now all I wanted was to bugger off again and deal with Du Pont and the green man before they escaped or someone found them.

'Have you had lunch?' Gennat asked.

'No sir.'

'Right, you and me alone, after we're done here. You're going to tell me what you've been up to all goddamned morning. Clear?' He glanced at Ritter. 'Give him the photographs.' Gennat locked eyes with me again. 'Hand this material out to the reporters and keep your mouth shut. And take off that damned hat.'

He pulled the trilby from my head, caught sight of my hair and clamped the hat back into place. He crossed to the lectern, muttering as he went. The PP was going on with the details of the case. Sounded like they'd got Kürten to talk despite my absence. I didn't know if that was good for me or not.

'... focus of our present investigations to gathering more evidence in the cases of poor Gertrude Albermann and the unknown victim discovered in Papendell on Sunday.'

'Apropos of which,' Gennat broke in, 'we are appealing to you good ladies and gentlemen of the press –'

'I don't see anyone from the *Volksstimme* here,' one of the local reporters exclaimed.

'Well, you won't,' his neighbour shouted, 'Düsseldorf's own Scarlet Pimpernel, that Andre Du Pont.'

'That's right, he doesn't need to be here, does he?' the first reporter said. 'He can just take the detectives out for beers afterwards, get all the information he wants.'

'Now now, people, we've gone over that,' Gennat said, wagging a finger and holding his cigar in the corner of his mouth.

'Yeah, yeah,' the first reporter said, waving his notebook, '*danger to society in need of a long course of treatment... attempted murder beyond doubt*, blah blah. Tell us something we don't know.'

'Hey, don't forget that *the cases of Ohliger, Scheer and Gross are still uncertain and wrapped in mystery*,' the second reporter said, reading from his shorthand.

'Ain't that what we pay a police force for? To solve mysteries?'

Ritter handed me a stack of photographic prints and shoved me at the reporters.

'No, we pay them to build fancy new headquarters on the edge of town and plunge the city into debt, didn't you know?' said the second reporter.

Bunch of snickering hyenas they might've been, but they had a point about the new headquarters being built down at Jürgensplatz. Damn thing was a publicity disaster, over budget and a year behind schedule already.

'Well why not, there's only a Depression on. It's not like it's a bad time for large-scale public works or anything,' said the first reporter.

'Excuse me, can you please shut up?' said a woman dressed in silk and pearls. She had a foreign accent I couldn't place and her dress revealed a lot of shapely stockinged calf muscle. I handed her some photos and tried a smile on her. She smiled back.

'As you can see,' Gennat said, 'we want you to take three pictures each. The first shows a set of house keys buried with the body. The second is a torn, silk summer dress she was wearing when killed. The colour is pink. The third is a straw summer hat of common design also buried with her. From the preliminary autopsy information that we have, this woman was most likely in her mid-twenties, with long, straight, fair hair. Caucasian. She was between one metre sixty and one metre sixty-five in height.'

I stood at one end of a row of chairs, passing photographs down the line. The reporters took what they needed from the pile and passed it on.

'We are appealing to friends and family, to anyone who might have known her or any witnesses who might be able to help us trace her movements in her last days of

144

life. We need to know who she was. According to our information, the woman was killed on Sunday 11th August last year, on the same meadow where we found her. We believe she conversed for some moments with a smartly-dressed gentleman on a park bench in the Hansaplatz on Thursday 8th August. She was next seen around one-thirty p.m. on Sunday the 11th, at which point...'

I switched off.

17.

The sun came out as Gennat and I entered the café. Light streamed through the floor-to-ceiling windows. A frayed poster of a bullfighter adorned the exposed brickwork of a nearby column, a splash of red, yellow and black against the clay and mahogany tones of the floor and walls. It was a recent national epidemic, this yearning to be from some other country. I got it, I'm not pretending I didn't, but hell, running away from problems ain't the answer to them. Besides which, things seemed to be just as bad all over as far as I could make out from those snippets of truth that did make it into the papers.

Post lunch rush, most of the tables were empty. Gennat selected one in the window. He sat and closed his eyes, his bulk and his bristling moustache giving him the air of a walrus sunning itself on the beach. How was I going to get him to listen to me now?

We ordered bockwurst and potato salad and a large beer apiece from the guy in the stained black apron behind the bar.

Gennat threaded his hands together and rested them on his stomach. He opened one eye. 'Not only did you disappear this morning when you knew we would need you, but you turned up late for the press conference. So whatever you've been doing, it had better be damn good.'

He broke off as the drinks and food arrived. He drank most of his beer in a few smooth gulps before starting in on his sausage, which he dipped in the mustard clinging to the side of his plate. The crunch of the sausage skin breaking as he bit into it made me wince, waxen corpses coming to mind. I fought my way through a couple of mouthfuls of beer before wiping my top lip and taking a deep breath, trying not to think of the green man waking up next to a garrulous journalist in a dark coal cellar. Christ, why had I left him with Du Pont? I hoped Vogel would be as good as his word, and get there in time.

I forced myself to concentrate. 'Last night I checked Kürten's confessions against the crime scene information, just as you asked.'

'How kind of you,' Gennat rumbled, his mouth full of food. 'Perhaps now you'd like to get round to telling me what conclusions you came to?'

'Kürten didn't kill Gross.'

'No?'

'No, it was the only confession where he got details wrong –'

'Forgive me for interrupting, but could I trouble you for your opinion on the other five cases?' Gennat's sarcasm was mallet-like in its subtlety. I tried not to betray my impatience.

'With all the others Kürten's recall was clear and detailed and it matched the existing evidence in every way,' I said. 'That's just the point. In the case of Gross he didn't know what he was talking about. Look, I don't have your experience, sir. This kind of maniac is new to me, but I've spent more time with him than anyone else on the department and I think he craves the notoriety. He doesn't want anyone else taking any of his glory. Does that make sense?'

'Yes, fine,' Gennat said. 'Then we stick with Stausberg for the Emma Gross killing, and everyone's happy.'

I sank some beer. It had a bitter after taste. I took a deep breath. 'But that's what I was doing this morning, sir. Checking with Stausberg. He didn't kill Gross either.'

'What?'

'Stausberg's murder confessions were forced. Now he can't even remember who he's supposed to've killed, much less how he was supposed to have done it.'

'Go on,' Gennat said, shovelling food into his mouth.

147

'What do you mean "go on"? Isn't it obvious?'

'Watch your tone, detective.'

I lowered my voice. 'Kürten didn't kill Emma Gross. And if Stausberg didn't do it then that means someone else killed her. We've got another murderer out there.'

'And of course you're about to show me the evidence that trumps not one, but two signed confessions from undesirables we already have behind bars.'

Gennat pushed his plate away, emptied his beer and gestured to the barman for another. He pointed at my glass and raised his eyebrows at me. I shook my head.

'And bring a pot of coffee too,' he called.

'It's Ritter,' I said. 'He forced Stausberg's confessions to clear his cases last year.'

'Oh Ritter, Ritter, Ritter.' Gennat slapped the top of the table hard enough to rattle the salt and pepper shakers. 'That's what this is all about, is it? I don't know what it is between you two, and I don't want to know. But if all this is just to prove Ritter wrong then you can drop it. What do you think the chances are of the public prosecutor and the attorney general pursuing this? Undermining the head of the Kürten murder commission? Thereby undermining the case against Kürten? And that's before we even consider how low Düsseldorf *Kripo*'s reputation has sunk with the press and the public. You think anyone in authority is going to risk it sinking any further?'

I started to speak but he shut me up with a raised finger.

'If you think I'm going to help you out you can forget it. Kürten gets transferred to Düsseldorf Prison at the end of the week and then Vogel and me are done here, off back to Berlin. So even if I wanted to help you I couldn't.'

The fresh beer and coffee arrived. Gennat downed the beer and wiped his mouth with the back of his hand before pouring the coffee. I ate in silence.

'You say you don't have my experience,' he continued, softening his voice, 'and that's true. When you've been in this business as long as I have, Thomas, you'll know that people don't really care who killed their loved ones. They only care that *someone* did. You understand?'

Ah, fatherly advice. The perfect blend of do-as-I-say and it's-for-your-own-good. This shit I could do without.

'What can I say to that, sir? You're telling me you don't care who murdered that woman?'

He passed me a cup of black coffee. He added milk and sugar to his cup before passing the sugar bowl to me. I ignored it and waited for his response. He had to come back at me with something, for Christ's sake. Hadn't I just accused him of lacking moral fibre? Or maybe he really didn't give a damn.

'You know, about that business in Hanover,' he said. 'Fritz Haarmann was a police informant. That's why Hanover *Kripo* weren't too keen on linking him to all the bones those kids found buried in the riverbank.'

Gennat took out his cigar case and offered it to me. I shook my head. He lit himself one and puffed smoke rings at the ceiling. Was he going anywhere with this or was he back to playing to the gallery?

'I had a high case clearance rate in Berlin,' he went on, 'good press coverage, and I'd been making noises about the need for a permanent homicide squad in the capital. Basically making myself a nuisance to the brass, who didn't want me undermining them. So the police president sent me out to prove myself by discovering and arresting this Hanover killer.'

He grinned. 'Or to fail in the attempt. I suspect he hoped the latter, then I would come back with my tail between my legs and drop all this homicide squad stuff. It was the parents of one of the young men who went missing. God, what was his name?' He clicked his fingers.

'Anyway, they hired this private investigator when it was clear the local *Kripo* didn't have the manpower or the expertise or indeed any interest in finding out what had happened to their son. He tracked the kid to Haarmann, and the rest was a matter of following the leads. Hanover got its werewolf, I got my homicide squad. Local cops went from pariahs to heroes, just like that. Luck, really, just like you getting that tip off from Maria Butlies.'

'The lucky part was Kürten leaving her alive,' I said.

'Well, quite. But lucky none the less. I'm afraid that's how it is with these serial killers.'

'Serial killers?' I said.

'Yes,' he smiled, 'it's a phrase I've been working up for a magazine article. Has quite a ring to it, don't you think? I mean, mass-murderer is all very well, but it's a little imprecise. Surely a mass-murderer is someone who kills several people at the same time, while what we have here is actually quite a different phenomenon – a killer who targets several victims, but in a series, one after the other.' He bounced his spoon in the air to illustrate his idea.

'No, my point was – and incidentally I'll be repeating it in my article – that traditional police work hasn't a hope when up against men of this stamp. Against the likes of Kürten and Haarmann all we can do is wait for them to make their mistakes and try to be there to spot them when they happen.'

A magazine article. I must've been the only mug in all of *Kripo* not treating the job as some kind of stepping stone to glory. He sipped more coffee and then topped up his cup from the pot. 'I phoned your watch commander today, told him you'd be free to return to normal duties as of tomorrow.'

'Oh,' I said. Now the end of my involvement in the case was in sight, I wanted to stay and see it through.

'Well, you can't be surprised, surely? Not after today.'

'I suppose not.'

I sipped my coffee. It was strong with a thick foam on the top.

Gennat blew his mouldy-leaf smoke at me. 'Of course, he reminded me that tomorrow and the day after fall on your days off. So you wouldn't be due back until Friday morning.'

His brown eyes sparkled.

'What are you saying, sir?'

'It occurs to me, thinking back over the Haarmann case, that the difference between a good detective and a bad one isn't just luck, it's also having the balls to keep pushing at a problem until that luck comes along. After all, you had one stroke of luck already.'

'Oh?' I said.

'Yes, who was it who picked up the Butlies case in the first place? For eighteen months, all of Düsseldorf *Kripo* tries to track down the Ripper, without success, and then the answer just falls into your lap? That's the kind of luck that clears cases. Maybe you're due some more of the same. Believe me, you keep pushing on this Gross case and you're going to need it.'

He rooted for his wallet. 'Lunch is on me, I think.' He passed me a couple of Reichsmark. 'And for God's sake get yourself a haircut and a shave. I might not be able to control what you do for the next two days, but I won't have you going round looking like a damned hobo.'

This was Gennat giving me permission to go rogue. And making sure I couldn't prove it. Talk about your political animal.

'Sir...' I began. I wanted to tell him about the green man, about Du Pont following me around. I wanted to ask his advice, since he was clearly in the mood to dispense it. But he spoke before I had the chance to go on.

'Oh, and let's have an end to this cavorting with Marxist reporters, eh? If there's one thing guaranteed to get you chucked off your little case – and off the department – it's that.' He took another drag on his cigar. 'Anyway, you wanted to say something.'

'Did you ever find out what happened to that young man?' I said after a second or two of mental fumbling.

'Mmmn? Which young man?'

'The one in Hanover whose parents hired that PI.'

Gennat shrugged and finished his coffee. 'Same as happened to all the others. Haarmann fucked him and tore his throat out.'

18.

The air felt cool on my smooth face and around my ears as I entered the lobby of the Hotel Adler. Vogel's hat I'd left in the barbershop. A tip, if you will.

The clack-clack-clack of a ceiling fan drew my eyes upwards. The spinning blades cast swirling patterns into the tobacco smoke hovering beneath them. Flies bobbed above the florid faces of dark-suited men occupying the chintz armchairs scattered about. In a smoked-glass mirror above a huge stone fireplace, a girl in stiletto heels tottered past a potted palm with brown spots on its leaves, on her way to a dark-suited lap. She just about kept time with the big band music crackling into the room from a concealed wireless. The girl was the only one paying any attention to the music. When I turned to watch her without the mirror's assistance she looked unreal, un-tinted and back to front.

The lamp fittings trembled in time to the sound of a train pulling out of the station half a block away. I approached the check-in desk tucked into the corner by the stairs. The girl behind the desk had eyes as black as tar and a white cap atop her black hair which drew my eyes to the round studs in her ears. She wore a small white pinafore over her dark street clothes. She also had a crooked back. My heart gave a tug and I wondered when it was I'd grown so soft.

'Can I help you sir?' the maid asked. Her hand rested on an open ledger on the desk.

You can tell me who killed Emma Gross for a start, I thought. What was I doing here? On top of my suspicion of Ritter's paperwork on the case, it was true that crime scene sketches and photographs were a poor substitute for standing there in the space where murder was done and picking up what you could from the dimensions and the objects in the room. But what could I hope to find more than a year after the fact?

'I very much hope so,' I said, for some reason putting on the same posh voice I'd used on the telephone with Berg. I flashed her my ID. Her eyes widened and she vanished through a door beside the pigeon holes. Another black mark against Kürten's confession: no wall clock. My watch told me it was a little after five p.m.

The door opened and another woman bustled out to meet me. The thick lenses she wore on a beaded chain around her neck magnified the blue of her eyes, and dark hair ran to grey at the sides of her head where it obscured her ears. She snatched the ID from my hand and held it up to her lenses.

'It is genuine,' I said.

'What is this about?' She rolled something hard around her mouth, making her lips bulge so that I forgot my first question. Either she was hooked on hard candies or she had a pair of false teeth that didn't fit.

'I'm here about Emma Gross.' I held out my hand for the ID.

'Don't know anything about that,' the woman said, looking at my battered face. Following my shave, the cut in my cheek was exposed to the air and it itched like crazy.

'This is the Hotel Adler?'

'Yes?'

'You are the manageress?'

'I am the proprietoress.'

'You were the proprietoress on the night of the 28th February last year?'

'Yes?'

'Well then you know plenty.' I consulted my notes. 'I'd like to see the room where she died.'

'Who?'

'Emma Gross.' I snatched back the ID.

'I don't know which room that was.'

'Are you in the habit of hosting murders at your hotel, Frau... ?'

'Frau Holz. And no I am not.'

'Seems to me you might remember a murder, even in a cum-cabin like this.'

The woman gasped and so did the maid, who raised a tiny hand to her mouth and watched Frau Holz for guidance on how to react.

Holz adopted a stage whisper: 'This is not a cum-cabin! And I'll thank you to keep such talk out of my hotel.' The woman's eyeglasses fell from her nose and swung in front of her blue satin blouse.

'Well what else do you call a place that charges by the hour?' I turned the ledger and flicked through the pages. 'And doesn't write those guests in the book?' A cum-cabin with pretensions was still a cum-cabin.

'We do no such thing here, officer, I assure you.'

A man and woman descended the stairs with a burst of loud giggling that pierced the lobby's relative hush. The woman had the man's overcoat on her shoulders, just covering her skinny arms and legs and her thin silk dress. She tipped a champagne bottle to her lips until froth spilled down her chin. The man belly-laughed at her and she laughed right along.

The man nudged me aside, slapped five Reichsmark on the check-in desk and moved off arm-in-arm with his floozy. He paused, clicked his fingers, delved into a pocket and slapped down a key attached to a large wooden block with the number 'twelve' stamped on it.

The man elbowed me and said, 'You look like you need help, friend. You want to borrow mine?'

He shoved his woman at me, if woman was the word for such a sack of bones. The floozy spat out champagne and slapped the man's shoulder and then the couple left for the street.

I wiped champagne from my cheek and flung the droplets at Frau Holz, who flinched. The maid busied herself, reaching up to put key number twelve back in its pigeon hole.

She stretched so far that her blouse came untucked. I resisted the urge to tuck it in for her.

'Okay,' Holz shrugged, 'so we do allow guests to have rooms by the hour, but we do not encourage... sexual congress.'

'So what do they do up there? Hold séances?'

'We offer discretion. What our guests choose to spend their time doing is of no concern to us. A view backed up by your vice squad boys, by the way, officer.' Her hand moved toward a cash register behind the desk and raised an eyebrow.

I waved away the implication. 'Save your money. I'm not vice. Was Emma Gross a regular here?'

'No.'

The maid flitted into the back room. The door clicked shut behind her.

'Is there anyone here who knew her? Who spoke to her?'

'I'd hardly encourage that, officer. Why, if I'd known she was a whore I'd have kicked her out.'

I looked back into the lobby at the girl in the stilettos. She wriggled in her florid gentleman's lap and played with his neck tie. In the trade the girls called their marks 'suitors' with ironic formality. She'd got herself an easy one here: guy was turning beet already, and he still had all his clothes on.

I turned back. 'Did you see the man she came in with that night?'

'Who?'

'Emma Gross.'

'When, the 28th?'

'Yes, the 28th.'

'No.'

'Was there anybody working here that night who might have?'

'I was the only one working the desk that night.'

'You're sure about that?'

'I answered enough questions at the time, officer, to be sure. Yes.'

'There's no way your maid might have walked in on her in the room?'

She put her eyeglasses back on her nose so she could glare through them at me. 'If Marta was in the habit of doing such things I am sure she would not still be working for me.'

'She was there that night too?'

'No.'

'Mind if I ask her?' I flipped up the hinged top in the check-in desk and reached for the door to the back room.

Frau Holz put out a hand to stop me. 'That is to say, she was not on the desk or cleaning the rooms or the hallways that night, officer. She was in the kitchen, helping chef.'

'And may I speak with the chef?'

She beamed at me. 'Chef is regrettably no longer in my employ, officer.'

'And your husband. Is he around to speak to?'

'He passed away.'

I read through my notes again. 'And you're sure you don't remember which room Gross was killed in that night?'

'That's right.'

'Make any difference if I ask your guests?' I turned and nodded at the men in the armchairs, taking a couple of steps away from the desk.

'Room thirty-seven,' Holz said. 'But it's occupied right now.'

I checked the ledger. No record of any occupants of room thirty-seven for the whole day, or the night before.

'Holding a séance, are they?'

Now Holz' reticence made more sense. I went up to the third floor. Thirty-seven was a short walk down the hall from the top of the stairs. I pressed my ear to the door. Groans, grunts and squeaking bed springs issued forth.

I tried the handle but the door was locked, of course. I knocked.

'No thank you!' called a man's voice. He sounded out of puff.

I knocked again.

'We're busy in here, thanks!'

I knocked again.

'Look, bugger off will you!'

I kicked at the lock. The screws keeping it in place separated from the wood of the door-jamb and the door swung open. The man and woman copulating within ran with sweat. She was on all fours and he was *schtupping* her from behind.

That's when I got my first surprise.

The man and woman were copulating on a divan across from the door, not the double bed against the right wall. It was the divan that was squeaking, not the bed.

And that's when I got my second surprise.

That was the same divan Gross had been lying on when they found her. I recognised it from the crime scene photographs.

The man on the divan heaved his deflating hard-on from inside his corpulent squeeze and got to his feet. This one wasn't florid. He had tan lines above and below his groin, and a heavy gut beneath a toned chest and muscular arms. The Depression didn't seem to be touching him at all.

The corpulent woman bent to pick up some clothing lying on the floor by the divan but the man pushed her down. 'Stay there,' he commanded. He sniffed a line of white powder from the dip in her back above her buttocks. He straightened, rubbing at his nostrils with his right thumb.

The man approached me, his penis shrivelling. 'Do you know who I am?' he said. He swept loose hair back on his head and curled his hands into fists.

My knee connected with his groin. He groaned and sank to his knees. I pulled his head back by his hair so he could get an eyeful of my ID. 'Do you want me to know who you are?' I said.

He shook his head as far as my fist would let it.

'Get on the bed.' I looked up at the whore. 'You too.'

157

They both of them did as I said. The man crouched in a foetal position. 'Now, answer my questions honestly and I won't have to take your names. Do either of you know the name Emma Gross?'

'Do I?' the man said, voice halfway between a choke and a sob. 'We paid extra for this room on the understanding that it was *the* room. That this is *the* divan. It's triple the price, you know.'

Footsteps echoed in the uncarpeted hallway. I pulled my Luger and trained it on the door as Frau Holz burst in with a wartime carbine in her hands. The barrel tipped down towards the floor and Holz' glasses tumbled from her nose at the sight of my gun.

'I heard... th-there w-was trouble,' she said. Behind her, the maid's dark head bobbed up and down.

'There will be.' I pulled the carbine from her hands and removed the magazine. I pulled back the turn-down bolt and ejected the cartridge from the breech. 'Charging extra for the murder room, Frau Holz?'

The woman ignored me and addressed the man. 'I'm sorry, Herr –'

He waved his hands in the air. 'No, for God's sake woman, don't tell him who I am.'

'Go downstairs and wait for me,' I told Holz. 'We'll discuss your gun permit presently.' I pointed at the door. She didn't budge. 'Move!' I yelled. My trench voice. She jumped, as well she might.

She left, but not without mumbling, '... right to defend myself on my own property...'

I shut the door. I conjured the crime scene photos in my mind, ignoring the sweat-slicked couple as I approached the divan and pictured Gross' slack body lying in the broken-doll posture in which they found her. But in which who had found her? I wasn't sure the file had mentioned that. But then, since Ritter had extorted or conned a confession to the Gross murder from Stausberg, just how valuable did I expect the information in the file to be?

158

'Did either of you know Emma Gross?' I asked, looking at the woman. She shook her head.

'Look, detective,' the man said, 'I think you might have got the wrong idea. This woman here is my... lover, you understand? She's not a *chonté* or anything like that. There's very little reason why she would have known a *chonté* like Gross. And I've never slept with one. We've only used this room a couple of times. Only used this hotel a couple of times before that. We weren't... seeing each other last year, so neither of us came here then. Does that answer your question?'

'I'd say so.' The long seat of the divan was upholstered in blue, studs holding the fabric to the dark wood. That was a lot of space for fingerprints to show up, but only one had. Did that mean someone had tried to wipe it down after the killing? Or was it more routine than that – that there'd been hundreds of smudges but only one clear, usable print? Why the hell hadn't I picked this up from the file when I had the chance? And then again, how much of this had made the file?

The naked man appeared at my shoulder. He stood a little taller than me, though the pain in his balls caused him to stoop.

'This is where she died, right?' he said. His eyes shone, though whether with simple ghoulishness or with the cocaine he'd sniffed off his woman's back, who could say.

'What do you know about it?' I said.

He held up his hands. 'What I read in the papers. That's all, detective, I swear. I heard it was Johann Stausberg that did it. The stabbing. Funny though,' he patted at the fabric of the seat, 'no blood. I mean, did they wash it?'

'No, they didn't wash it.'

'So is this a different divan or what?'

'You know, you can go ahead and get dressed any time you like,' I said.

He looked at me with a puzzled expression. 'I'm hot,' he said finally. 'Aren't you, darling?' He turned to his

159

woman. She was scrabbling amongst the clothes on the bed. If she was looking for her underthings she wouldn't find them there: panties and bra lay twisted at my feet. I scooped them up and passed them to her. As she smiled, a tear tracked mascara down one of her cheeks. She looked older than the man. I did wonder then about them, about the nature of their relationship, who they were married to. Two wedding rings lay beneath the divan next to a man's wrist watch.

'Okay folks, I'm sorry for the intrusion,' I said. 'I needed to... get a look at the room.'

'Why?' the man said. 'What's so important about all this now?'

'You've read about the arrest of the Ripper?'

His pupils, already dilated, widened until they consumed his irises entirely. 'I see,' he said. 'Wow. Come on, darling.' He took one of the half-dressed woman's hands in his, kissed the bridge of her flat nose and smoothed her hair.

'Can we go now Fritzie?' she said.

I tried to look as though I hadn't heard anything as I left the room and went downstairs. Okay, so I'd seen the murder room, but what had that got me? One thing I was fairly sure of. Frau Holz had altered nothing since Gross' murder, so at least everything was still as it had been back on the 28th February 1929. That confirmed what I'd picked up from the crime scene photographs beyond any doubts I might still have had that Kürten had not killed Gross. It just hadn't given me any evidence to prove Stausberg's innocence. For that I'd still need him or his mother to change their statement. And nor had the room given me anything pointing to the real killer.

Well, I'd put it off for long enough. It was time to call Vogel.

I approached the check-in desk with the carbine slung over my arm. Frau Holz was still there, as was Marta, sitting on a stool behind the desk and munching on a bread roll. I needed to talk to her without Holz being within

160

earshot controlling her every response.

'Frau Holz,' I said, 'perhaps you'd be so good as to fetch me your permit.'

The older woman reached for the carbine and I pulled it out of her reach.

'The permit?' I said.

'I've lost it.'

'Unfortunate.'

'Well, it might be in the office somewhere,' she said.

'That's the spirit. I'll wait. In the meantime, Marta, I need to use your phone. Perhaps you can show me where it is.'

'It's right over there.' Holz pointed to a booth by the lobby entrance.

'I'll need to speak to Marta, Frau Holz. Now, off you pop and find that permit, eh?'

Holz retreated to her office and I took Marta with me to the booth. I picked up the receiver, connected with the operator and asked for police headquarters. A desk sergeant took the call and told me Vogel wasn't there.

'But he did give me a message to give you, Detective Klein, in case you called.'

I pressed the earpiece tightly to the side of my head. 'Yes?'

'He said to tell you your prank was very funny.'

'What?'

'Oh, and the next time you want to ask him for a real favour, he says you can shove it up your *arsch*.'

'*What?*'

'Don't ask me, detective. That's all he said.'

I hung up. Clearly, something had gone wrong. Had Du Pont and the green man cleared out of the cellar before Vogel could get there? If so, where was Du Pont? Had something happened to him?

Marta cleared her throat, a reminder to keep my focus. I turned to her and tried putting on a smile that wouldn't show the strain I was feeling.

'You knew Emma Gross, didn't you Marta?'

161

She nodded. I didn't say anything, and after another short while she stopped nodding and said, 'Yes.'

'Was she a regular guest here?'

'Yes.'

'Did you speak to her often?'

'Just sometimes.' She smiled. 'She would give me chocolates sometimes. Sometimes spare change. She was nice, I liked her. After she had noisy... suitors...' Those liquid black eyes appealed to me not to judge her for slipping into hooker slang. I smiled and leaned closer to encourage her to go on. 'They were bad sometimes. They hit her I think, though she'd never say so. After those times she'd give me money or sweets or fruit. She was nice.'

'Are you sad she's dead, Marta?'

'Murder is a terrible thing isn't it, detective?' Her words spilled out as though she'd been waiting a long time for someone to say them to.

'Did you see or hear anything that happened that night?'

'No...' Her tone suggested she had more to say, only she couldn't find a way of saying it. I needed to hit upon the right question to open her up.

'Who discovered Emma's body that night?'

'Her friend.'

'Friend?'

'Yes, another... night worker, like Emma was.'

'A girl in the same business, you mean?'

She nodded.

'What's her name?'

'Trudi something. Something with an "S" I think.'

'She a regular too?'

'She was.'

'But not now?'

'No, not now.' Marta's frown went deep.

'Would you know where I can find Trudi?'

Marta took me back to the check-in desk, ducked beneath it and came up with a match book, which she gave to me. A name was printed on it: *Willi's*. Beneath that was an address.

'It's a bar,' Marta whispered.

'Thank you, Marta.' I wanted to give her some spare change or some chocolate too, but I couldn't. If this lead went somewhere and it came out that she'd had money or sweets from me then a defence lawyer could call bribery. I'd seen a few cases laid low that way. Instead, I patted the back of Marta's hand and she beamed at me.

Holz clearly hadn't found her permit, since she was still in her office. Assuming she'd really had one and wasn't just playing for time. I checked my pockets for the carbine magazine, then I left it and the gun on the desk and walked out of the hotel.

Permit be damned. I had to go check that cellar for myself.

19.

The coal cellar door hung open on its one remaining hinge.

I whispered for Du Pont. No one answered, so down I went, waiting at the bottom of the concrete steps for my eyes to adapt to the gloom. The moon lit part of the way. That was enough to see by. The back stalls of the cellar were empty of anything bar the coal they were supposed to hold.

No Du Pont. No green man.

I waited. What for, I couldn't say. But I waited anyway. Then I looked around for any trace of what might have happened.

There was nothing of use there. Certainly no clues as to where they might have gone. All I could see were traces of police footwear that had stirred up the dust. At least it looked as though Vogel had been as good as his word. But that was a bad thing, of course. For not only did Vogel now think I'd been playing games with him, but the two men I'd left down there were missing.

Now I had an angry Commie reporter and a mystery thug with a broken wrist out roaming the streets. Well, Du Pont was a talker. If they'd gone off together, there was no way he hadn't got some information out of the green man. Or so I hoped. Though even that slender hope would come to nothing unless I could track down Du Pont.

I returned to the steps, hand on the Luger in my pocket in case of ambush. I trod on something soft. I raised my foot and looked down. I'd stood on Du Pont's flat cap. I squatted and picked it up. It was damp. I held it under a shaft of moonlight and saw a dark patch. I noticed similar dark patches on the floor. To my battered mind they looked like blood spatter.

***

Call it tiredness from the fact it was just after midnight, but I missed the front door of Willi's the first two times I walked past. The third time I noticed the 'sign', a small imperial flag with the word *Willi's* stitched into the fabric. The flag jutted into the street at an angle.

I pulled open the door, got a blast of warmth and humidity and harsh jazz music and a smell that was probably stale beer laced with tobacco. Or sweat laced with tobacco. Or maybe all three. Willi's was a step-down bar, the stairs winding deeper even than those of the accursed coal cellar.

I descended the steps. At the bottom, I brushed through a black and white curtain into a low-ceilinged room filled with round tables. A bar lined the left wall and the music was louder here. A piano tinkled atop a foundation of drum and double bass, with some brass or woodwind or something on the side.

The band sat at the back of a small stage at the far end of the room, the lights thickening the tobacco smoke so that the musicians looked like bow-tied genies on the lam from their Baghdad oil lamp internments. A woman danced on the stage in front of the band. She was naked but for the spiked imperial army helmet and – I kid you not – false Kaiser Bill moustache she wore. Her dancing was uncoordinated but that didn't matter much because the crowd at the tables wasn't really looking.

Waitresses bustled through the room with trays of drinks, this Trudi somewhere among them. They wore the same whole lot of fake-moustachioed, spikey-helmeted nothing as the girl on the stage. It was a distinctive look, there was that going for it.

The barman noticed me as I approached the bar. I sat on a stool and met his gaze. He smoothed his waxed moustache with meaty fingers, his clean-shaven head reflecting light from the kerosene lanterns on every table.

I pointed at his face fur. 'Yours fake too?'

'What do you want here, detective?'

'How about a drink?'

'Aren't you on duty?'

'What do you care?'

He thought about this, rubbing the stubble on his jutting chin. He pulled a small beer from the tap and set it down in front of me.

'Now,' he said, 'what do you want?'

'I'm looking for a woman who works here. She's called Trudi.'

'This Trudi have a last name?'

'Does she need one? How many Trudis do you have?'

'I just don't want any trouble from a dumb bull like you.' He leaned on the bar. His baggy linen shirt did little to conceal the web of green tattoos covering his taut triceps or his thick chest.

'The only way we're going to have any trouble here is if you keep talking to me that way.'

The barman lit himself a cigarette. 'She'll be getting changed about now.' He moved down the bar and left me with my beer.

I sipped it. It tasted sour.

A girl wandered over. She had long blond hair under her spiked helmet and her moustache was full and thick and black.

'Hey Bern, you got a pad for me?' she said to the barman.

He handed her an order pad and nodded at me. 'Guy here wants to talk to you.'

The girl looked me up and down and shook her head. 'I don't think so, Bern.' She laughed. 'You'd better give him his money back.'

Bern touched her arm as she went to walk away. 'He's a bull.'

She looked again. I let her look while I took in a few

details of my own in the back bar mirror. Someone, and my money was on Bern, had taped two glossy photographic prints to the mirror. One was of our dear departed Kaiser Wilhelm II, the other of our glorious president, Field Marshal Paul von Hindenburg.

'You been in the wars, soldier?' the girl said, suddenly up close.

I took a deep breath but my sinuses were still too swollen to make out what scent she wore, if any. I looked her up and down. Not even any jewellery, though she had a mole on one hip and a small red scar to the left of her belly button.

'How does the moustache stay on?' I said.

'What do you mean?' she said, fondling it. 'This is all natural. It's my hair that's fake.'

'Nice.' I glanced at her blond crotch, a reflex action.

'Thanks. I get that a lot.'

'Not sure about the helmet though.'

'Look, I need to get along and earn my tips, so do you want to come to the point?'

Her eyes were blue, not brown. This would be a cinch. I took a quick sip of beer.

'You knew Emma Gross?' I said.

She folded her arms, a move that emphasised what little cleavage she had. 'Why are you here bringing this up now? Emma's death was more than a year ago.'

Her pale skin was colouring up beautifully. This wouldn't be such a cinch after all. I was turning soft, remember.

'We've reopened the case. We don't think we got the right guy last time.'

'Oh yeah, who's we? Cause that detective I spoke with last year, he wasn't worth shit.'

'And who was that?'

'What, you think I've got nothing better to do than sit around remembering detectives' names?'

'Why don't you just relax and tell me what you know, and this'll all go a lot smoother.'

167

'Are you threatening me now?'

'No, I –'

'Bern, did you hear that, this guy's threatening me.'

Bern rubbed a hand over the stubble on his head. I put my palms down on the sticky surface of the bar.

'Look, Trudi, no one's threatening anyone,' I said.

'You got someone for the murder already. Why would you want to go hunting for someone else?'

'Did Emma have a boyfriend?'

'Oh man...'

'Yes or no.'

'No.' Something in her face told me there was more.

'But?'

'But what?'

'She didn't have a boyfriend but there was... someone, right? A girlfriend?'

'Christ on the cross, Herr Detective, not all prostitutes are dykes, you know.'

'So tell me. She had someone, but not a boyfriend?'

Applause from the tables drowned out her words. The woman on stage twirled on her heels as the band syncopated its tune all to hell. Trudi moved closer. One of her pink nipples brushed my jacket sleeve but I put that down as a mistake.

'There was some guy,' she said, raising her voice, 'some suitor she had regular. I never knew his name, though God knows I tried to find out. But she wouldn't say. Then it all went... different somehow. I don't know. We didn't talk for a long time.'

'But you worked the same hotel. The Adler? Worked the same streets around the station, right?'

Trudi went over to Bern, who was keeping his distance. She took his cigarette from between his lips and jammed it into her own mouth and smoked off more than half of it in a couple of puffs. Hell of a trick, though hardly surprising given her former calling.

She came back with the cigarette burning in her fingers and said, 'Yes.'

168

'So you saw her around even though you stopped talking so regularly?'

'Uh-huh.' She took another drag. The cigarette was down to the end now.

'About how long before she died did she stop talking to you?'

'Couple of months. Sometime after Christmas. We'd had a nice Christmas together. Worked all through but on the 24th, the evening, when we gave each other presents. It was nice, you know? Something to remind us of home?'

She smiled, gazing into the distance, seeing beyond the confines of the cellar bar in its faceless city street. 'It wasn't like she stopped talking to me, if you get me. She withdrew all round, didn't really talk to anyone so much. I don't know what it was, but it wasn't long after she started with this regular suitor. I think that was something to do with it.'

'Two months isn't that long a time to go without regular contact,' I said.

Her eyes flashed lamp light at me. 'It is when you've been so... it's a hell of a long time in streetwalker years, bull.'

'Were you two lovers, Trudi?'

She dropped the smoking stub and ground it out under her heels. Funny, I hadn't noticed she'd been wearing shoes earlier.

'Okay, it doesn't matter. This regular guy, you never saw him?'

'I might have done, but I wouldn't know. Never one for taking it easy, our Emma. There was never any one guy I noticed her with more than any other.' She locked eyes with me. 'They all get to look the same, after a while.'

I held myself still. 'You found her in room thirty-seven that night?'

She shook her head and sighed the last of the smoke from her lungs. 'Next morning. About six.'

'How'd you know she was in there?'

'I had a suitor the same night. I saw her go upstairs.

169

Didn't see her come down. In the morning I saw the key for thirty-seven was still missing from the pigeon hole and I went up to knock on the door. It was open and she was inside.'

'Did you see the suitor she went upstairs with?'

Trudi looked up from staring at the floor. 'No, damn it!' She said, 'You think if I'd seen him I wouldn't have shouted it out loud to the world?' She gave a disgusted grunt and waved me away. 'But I told you all this before.'

'Me?'

'No, that other detective.'

'Dark hair, buck teeth?'

'That's right.'

'Name of Ritter? Inspector Michael Ritter?'

'Well, Inspector someone-or-other. Beyond that I don't remember. But the teeth, yeah, that sounds like him. He didn't seem all that interested so how'm I supposed to believe you'll be any different?'

'Trudi, if you know something –'

'Frieda,' she said. 'Frieda Brandt. Find her.'

Trudi lifted a drinks tray from behind the bar and moved off with her sights on the tables.

'Who is she?' I called.

'Emma came to me that night, the night she died. We had a talk. There was a lot going on. Find Frieda Brandt. If anyone can tell you more, she can.'

'Where do I find her?' I called.

'If I knew that I'd tell you,' she called back.

Bern had crept closer over the course of the conversation. Now, as I looked at him, he shrugged.

'Another beer?' He pointed at my glass.

'No, save it.' I pushed off the stool and got to my feet. 'Tastes like shit, anyway.'

'You're breaking my heart, bull. Do you want to try some other place next time?'

The girl on stage had finished her act. The band stopped playing. The drummer gave a circus roll and the girl whipped off her fake moustache to a smattering of

170

applause. Many of the drinkers sported fake moustaches too. What some people would do for fun.

I headed for the curtain, in reality a large black-and-white imperial banner, the bigger brother of the one hanging above the door outside. So now I had another name but no idea of how the woman who owned it might be connected to the case. Of course, the best way of finding that out would be to find her. I had the feeling that would be easier said than done.

20.

First thing you did when you wanted to find someone in Düsseldorf? You hit the residential records. Each precinct house kept records of who lived in its precinct; whenever anyone moved, he had to notify his local precinct before registering his new address with whichever precinct he'd moved to.

Two snags. First, not everyone bothered to register. Second, there was no central department to coordinate these records. If I wanted Frieda Brandt's address I'd have to visit each and every precinct until I found it.

Unless...

I took a bus to my precinct. If not for the sign above the door and the bars on the ground floor windows, the station house would have been impossible to distinguish from the five-storey apartment buildings either side of it. It had the same weathered, unwashed façade, the same number of high windows, the same three steps leading from the street to the door. As I walked up the steps, the place felt like home, albeit the kind of home you never wanted to go back to.

I pushed through the door into the waiting area. Two *Schupo* were wrestling a citizen to the ground beneath the information board. A couple of the posters had come loose and floated to the tiled floor. The citizen was babbling the way habitual drunks do. Despite my busted nose, the smell of weeks-old booze-sweat made it through and I had to hold my breath as the *Schupo* hauled the man to his feet and to the cells in the basement.

I greeted the desk sergeant, a tall, dark-haired man with mutton-chop whiskers who'd only worked on my shift a couple of times. He loomed from the front desk. The clock on the wall beside him told me it was twenty to one in the morning. Aside from the echoes of the drunk yelling on his way to the cells, the place was quiet enough to hear the clock ticking. The sergeant had been filling in a form. I handed him my ID.

'Captain's not about I suppose?'

The sergeant glanced at the clock and then gave me a look.

'All right.' I held up my hands. 'Stupid question. I need to leave him a message, then. I'll go and take it to his office.'

He shrugged, emphasising the breadth of his shoulders. The electric lamp overhead made his oiled hair gleam.

'Kaufmann's running the squad tonight,' he said.

'Thanks.'

'He's out on a burglary though. Only just gone, so if you need to speak to him...'

'I should be okay, thanks.'

Andreas Kaufmann, a detective on the opposite shift to mine. I'd worked with him a couple of times. He was a competent man. Better, he'd be out for the next couple of hours, which gave me the time I needed. I walked past the desk to the stairwell, pushed through the door and went up the stairs. I went up to the second floor. At the end of the hall was the captain's office. I headed for that and opened the door.

It wasn't locked. It was never locked, for one simple reason. It was the only room in the building with a telephone. It had to be kept open in case the night watch commander had to make a call.

The large desk looked small against the size of the office, which stretched across the building. There were two windows on opposite sides of the room, one looking out onto the street, the other looking over the courtyards of apartment buildings. Filing cabinets lined the wall behind the desk. The telephone sat on the desk blotter, its thick rat's tail cable running into the chipped plaster of the wall. There was a small leather-bound address book nestled between empty paperwork trays. I turned on the desk lamp and a moth started flitting around the light. I swiped at it and missed.

I opened the book. Each precinct number was listed under 'P'. Made sense.

I lifted the phone's handle from the cradle and waited for the line to connect, the moth flapping at my face. When the operator came on, I asked for the first precinct number on the list. The operator connected me. Eventually a yawning voice answered the phone and I asked the man on the other end to look through his residential records for a Frieda Brandt and to call back if he found anything. I repeated this process ten times, then I hit the records room down the hall.

An hour later, I'd got six negative phone calls and a big fat *nichts* from the precinct files. Whoever this woman was, she didn't live in Flingern, and never had. No, nor Grafenberg, Unterbilk, Oberbilk, Friedrichstadt, Altstadt or Derendorf either.

The phone rang again and I went to answer it.

'Hello?' I said into the receiver.

'Hi, is that Detective Klein?'

'Yes, Klein here.'

'Hello?'

The line buzzed and crackled and the sound of faint voices filtered through.

'Hello?' I said.

'Hello? Are you there?'

'Yes, can you hear me?'

'Yes, I can hear you. Can you hear me?'

'Yes, fine. Do you have any information for me?'

'Yes,' the other cop said. 'We've got an address for her here in Flehe. Fifty-five Uedesheimer Strasse. It's near the park.'

I thanked him and hung up.

21.

It was too late to rely on public transportation, so I took a cab out to Flehe. Every so often during the drive I'd look back to check if the green man was following me. If he was, I didn't see him. The Rhine curled up under this district of the city, giving it a cut-off island feel. The houses we drove past were large, three or four storeys high.

The cab pulled up outside number fifty-five. I paid the driver and opened the front gate as the cab drove off. The gate carried three post boxes, suggesting this house was broken up into flats. Sure enough, there were three buzzers by the door, each one bearing a different name. None of the names was Brandt. Of course, maybe Brandt had been the woman's maiden name. Maybe she'd married. Maybe, maybe, maybe. The cogs of police work are oiled with maybes.

Or so I told myself as I pressed the buzzer for the ground floor flat. I kept my finger on for several seconds. Then I buzzed again. It was quarter-to-two in the morning. Area like this, no autos about, nobody out walking the streets, it was a safe guess that I was waking the inhabitants.

I waited two minutes then buzzed again. A light came on inside the house. A shape lumbered between the light and the glass panel in the door, then the door opened. A middle-aged man stared at me with puffy eyes and mussed brown hair and a paisley patterned dressing gown that was too short for his smooth, hairless legs. He was still tying the belt around his thick middle.

I held up my ID and checked the name on the buzzer. 'Herr Weber?' I said.

He grunted.

'I'm looking for Frieda Brandt.'

'Well she doesn't live here.'

I waited for him to add anything. He didn't.

'She used to live here,' I said. 'She's registered at this address.'

'Oh, right.'

Another shape hovered behind Weber.

'Honey? Who is it?' A woman's voice.

Weber turned back and said, 'Just get on with the coffee, will you?'

'But who is it, Uli?'

'It's the police.'

'What do they want?'

'Yeah, what is all this about anyway?' Weber asked me.

'I told you,' I said, 'Frieda Brandt.'

'What's she done?' Weber said.

'Frieda? Oh, she was nice,' said the female voice.

Weber huffed and threw open the door and gestured for me to come in, so in I went, through the vestibule and into the ground floor apartment. African art and masks hung on the wall, the overall effect one of dark wood and white animal hair. Frau Weber was small and round and had deep wrinkles around her eyes and mouth, though the rest of her face was smooth.

'You're having coffee at this time of the morning?' I asked her.

She nodded while her husband said, 'Well, I'm awake now. I won't be able to sleep again, not for hours. And I've a lot to do tomorrow, so I might as well get started.' He didn't bother to keep the annoyance from his voice.

I nodded at the African artefacts on the walls. 'And what is it you do, Herr Weber?'

'Uli teaches at the university. Don't you, sweetie?'

Weber had pushed past to the kitchen where it sounded as though a coffee pot was bubbling on the stove.

'Lecture, dearest,' Weber called back, 'I lecture at the university, I don't teach. There is a difference.'

Frau Weber rolled her eyes at me, but she was smiling.

'Frau Weber, you knew Frieda Brandt?'

'Oh yes.' She finger-combed her shoulder-length dark hair and rearranged her thick cotton robe. She called out to the kitchen: 'Don't you remember, sweetie? We took the flat from her.' There was a grunt from the kitchen. Frau Weber added. 'She was so helpful, taking us through the rental contract and pointing out what the landlord would and wouldn't do, all that. It was most helpful. Yes, she was nice.'

'Do you have any idea where she moved to?'

'Oh, I'm sorry. She didn't say.'

'How long ago did you move in?'

'About a year and a half. Actually, probably closer to two now I think about it.'

'In 1928?'

'Yes, that's right. After the summer it was. Say September or October.'

'Is there anything else you can tell me about Frau Brandt? Where she worked, perhaps? Whether she worked? Was she married? Did she have any children?'

Frau Weber gave a girlish giggle. Her face crinkled for a brief second before settling down again. 'She certainly wasn't married. I got the feeling she didn't have much time for it. And she didn't talk about children, not the way people do when they have any. It's possible, but I didn't see any photographs of her family at all.'

'So she worked?'

The sounds of percolation had gone and my mouth watered at the thought of fresh-brewed coffee. Weber came through with a cup for his wife and another for himself. He didn't offer me any.

'Yes, she was some kind of nurse wasn't she?' Frau Weber asked her husband who shrugged.

'What kind of nurse, do you remember?' I said. 'Did she work in a hospital, or in a dentist's surgery perhaps?'

She shook her head. 'I'm afraid I don't know that. We really only spoke together over a matter of days, detective.'

She paused. 'Did you want some coffee?'

Uli flinched. I was tempted to say yes just for the look on his face.

'No, thank you Frau Weber. You've been most helpful.' I looked at her husband. 'Sorry to disturb.'

'Any time,' he grumbled.

'By the way,' I said, 'did you rent the flat here through an agency or with the landlord directly?'

'Through an agency,' Uli Weber said.

'You remember which one?'

'Yes thanks.'

Frau Weber gave her husband a playful slap and said, 'It was Bauer and Bauer. It's not far down the road here. They have an office on Achener Strasse, on the square. It's a five minute walk. But we see the landlord from time to time too. He stops by if we have any maintenance trouble.' She disappeared through another door.

'Don't go making a mess in there, you hear?' her husband called out. Then, to me: 'That's my study.'

Before I could say anything there was a crash. Herr Weber flinched again and put down his coffee. He bustled into the study after his wife.

A few seconds later Frau Weber emerged clutching a compliments slip with a torn corner and handed it to me. The printed address read: *Herr Dornfelder, 12 Bucherweg, Meerbusch.* Meerbusch was a suburban town to the north west of the city on the other side of the Rhine, an area full of charming woodland and exclusive restaurants, as the local estate agents would probably have put it. One of those parasitical moneyed places that skimmed off the sweat of the labour toiling within the city proper, as Du Pont would probably have put it. All a matter of perspective.

'You sure you don't need this?' I said, waving the slip.

'Oh no, you take it detective. Anything to help. We have more anyway.' She beamed at me.

'Where's your local post office, Frau Weber?'

'Oh, gosh. There's one north on the Achener Strasse.

It's pretty far. Long street, that Achener Strasse.'

'How old was Frau Brandt?'

'Late forties, I would guess. But I'm not that good on people's ages, I'm afraid. She had quite a lot of grey in her hair and she didn't colour it.'

'How tall would you say she was?'

'A little taller than me. Not much.'

'And you're what? One metre fiftyish?'

'One fifty-four.'

'What kind of build did she have?'

Frau Weber chuckled and patted her belly. 'Certainly not like mine. She was thin. Especially in the face. Liked to wear loose clothing though, so it's hard to say for certain. You sure you didn't want any coffee?'

'Well...' I said. Herr Weber came crashing out of his study and gave me the mother of all scowls.

I declined the offer and left the house with a grin on my face, a little closer to Frieda Brandt, but not much. This Dornfelder was miles away and if I kept spending on taxis I'd be broke before dawn. Dornfelder could wait. The letting agency would, of course, be closed until morning, so they would have to wait. All this hassle for the forwarding address of a woman whose connection to Emma Gross I knew nothing about.

Trudi's hot lead had cooled and I'd run out of excuses. It was time to see if I could find Du Pont.

179

22.

It took me almost half an hour to find a cab in empty Flehe, but ten minutes after that the driver pulled up outside the *Volksstimme* offices. I paid him, swearing that would be the last taxi I shelled out for that night.

The offices of the newspaper occupied the first floor of the four-storey building, where the absence of lamp light suggested business was done for the night. Ditto the silence coming from the basement printing presses. Light spilled onto the pavement through the plate glass window of the bar on the ground floor where, by contrast, the night's business was just ratcheting up.

On the inside of the bar windows the staff had pasted a mock-up of the last edition to go out, blown up to poster size.

KRIPO IGNORE EVIDENCE, INSIST ON GUILT OF STAUSBERG

the headline read.

I entered the bar without bothering with the rest of the story, though I noticed it didn't carry Du Pont's byline.

Chatter filled the place, every table crowded with boisterous groups. One couple at a round table next to the toilet door were an exception, two young women holding hands across the table, fingers entwined between tall glasses of coffee topped with cream. They gazed silently into each other's eyes, two women in the same room with nothing to say. What were the odds?

I went to the bar. A young man dressed in black and sporting patchy whiskers came over. He sized me up before smiling a smile I would have sworn was genuine.

There was I, a cop in a Commie bar, and this was the first person all day who hadn't taken me for a bull as soon as clap eyes on me. Still, he couldn't have been more than twenty years old, if that. Time yet for life to grind him down.

'What happened to your face, friend? Trouble with the bulls?' When the word 'bulls' left his lips, he came off like he was mimicking the dialogue in some gangster picture.

'You could say that,' I replied. I ordered a coffee. 'Du Pont about?'

'Who? Andre?' the young guy scratched his beard. 'Haven't seen him all evening. Or Ruth either, for that matter.'

'I've got that scoop for him if he wants it,' I said, wondering who the hell Ruth was.

'Well, I suppose he must be staying home tonight.'

'But he left a message for me to meet him here. Don't tell me he's forgotten!'

The young man squinted at me and didn't say anything. If there was a time for him to make me then this was it. He scratched his beard, dislodging white flecks that settled on his dark pullover.

I made a show of glancing around, checking for bulls.

'This is dynamite stuff. Links in with the Stausberg story, you know? He's going to want this pretty bad. But I can understand you being cautious.' I got up and went through the motions of getting ready to leave. 'I mean, I can always peddle this stuff to someone else...'

'All right, all right,' the guy said, pouring coffee from a large steel urn into a cracked cup. 'Jesus, you sound just like him.' He handed me the cup and said, 'Two blocks over. Go out the door, turn right down the side of this building the two blocks, then turn right. It's number twenty-one, on the right. He's got ADPont on the door, like that.'

The guy even wrote *ADPont* out for me on a pad and handed me the slip of paper. I took a sip of coffee and struggled to swallow it. I stayed there for a few minutes and forced down another couple of scalding, weak mouthfuls. As soon as the bartender turned his back I left.

A two-minute *schlep* took me to Du Pont's building, where I pressed his buzzer on the outer door. The name-plate gave the apartment number as three, fifth floor. The door clicked open and I took the stairs at a trot.

Du Pont's apartment door was open when I got to the fifth. My hip ached and I was out of breath. I pushed open the door to the refrain of a trembling female voice:

'Andre? Andre, did you lose your keys again?'

The girl standing in the apartment hallway in a cling-ing night dress opened her mouth in a neat, round 'O' when she saw me. She was young enough to've still been in school, though her bosom suggested that, if so, she'd be getting a lot of attention from her male classmates. Freckles dotted her face. Her hair was dark and thick and tangled with interrupted sleep.

'You must be Ruth,' I said.

'Who are you?'

'A friend of Andre's. He's not here, I take it?'

'No.' Ruth vanished through the nearest doorway and re-emerged with a blanket across her shoulders.

'Damn. I was hoping he would be. I haven't seen him since just before lunch.'

'You saw him at lunchtime?' Her eager tone told me the last time I'd seen him was more recent than the last time she had. Oh dear. That suggested Du Pont really was missing.

'More or less. What about you?'

'Well, he got up about six and he was gone before I left for lectures.'

'You haven't seen him since?'

'No. It's not like him to stay away like this. Well, of course this is exactly like him, but not without sending me some kind of message to let me know where he is.'

'So you don't know where he is?' I said. She shook her head. What if something had happened to him? What if the green man had killed him or kidnapped him or something? Okay, so Du Pont had betrayed me for a good story and what happened to him I couldn't care less about, but what might he write about me if the green man had tried to kill him, and failed?

I rubbed my eyes, forgetting about the bruising yet again. The pain shot through my skull and woke me up some.

'Do you have any cognac?' I asked.

'Of course. This way.'

Ruth led me to a living room. The room must have been at least ten by ten, the floor done out in parquet and scattered with rugs. Two large couches faced each other on one side of the room, a long oak dining table and chairs filling the other side. Behind one of the couches was a chrome and glass drinks trolley piled high with bottles. Ruth selected one that was full of dark honey-hued liquid. She poured a healthy dose into a snifter and handed it to me.

I gulped half the drink and then sat on the corner of the couch by the trolley. The cognac warmed my throat and made me gag at the same time, which was some measure of the day I'd had. Through the windows, church spires and a couple of taller apartment buildings provided most of the ingredients for a good view. And was that the roof of the town hall in the Altstadt a little further off, lit up by street lamps? Not a bad place, this. It put my shitty single room to shame. If this was how Communists lived, bring on the revolution.

'Do you think something's happened to him?' Ruth said, breaking my cognac-induced trance.

'I do,' I said, before I'd given myself time to think it over. I could've kicked myself for the look of worry that crossed the girl's face. 'You been seeing him long?' I asked. 'We've known each other a good while, but he never mentioned you.'

'A year,' she said, pouring a drink for herself. 'Just over.' She drained her glass and then clutched it close.

I got up and took the glass from her, poured her another drink and gave it back. She put some effort into trying to smile, but the effect was all effort and no smile. Killer dimples, though.

Brown eyes, of course.

'You don't suppose...' she began. 'Look, I don't want to go to the police about this, but I'm worried, and you're a policeman, and here you are looking for him. Would you find him for me?'

'I'll do what I can.' I finished my drink and set my glass down on the trolley. I went over and tousled her hair before leaving the apartment. I'd wanted to kiss her on the cheek or something, but she'd looked so young that it hadn't seemed right.

I couldn't help wondering how a slob like Du Pont had ended up with such a knock-out.

23.

There were four hospitals on the city side of the river. Two were out east, in Grafenberg. The medical academy research and teaching hospital lay south, at the very edge of the city's Bilk district. The nearest and smallest of the four hospitals, St. Vincent's, was a half hour walk north to Derendorf. It didn't take me long to decide where to go. I headed north.

St. Vincent's turned up negative for Frieda Brandt's employment records or admissions of men matching Du Pont's name or description. So, where next? The coal cellar had been closer to Grafenberg, but the academy hospital was closest to Brandt's old address. It was a question of priorities. I thought of Ruth's sleep-tangled hair and freckles and struck out east. Hell, I had all night. What else was I going to do? Sleep? Grafenberg was only forty-five minutes away by foot from Derendorf anyway, half the distance of the southerly option.

When I got to the Grafenberg woods, I took the Bismarkweg through the trees to the hospital complex rather than stick to the main road. My watch told me it was four a.m. The night air felt warmer than it had for weeks, and the wind had died away completely.

The bushes rustled ahead of me. No breeze meant something was moving about in there. These woods had been one of Kürten's play areas. How many victims would it turn out that he'd raped and killed among those trees? How many other Kürtens were out there doing the same right at that moment?

I emerged from the wood and moonlight bathed my face. The hospital complex spread itself before me, perhaps a

185

score of buildings dating from the eighteenth and nineteenth centuries, tall brick structures comprising their own village: the march of modern progress against the fairytale nightmares of the pre-modern age. Civilisation amid the forest.

A sign at the front gate pointed out the main reception not twenty metres away, in one of the largest of the hospital buildings. I went up a short flight of steps and pushed through the revolving door.

I flashed my ID at the nurse, or receptionist, or whatever she was who sat at the front desk. She wore sombre office clothes, so she probably wasn't a nurse. There was a faint medicinal smell in the air. Off to the left was an area full of open seating where a knot of patients sat reading magazines. One of them shuffled in her seat while another one raised a fist to his mouth and coughed.

'I'm looking for a man who might have been admitted here earlier today,' I told the woman at reception. 'Well, technically any time between yesterday and this morning, I suppose I mean. You know what I mean, right?' She nodded. 'Good. Name of Du Pont, Andre Du Pont.'

'Can you be any more precise about the time?' the woman asked. She had a deep, calm voice that failed to match the scowl on her face.

'Anytime from one p.m. yesterday. That's as precise as I can manage.'

'What injuries did he have?'

'I don't know.'

'Missing persons, is it?' she said, reaching for an admissions folder in the filing cabinet next to her chair.

'Pretty routine, but he's a possible witness and I need to interview him.'

'Well, I shouldn't think we would allow you to trouble him at this time of the morning.' She flashed me a brief smile. 'That's if he's here. Let me see...'

She flicked through paperwork. There looked to be a lot of it. 'Couldn't be any more precise, could you?'

'Sorry.' I shook my head and tried to look sympathetic.

'I mean, that's over twelve hours... Oh, here we are.'
The surprise in her voice matched the surprise I felt.

'No, really?' I said.

'Yes, looks like. Andre Du Pont. Lives in Stadtmitte?'

'That's right.'

'Okay, let's see. Picked up on Grafenberger Allee, admitted to A&E at three-thirty yesterday afternoon. Multiple bruises, minor cuts, it says on this form. Some kind of difficulty talking, like he was drunk or something.'

'Drunk?'

'Well, those are just the initial notes, you understand. Looks like he's sustained quite a battering.'

'Thank you. Where would he be now?'

'P ward, according to this.'

'P for Placid?'

'I'm sorry?'

'Don't worry. Just a bad joke. Which way is P ward?'

The woman pointed to a series of signs tacked to a nearby wall. P ward was signposted to the left, past the open waiting area. I scanned the signs for indications as to where employee records might be. As I'd expected, there wasn't a sign for that.

'Before I go, I'm also looking for a nurse called Frieda Brandt. She's about one metre fifty to one fifty-five in height. Slim build. In her late forties. Greying hair.'

The woman shook her head. 'I don't know everyone here. I tend to work nights more often than not, but that's not a name I recognise.'

'Do you have an employee records department?'

'It'll be all locked up this time of night.'

'And who do I speak to to get the key?'

'I'm not sure.'

'Why don't you find out for me while I go and talk to my witness?'

The woman gave me a dirty look, but I got a laugh out of her when I blew her a kiss.

P ward was quiet and dark, the only light coming from

the nurse's station, a separate little room at the entrance to the ward. Two nurses sat in the station on small chairs, drinking coffee from cups resting on a card table. They were in the middle of a game.

'I'm here to speak to Andre Du Pont,' I said, showing them my ID.

The nurses looked at each other, then at me.

'He's an important witness in a case. You've heard about the arrest of the Ripper?'

That did it. The nurse closest to me leapt to her feet and straightened her starched headgear before beckoning me onto the ward with her.

'I can't make any promises that he'll be awake,' she said, rubbing her left earlobe. She was small and dark and had a fuzzy moustache outline clinging to her top lip. I was tempted to ask if she ever moonlighted at Willi's.

'Don't worry,' I said. 'I can wake him if necessary.'

I followed the nurse the length of the ward. Beds jutted into the room from both walls. Each bed we passed had a night stand and a lamp, and each bed was occupied. Most of the occupants slept, though some fidgeted.

Du Pont was in the last bed on the left. His lamp was off. The nurse bent down to switch it on. The sudden light made Du Pont blink: he'd been lying dead still and watching my approach. His brows formed an angry V and a large bruise bloomed at his left temple. Another bruise marred his jaw and left cheek. His beard looked crooked somehow, and blood crusted on his chin. When he scratched his face I saw that the back of the hand was bruised and one of his fingers was bandaged to a splint.

'Thank you, nurse,' I said. 'I'll call you if I need you.'

The nurse paused, looked at Du Pont, put the case notes down on the night stand, and left.

'How are you, Andre?'

He said nothing.

Okay, so he was angry with me, I could understand that. After all, I'd given him at least one of those bruises. And the split lip.

188

'You know who sent me after you?'

Nothing.

'Ruth.'

He blinked. He shook both hands at me. After a few seconds, I realised he was making a writing gesture, miming a pencil on paper. I handed him my notebook and pencil. He scribbled on the page and gave me back the notebook. HOW IS SHE? I read.

'Worried about you, my friend. How long you going to be in here, did they say?' The book changed hands again.

NOT YET

'So what's with the scribbling?'

JAW WIRED SHUT

I laughed. That explained the crooked appearance of his beard, and the trouble speaking the receptionist had mentioned. Du Pont glared at me.

'Oh come on, Du Pont. To anyone who knows you, that's funny.'

He started to write something, then scratched it out so hard he tore a hole in the paper.

'Did the green man do this to you?'

?

Oh yeah, that's right. Green man was just the name I'd given him in my head. No one else would know that was how I thought of him.

'The guy we tied to the railings. The one with the gun who followed us. Did he do this?'

YES

'Why?'

Du Pont rolled his eyes and wrote: THE HELL SHOULD I KNOW? HE DIDN'T SAY

'He didn't say what he wanted?'

Du Pont shook his head. HE ASKED IF THE STORY I WROTE ABOUT GERTRUDE ALBERMANN WAS TRUE

'Which story?'

MONDAY'S STORY YOU IDIOT. THE ONLY ONE I WROTE ABOUT HER

189

'Oh, the one with the made-up interview with me? That the one you mean?'

YES

'Did he say anything else?'

HE'S ANGRY AT YOU FOR HITTING HIM AND TAKING HIS GUN

'Anything else?'

I'M ANGRY TOO

'I mean about the Albermann girl. Come on, Andre, you're the best damn reporter out there. If anyone could've got information out of this guy, it's you. You didn't get his name, I suppose?'

NO. ACCENT LOCAL. HAS A TEMPER. LIKES TO KICK. WEARS STURDY SHOES. THAT'S IT

'You didn't see what brand of shoe he was wearing?'

THE KIND THAT HURTS

'So was he following me or was he following you?'

Du Pont shrugged.

'I got a lead on the Emma Gross case,' I said. 'Does the name Frieda Brandt ring any bells?'

Give him his due, he thought it over for a while. Then he shook his head and scribbled some more in the notebook.

WHAT ELSE YOU GOT ON HER?

'I think she used to work as a nurse. Used to live down in Flehe, near the park, but that was at least eighteen months ago.'

SOUNDS LIKE A WELL-PAID NURSE. SHE UNREGISTERED?

'Yes.'

WHAT KIND OF NURSE?

'I don't know yet.'

WHAT KIND OF DETECTIVE ARE YOU?

'I found you, didn't I?'

We stared at each other. He didn't write anything for a couple of minutes and I stood in silence, waiting. He sighed, and wrote:

CAN YOU FIND OUT WHEN THEY'LL LET ME GO?

TRY AND TELL RUTH. TELL HER I'M OK?

'No problem,' I said.

CAN YOU TELL HER I'M THINKING OF HER?

His eyes held no embarrassment, and nor did he shy away from my gaze. He scribbled some more.

HEY, I WOULDN'T ASK BUT YOU'RE THE ONLY ONE KNOWS I'M HERE

'Okay, Du Pont, I'll do it.'

I'LL GET YOU BACK FOR THIS IF IT'S THE LAST THING I DO

I took the notebook and pencil and pocketed them. I laughed again, couldn't tell whether or not he was being serious.

'Andre, my friend. If you try and get me back for this, it *will* be the last thing you do.'

He turned away from me. I switched off his lamp and walked back through the ward to the nurses' station. The small, hairy-lipped nurse was there. Her colleague had gone off somewhere.

'Any idea when he'll be okay to go home?' I said. 'He's missing his lady friend.'

'Should be some time tomorrow morning. Thursday morning, I mean, not later today. The doctor wants to check for concussion. If he's got concussion then I can't say. That's up to the doctor when he sees him.'

'Thank you, nurse.'

I went back to the woman at the reception and she rang a bell. A janitor came round the corner with a set of keys. He must have been nearing pensionable age. He looked fragile enough to break if he tried any cleaning. He led me to a door located down a flight of stairs and a good ten metres of dimly lit hallway. It was warm down there, but that was where the positives ended. This floor hadn't been swept in a while, and were those mouse droppings or dead insects littering the skirting board?

I waited while the old man unlocked the door and opened it with a flourish. I thanked him and entered the room. The room was full of dust, as well as paper and wooden cabinets and cardboard boxes that were collecting dust. Also cobwebs, which of course were collecting dust too.

I left the room two hours later with a running nose, running eyes, a sore throat and no goddamned information on Frieda goddamned Brandt.

24.

I came up empty for Brandt at the Gerresheim Hospital down the road, too. By then it was after six in the morning and I had a nice, ripe headache to lay beside my sore throat. Sick of walking at that point, I threw prudence to the wolves and took a cab south.

Twenty-five minutes of desultory cabbie talk about the economy later, we pulled up outside the Moorenstrasse entrance on the north side of the academy hospital complex. I went in, found the main reception and repeated my now over-familiar spiel about Brandt.

A white-coated doctor sidled up and cleared his throat. He'd yet to break into his fourth decade of life. His chin looked so smooth that, on reflex, I scratched at my five o'clock shadow.

'Excuse me,' the doctor said, 'but you were asking about Frieda?'

'I was. That is, I am.'

His smile spread across his face quicker than red wine on a white table cloth. 'Thank God, is she okay?'

'Well, that's just the point, she seems to have disappeared. I'm trying to locate her.'

'Oh, damn. I'd hoped it was good news. Or at least news.'

'Doctor, if there's something you can tell me, I'd be grateful. Anything could help.'

The doctor checked his wrist watch.

'It's important that I locate Frau Brandt as soon as I can,' I said.

He handed the file he'd been holding to one of the three receptionists at the front desk. We walked down a wide hall and around a corner.

He opened a door and led me into the room beyond. The room was small, carpeted in blue, with overstuffed sofas and armchairs lining the undecorated walls. Outside, the sun had risen high enough that its rays were peeking through a window that looked out upon meadows and trees and the beginnings of yet another road begun before the stock market crash in New York the previous October had made finance so hard to come by. The fringes of the city were full of such unwound civic threads, all thanks to the machinations of faceless men in a crowded room in a faraway city where they didn't even speak the same language as me. Maybe political nuts like Du Pont had it right, after all. There were plenty in the labour unions, and plenty more sleeping rough in the streets and empty warehouses down by the docks, who would agree with him. Me? I didn't have the energy for all that. I had too much to do looking after myself, and I wasn't doing such a hot job in that department either.

'Would you like coffee?' the doctor asked.

There was no point resisting. I collapsed into the nearest sofa with a yawn. My body was too tired to carry it through though, and I stretched without managing to work out any of the tension in my legs or shoulders. The doctor went through an open door into an adjoining room. He lit the stove and put some coffee on to boil.

'Milk and sugar?' he asked.

'Neither.'

'Good man. Nor me.' His speech seemed old-fashioned for such a young man.

The doctor wiped his fingers on a stained piece of cotton that might once have been a towel. I hoped he washed his hands before surgery. When he came back into the sitting-room, his white coat was unbuttoned. He was wearing suit trousers and waistcoat beneath, and a white shirt topped off with a high collar and a blue-and-white striped neck tie. A pink scar slashed across his forehead, a scar that I'd taken at first to be a mark from wearing a hat that was too small.

194

'You have information for me, doctor?'

He sat at the other end of my sofa and turned towards me, fiddling with his wedding ring. 'It's not good news. Frieda left the hospital under fraught circumstances.'

'Would you care to elaborate?'

'She was a good nurse, a damn good nurse. In fact, she was a midwife, and I think the best in the hospital. I'd just qualified when I arrived here back in 'twenty-four. Even fresher-faced then.' He stroked his chin to emphasise the point. 'Oh, hold on.'

He leapt up and into the kitchen, made the coffee and returned with two steaming cups of the stuff in under two minutes. His clipped movements were neat and precise. Of course, he was too young to have served in the trenches. Perhaps the military bearing ran in the family.

A midwife, though. That stirred something in me. I didn't like the sound of it.

I sipped my coffee and scalded the roof of my mouth sufficiently to jolt me awake. Coffee spilled onto my crotch.

'Oh, look out fella,' the doctor cried. 'You want a towel for that?' He groped for the kitchen, halfway to his feet. I thought of the stained towel.

'No doctor, please, don't trouble yourself. Just clumsiness, is all.' I patted at my overheated testicles with overheated fingers and hoped I hadn't done myself too much damage. I shifted in my seat and moved to a drier spot, crossing my legs to cover the stain. Well, I was awake now, damn it, and my guts were aching too, but what the hell had set that off?

'Where was I?' the doctor said.

'Midwife,' I prompted. 'Damn good one.'

'That's right. I'm an obstetrician. Dr Flensburger. Julius Flensburger.'

'Detective Thomas Klein.'

He extended a hand and we shook.

'Glad to know you, detective,' he said.

'So, Nurse Brandt?'

195

'Yes, quite right. Back to the point. Nurse Brandt pretty much held my hand through my first year and kept on dispensing advice for the next few. Until it all started to go wrong.'

'How do you mean wrong?'

'Little things at first. Showing up in the odd stock take, you know. A phial here, a phial there. Small enough to be clerical error, so it went without comment. Her work continued fine. Top notch, in fact. If you could get Frieda in for your births then you damned well asked for her, and every one of us would breathe a sigh of relief on coming in for our rounds if we saw her name on the roster.'

He sipped his coffee. I sipped mine. It was strong and thick and I had to stop myself draining the contents of my cup all at once and then asking for more.

'By – when was it, now? – winter of 'twenty-eight, I think, it was obvious we had a problem. Not just the odd phial, but at least half a dozen in several stock takes, even a whole batch in one. So we upped the number of stock takes and rotated the duty to be sure.'

'Forgive me doctor. What was going missing?'

'Oh of course, you wouldn't know, would you? I do apologise.' He took another sip and I had to wait for him to swallow. 'It was our morphine stocks.'

A junkie midwife. I liked the sound of that even less than plain old midwife. 'I see.'

'I'm sure you do. So we started locking the stuff in a special cabinet and restricting the keys. The bursar of the academy looked through the records and noticed that phials went missing every time poor old Frieda was on one of her shifts. He came to me with this and of course I wouldn't hear of it, was all for boxing his ears and sending him out on a stretcher. But he kept on about it and he ground me down and so we agreed in the end to an experiment.'

I finished my coffee and rose to put the empty cup in the kitchen. Flensburger went with me and took the cup.

'Let me, old man. Don't bother yourself about all that.'

He went into the kitchen. 'You didn't want any more did you?'

I toyed with saying no, but who was I fooling?

'God, yes please.'

'Ah,' his grin split his face, 'I see you like it strong too. This is full Julius strength, this brew. Stuff of life to us doctors, you know, specially this time of a morning. Well, you must know how it is yourself, detective, eh?'

He handed me another cup. I rested this one on the arm of my sofa as Flensburger seated himself.

'So where was I?' he said.

'An experiment, you said. To do with the missing morphine.'

He clicked his fingers, the diamond in his wedding ring twinkling in the light. 'That's it, yes. So I consented to this crackpot scheme whereby old Koch – that was the bursar's name, silly old ass – would hide out in the stock cupboard on one of Frieda's shifts and wait for her to come and steal the stuff. And damn me if he didn't turn out to be right. There she was, red-handed, arms full of phials. Of course, silly old Koch grabs her arm so she drops all the morphine, doesn't he? So we still lost that batch even though we'd found our thief.'

He shook his head and drank his coffee. That seemed to be the end of the story for him.

'What happened next?' I said.

'Well, she was struck off, wasn't she. Cast down never to darken our door again, that sort of thing.'

'And you haven't seen her since.'

'No. Well...'

'Yes?'

'There was one time I was coming out of a nightclub in the Altstadt at about four in the morning and I fancied I saw her in the street then as I drove by in a cab with my wife. But it was only for a couple of moments, and she seemed to be arm-in-arm with some kind of... *beinl*. Streetwalker, you know? Rum thing, so it probably wasn't her after all.'

197

'When was this?'

'About four in the morning, I told you.'

'No, I mean how long ago. What night was it?'

'Oh, well it was a Friday. That's for certain. My wife and I only go out Friday nights. If I'm off duty, which isn't often, let me tell you. So rare is it, in fact, that you'd think I'd remember it all a bit easier, eh? Thank God for the coffee, is all I can say.' He drank some more and swished it around his mouth while he mulled. 'Only a few months ago. Before Christmas, but not that long. Let's see... was 21st December a Friday?'

'No, that Friday was the 20th.'

'Well then, that must be it. There's your answer.'

'Which street was this?'

'Oh, but it can't have been her.'

'Just in case, sir. If I run out of leads then this might be all I have to go on.'

'But I mean, arm-in-arm with a prostitute? What in God's name would possess her to stoop so low?'

'What indeed?' I asked.

He frowned. 'I'm not sure. The nightclub was that Blue Hake place on Königsallee. I can't remember which street I thought I saw her on, but it was one of the ones just around a corner, if that's any help at all?'

'Where do you live, sir?'

'Oh, up in Golzheim.'

I jotted that down and put my notebook away. That meant the taxi would have headed northwards, which might cut the number of streets I'd need to search for Brandt if it came to that. I stood and slung coffee down my throat. That second cup was even tastier than the first.

'Tell me doctor, the hospital keeps records of the employees?'

'Oh yes.'

'And it would still have Frieda Brandt's file?'

'I believe so. I can check for you with the front desk.'

'That would be most helpful, thanks.'

198

Dr Flensburger was true to his word, and thirty-five minutes later I left the hospital with a photograph of Frieda Brandt taken from her employee file. In exchange, I promised to supply the good doctor with whatever information I could about the former midwife's whereabouts.

Whatever Brandt's significance to the Gross case, I was edging closer. I just had to hope that wherever this lead took me, the green man wouldn't be there with another gun-shaped piece of metal in his fist.

25.

The St. Rochus hostel was located behind the church where I'd captured Kürten. By contrast with the pretence of the church's domed neo-Byzantine architecture, the hostel was a brick building that looked its age, which was late Kaiserreich.

Drug addicts, the diseased, the widowed, the mentally ill, prostitutes trying to go straight, these hostels were their last port of call on the journey to starvation or begging on the streets, or back to walking the streets. I'd tried the St. Gertrude women's hostel and come up empty. If Brandt wasn't at St. Rochus then I'd have to try something else. My vision was getting grainy and sluggish, just like the last time I was in the vicinity. God was trying to tell me something.

The hostel's high arched gateway faced onto a street encircling the small public park behind the church. A few lonely pedestrians crossed the park. Auto engines rumbled from the busy square on the other side of the church. I approached the hostel gate, one door of which stood open. The brass plaque set into the brickwork next to the gate read:

You once cared for sufferers of the plague and were always ready to help others by kind service and fervent prayers. You had no home and you died in a dungeon. Please grant us the cure we seek and help us become healthier in spirit.

Some would've found that uplifting, I supposed.

I knocked on the open door. A youngish priest in his middle twenties drew near. He wore a black buttoned-up robe, or cassock, or whatever the he... heck they were called, that reached down to the ankles. He touched his white collar with thin, pale fingers. His hair was short and dark and well-combed and it shone in the morning sunlight. He angled his head and he didn't say anything.

'Oh shit, you haven't taken a vow of silence have you?'

He smiled. 'No, my son. I'm a priest, not a monk.'

My son. The guy was ten years my junior. Five, at the very least, if he was older than he looked. I held the photograph of Freida Brandt in one hand and my *Kripo* ID in the other. The priest pursed his lips, glancing at both items in turn with steady grey eyes. His lips formed a perfect, feminine cupid's bow.

'I'm looking for this woman. A former nurse named Frau Brandt, though she may be registered under another name.'

'Has she done something terrible?'

'I'm not sure.'

'Well then why did you ask if she registered under a false name?'

'Is anyone registered here by that name?'

'We don't take names here, my son. We offer refuge.' He steepled his fingers in front of his lips. 'Sometimes that may include refuge from oneself.'

That sounded more like the French Foreign Legion than anything else. 'It's a little early in the morning for theology, father,' I said.

'It's never too early for a little theology, my son. Or too late.'

'It is for me. May I ask around inside?'

He considered this for a moment and nodded. 'If the lady is unwilling to go with you then we will of course have to step in.'

'She is here, then?'

'Ah.' He smiled again. 'You misunderstand me, but then I was not clear. I meant that, in the event that she is sheltering here, and, if so, in the event that she prefers not to accompany you, we would, hypothetically, feel compelled to respect such wishes.' He cast his eyes skyward.

So did I, though for different reasons, I suspect.

'You just out of seminary, by any chance?'

'Why yes, my son. How did you know?'

'Divine inspiration.'

I left him and strode into the building over floorboards that had been polished to a wicked sheen. Perhaps that was how those in receipt of the hostel's charity repaid its kindness.

A sign for the dormitories pointed to the right. The sounds of bubbling liquid and hissing steam assaulted my ears. I passed an open door to the kitchens, got a flash of pots and pans and women wearing white coats beneath rose-red cheeks and sweating foreheads. I kept going.

The hallway ended at a T-junction. Right to the men's dormitory, left to the women's. I turned left. Ten metres further, the hallway opened up into a large, wood-panelled room.

Narrow single beds lined the walls, the beds arranged so close together that they resembled a military barracks more than a hospital. A double row of beds, each row facing out towards the walls, ran up the centre of the room, a small metal chest nestling at the foot of each bed. Women of differing ages crowded the room while a gaggle of nuns helped the older and less physically able to dress themselves.

Voices echoed beneath the high ceiling: a whole room full of garrulous females. If I got any sense out of this lot, it'd be a miracle.

I stopped at the nearest bed. A young girl paused with her arm halfway through the sleeve of her blouse. I avoided gaping at her partially exposed breasts. Tried to, that is. I wasn't successful, but I did feel bad about that. I showed her the photo and ID in combination, as I had with the priest.

'Do you recognise this woman?' I asked.

The girl shook her head. I moved from bed to bed, first checking the occupant for any resemblance to the picture, then asking them if they knew Brandt, then looking around the room to see if I could see her. After a minute or so, the room quietened and each pair of eyes tracked my progress. None of the women, once dressed, tried to leave. Each waited her turn, no doubt eager to discover what this dumb bull might want from her.

It took me fifteen minutes to cover the whole room. None of the down-at-heel hostellers recognised Brandt from my photo, and nor did the nuns, though I had been offered a few hard luck stories and some scraps of useless gossip about feckless husbands and lovers and the like. I thanked them all through gritted teeth and left the dormitory. I walked back past the kitchen to the gate.

The young priest laid a hand on my arm as I was about to step through to the outside world.

'Will you not stay for breakfast, detective? You look as though you could do with some.'

My belly betrayed me by rumbling. I was forced to concede my hunger and it felt like a defeat. In a way it was. How was I going to track Frieda Brandt now? By asking at various post offices whether she'd left a forwarding address? By looking to see if she'd rented a post box somewhere in the city? By checking to see if she had an account at one of the city's banks? By staking out Altstadt night clubs in the hope she might perambulate past arm-in-arm with a *beinl*? This was shaping into a job that would take a whole detective squad several days to accomplish. I had to be back on my shift in a day or so. Maybe some food would help me think.

The priest took me to the dining room, another large space filled this time with rows of wooden benches and trestle tables worn smooth by the passage of time and the caresses of thousands of destitute buttocks. The room was half full of men and women both who sat in same-sex clumps under the watchful eyes of the white-haired priests at the top table.

I chose an emptier table and sat down. The young priest served me porridge, ladling the stuff from a large pot into an enamel bowl laid out on the table. I got a wedge of dark bread to go with it, then the priest floated off.

I set to, my hunger so deep that it hurt. The porridge tasted of oats and smoked bacon, a strange combination that tested the boundaries of what I defined as 'food'. Although it wasn't much, I couldn't manage more than half my bowl and a couple of bites of bread before I felt full. The meal dried my mouth, though I was able to wet it again with a cup of weak coffee dispensed by another priest. The coffee had a strange nutty aroma. Nor did it taste much like coffee. Ersatz stuff, probably.

If ever a breakfast was designed to motivate one out of poverty, this was it.

I got an itch at my temple and looked up. A young woman with dark hair and acne-scarred skin was glaring at me from a nearby table. I must've spoken to her in the dormitory, but I'd spoken to so many. She certainly hadn't told me anything useful, else I'd have remembered her. I ignored her and finished my pretend coffee. When I looked again, she'd gone.

I got up, feeling sick from the porridge, or from the too-sudden abating of my hunger, and I waddled to the exit. This time the young priest wasn't there. I stepped into the street and lit one of my cigars. I was taking a puff when someone tapped my shoulder.

I jumped and swallowed a great gob-full of smoke. I choked and dropped the cigar on the cobbles. I spun around, hand clasping the Luger in my pocket, but whoever had been there had gone.

I turned back to my cigar. The acne-scarred, dark-haired girl crouched on the pavement, cradling the smoking cigar in her hand and suckling on the end. I bent over and took it from her.

'I suppose that was you tapping me on the bloody shoulder,' I said.

'Yes sir.' Her voice sounded hoarse, like she'd been ill. Or maybe she was a drug addict of some kind too, like Brandt.

'You had a reason, I take it?'

'Yes sir.'

'You can say something other than "yes sir", can you?'

'Yes sir.'

'Glad to hear it. I'm going to go in this direction now,' I pointed past the church, 'though you're quite welcome to follow me until you decide to speak up.'

'It was that woman, sir,' the girl said. 'The nurse you were looking for?'

'Yes?'

'I know her. Or, that is, I did know her. Or, I don't know, met her might be a better way of saying it.'

'How?'

The girl took my hand and led me into the park. She sat on a wooden bench beneath the shade of a tree and she pulled me down next to her. She was thin, a loose skirt and sweater doing nothing to hide the sharp edges of her shoulder blades. She looked around before whispering.

'She helped me with a problem.'

'What sort of problem?' I couldn't bring myself to whisper, but I pitched my voice low nevertheless.

'I was pregnant. I was ill, and I couldn't support a kid. So I found out about her and she sorted it for me.' I opened my mouth to ask a question but she put a finger to her lips. 'You won't tell them at the hostel, will you?' she said. 'I wouldn't want them to know. They've been all nice to me and everything, letting me stay there for nothing and all, but I know what I did is against the Lord's teachings.'

Not to mention the law, I thought, though I didn't say it. I was in no position to judge. Exactly the opposite, in fact.

I took her hand and squeezed it. 'Don't worry. I understand. But tell me how you got in touch with her, would you?'

'There's a shop, out in Flingern. A pharmacy. It's on a corner. You go there and say you have a menstrual irreg...

well, a menstrual problem but that you heard there's a woman there who works miracles and can take away the problem. They ask you who told you about the miracle cure and you tell them. Then they ask you to go away and come back in half an hour. If they like the look of you then she comes and leads you up to a room in the building above the shop. You have to pay, like. She doesn't do it for free.'

'How much?'

'She did mine at a discount, she said. Fifty Reichsmark.'

'Where'd you get that kind of money?'

She shrugged. No point pushing it and making her clam up, so I dropped it.

'How long ago was this?' I said.

'Couple of weeks.'

'What's the name of the pharmacy?'

'Oh, I can't remember. But it's on the corner of Hermanstrasse and Lindenstrasse.'

I patted her hand. 'I know it. What's your name?'

'Why?'

I held my hands up, palms out. 'I need to know so I can tell them at the pharmacy.'

'Oh yeah,' she said.

'And I want to thank you properly.'

'Well...' She trailed off and I turned to look at her. She took the cigar from me, leaned over and latched her lips onto mine. My mouth opened in surprise and she stuck her tongue into it. Her tongue plunged to the back of my throat as though searching for any lingering morsels of breakfast, or trying to make me throw my breakfast back up, perhaps.

I seized her hips and threw her off. She landed on the grass at my feet. She rubbed her bony rump and screwed her face up at me. I didn't know if she was going to shout or cry.

'Don't you want me?' She pouted, or tried to. Her lips were in no state to carry off a pout.

'Well, no.'

'Oh.' She thought about this. The thin skin of her forehead creased with the effort. 'Then why did you stroke my hand?'

I pulled her up by her arm and sat her back on the bench. 'Well, I... didn't realise you'd take it that way.'

'How else is a girl in my station supposed to take it? You were the one wanted to know how I'd made that money, weren't you?'

I plucked the squashed remnants of my cigar from the grass, puffed on the end a couple of times to get it going again, and held it out to the girl. She smiled and went to take the cigar from me. I pulled back.

'So, what is your name?' I said.

She eyed the cigar. 'Sophie Ackerman.'

'Thank you, Sophie.'

I gave her the cigar and then I stood up. Across the park, a dark-haired woman ripe with curves was looking right at me. Took me a few seconds to work out who it was, and then my heart cringed. Gisela. No doubt on her way to morning mass. A couple of months after Lilli's death it had started, Gisela's attending mass every day.

The old hot needle back to resume its jabbing in my gut, I set off in her direction. That galvanised her. She turned and rushed off, heading for the tower entrance at the front of the building. Damn it, had she seen that girl canoodling with me? Had she, in fact, interpreted it as my canoodling with the girl?

I sped up and called her name. That stopped her. She hunched over as though I'd go away if she didn't look at me, but she waited all the same. When I got close I reached out to touch her, but I couldn't. She wasn't mine any more. Of course, she never had been, but she wasn't the woman I'd loved is what I meant, though I loved her still despite that. Was it only thoughts of Lilli that made me feel this way? I was chewing the inside of my cheek now.

'You don't have to explain yourself to me,' Gisela said, her voice soft but unwavering.

'Gisela, I'm sorry –'

'No,' she cut me off. 'You think you can apologise for what we did?' She backed away, closing the gap with the church wall. 'There is no apologising for what we did!' She lowered her voice. 'All we can do is beg the Lord for forgiveness and hope that He is listening. It's the only path to salvation, Thomas.'

She turned her back on me and headed off once again.

'Don't you remember that summer, Gisela?'

She stopped.

'The time you locked me in the wardrobe when Michael came home early? You remember that? How we laughed for hours the next morning once he'd gone back out to work, and you sneaking food in to me overnight. How you managed to persuade him you'd lost the key I'll never know.'

'Don't,' she said.

'Or the time we went swimming in the lake and ended up covered in mud, getting funny looks from the people we passed all the way back to the city? We were always laughing, Gisela, don't you remember?'

She rustled in her purse and turned back to me with her rosary beads in her hand. Her eyes were dry and she held the beads out as though to ward me off.

'There is no space left in my heart for laughter, Thomas. Is there really any in yours?'

'I'm sorry Gisela.'

'That's not enough, Thomas, don't you see?' And she turned away again, hunching her shoulders against me. 'I'll pray for you,' she said as she went.

'I gave her a name, after,' I called, but Gisela began to walk faster. 'Don't you want to know what I called her?'

But she'd turned the corner of the building and gone. I could have caught up with her, but where would that get me? She'd been lost to me a long time ago. There was nothing I could do about it now, and there was no point getting sidetracked. I left Gisela to her praying in the church and I left the acne-scarred girl to her cigar in the park while I headed east to a pharmacy in Flingern. The jabbing in my guts was making my knees wobble, but I didn't care. I kept on chewing my cheek, not to cover the pain now but to add to it, to mingle with it, and I welcomed it as I kept on walking.

26.

Sunlight sparkled in the windows of the corner building across from me. Behind one of those windows Brandt helped women with their menstrual 'irregularities'. Was I really up to it, to speaking to her, knowing what she did to fund her morphine addiction? The killing of unborn innocents, of countless Lillis like my own?

A couple of autos trundled past as I crossed the street. The pharmacy took up all of the ground floor, the plate glass windows either side of the door displaying seasonal allergy remedies. Beneath the painted sign of the green cross and above the door was the name *Mahler's Pharmacy*. Flingern was my district, my precinct, and I'd had no idea this place had existed as anything other than a pharmacy. What kind of detective did that make me?

I pushed on the glass panel of the door. It didn't budge. It was only eight a.m., and a 'closed' sign quivered on a chain on the inside of the door.

I pushed again but this door was definitely locked. I tried to look through the windows, but the sun shone off the glass, making it difficult to see inside. I shielded my eyes and peered in. Behind the counter were shelves of herbal teas and cold remedies, racks of skin lotions and ointments and hair products, a cash register, and a thick curtain hanging in a doorway. Surely someone should have been in the shop getting ready to open? I knocked on the door. Then I caught sight of a bell push. I pressed it, twice.

A couple of minutes went by, and still no one entered.

An auto backfired in the road behind me. I jumped. Down the street, some men in shirt sleeves unlocked the back of their dray cart and began unloading beer barrels. Across the way a grocer bellowed his best prices at passers-by. Apparently, the asparagus was good, but given the lateness of the season, I doubted that. Next door to the grocer, a lady newsagent smoked a cigar and held a *kaffeeklatch* with customers who flicked through their morning papers.

The sun had brought them all out, these people, and brought all their noise out with them. I looked at the windows above the pharmacy as though looking would help me hear any commotion up there.

I rang the bell again. This time I leant on it without pause and finally someone dragged aside the heavy curtain; a bald man wearing a shapeless white coat.

He waved me away, flipping up the hinged counter top and approaching the door. 'We're closed,' he said, his voice muffled. 'Please go away.'

I pressed my ID to the glass and his eyes widened. I pressed my Luger to the glass with my other hand, shielding it from the street with my body.

'Open the door,' I said, 'or I'll break it in.'

The man's eyes popped. He ran back to the counter, opened the cash register and withdrew a set of keys. He came back and opened the door, glancing up and down the street as he beckoned me inside.

'What do you want?' I don't think he realised he was whispering.

I put away the gun and showed him my photo of Brandt. He took a deep breath, shuddering when he let it out. I pointed up at the ceiling and he nodded.

'Now?' I mouthed.

He nodded again.

'Stefan?' came a voice from behind the curtain. A woman's voice. There was some urgency in it. 'Who was it, Stefan?'

The man ran for the hinged counter top and the curtain beyond it. I couldn't have him warning Brandt so I tripped him. His head smacked against the counter and he slid loose-limbed to the floor.

I went after him and turned him over. His eyes were closed. Blood dribbled from a gash in his forehead and his breathing came out heavy, close to a snore. He didn't move, even when I slapped his cheeks.

'Stefan?' That woman's voice again, but louder this time.

I grabbed the front of Stefan's coat and dragged him behind the counter. I knelt and rooted through his pockets for the door keys. I found a selection and returned to the door, trying two keys that didn't fit before the right one slid home in the lock. I turned the key and pulled down the roll blind that hung on the inside of the door.

'Stefan? Have they gone? I need help up here, damn it!'

I flung back the curtain. Behind it lay a short, dingy hallway that ended in a set of lamp-lit stairs going up. A dark shadow fell on the stairs. The middle-aged woman casting the shadow ran a hand over her drawn face and through her greying hair. The face matched my photo of Brandt.

'Who are you?' she said. 'Where's Stefan?' Then, 'You're police, aren't you?'

She gripped my jacket sleeve and pulled me up the stairs behind her. The stairs turned back on themselves, pitching us into a wider hallway that was filled with sunlight from the two large rooms at the far end. Brandt dragged me into a room on the left.

This room was west facing, so it wouldn't have got any light anyway at that time of day, but to add to the natural gloom the curtains were shut tight. A girl lay on a single bed against the wall. Her dress was rolled up to her midriff so that she was naked below the waist.

'Look,' Brandt said, pitching her voice low so the girl wouldn't hear it, 'you may be a bull, but if we stop now she could die. You want that?'

I shook my head, struck dumb by what I was seeing. At the sound of Brandt's voice the girl looked over at us, and at the sight of me she sat up like a shot of electricity had just passed through her.

Brandt crossed to the girl and pushed her back down, making lots of loud shushing noises as she did it. Then the midwife turned to look at me over her white-coated shoulder. 'Shut the door.'

I shut the door.

'You ever been present at an abortion before?' Brandt asked.

Oh, Jesus God, yes. I rubbed my belly scar, my guts hot as molten lead and twice as heavy. She looked puzzled for a moment, then came and shoved me towards the head of the bed, where the girl's long hair was tangled in the brass bars.

'Hold her shoulders,' Brandt barked.

'I can't,' I said, backing to the door.

The midwife stepped close and whispered, 'I don't know what you've done with Stefan but this is a two-person job. Without a steadying pair of hands this girl could injure herself. Do you want that to happen?'

She took my wrists and dragged me back to the girl. She pressed my hands to the girl's shoulders. The nurse's expression told me not to pull away or make a fuss that might upset her patient. I kept my hands in place and the girl went still. Her eyes blazed up at me, and in that dim light they could've been any colour. Just so long as they weren't brown, like Gisela's.

'And for God's sake don't stare at her. She's worked up enough as it is.'

Brandt parted the girl's legs. The girl kicked out and Brandt veered back. I pressed harder on the girl's shoulders as the midwife waggled a finger at her.

'Let's have no more of that, missy, otherwise we'll be strapping you down.'

The girl stopped moving and allowed the midwife to part her legs. Brandt leaned over the girl and held her with a look.

'Be still. This will be over soon.'

She crossed to a wooden table and hefted a rubber balloon that had a curved glass nozzle attached to one end.

The balloon bulged with liquid. Brandt made soothing, shushing noises and inserted the nozzle between the girl's legs.

The girl looked into my face again. Sweat rolled down my back and I shut my eyes.

The girl tensed and gave a whimper. That meant Brandt had pressed on the balloon and injected the liquid.

I found I was making shushing noises too, still keeping my eyes shut.

'Almost there now, missy,' Brandt was saying.

Then the girl groaned. My eyes flicked open. She was trying to curl up. I pushed at her hip to keep her still, got my hand caught in her dress. Brandt had been refilling the balloon syringe. She put it down on the table and hurried over, shushing and soothing again.

'It hurts!' the girl said, and the childish edge to her voice slapped me cold. Just how young was she?

'It will hurt, dear. But it'll be over quick, I promise. Just one more.' Then Brandt turned her eyes on me. 'Hold her still.'

She went back to the table and picked up the balloon syringe. I moved my hand from the tangle of fabric at the girl's hip and pressed harder on her shoulders.

'Help me,' the girl whispered.

I screwed my eyes shut. The girl groaned again as the soap water – or glycerine, or Lysol, or carbolic acid, or whatever the hell kind of liquid Brandt preferred – ate up the baby inside, cleansed it of life. Then the girl stiffened – the nozzle going in again. But I wasn't thinking of the girl beneath me. I was thinking of Gisela, the spare room of her house – she hadn't wanted to move to do it, which set me back a fortune with the doctor I'd got hold of – and the same groans of pain. The begging for help, the tears, the grinding, curling, reflexive hurt of the whole thing, burned into my memory.

It hurt. Of course it hurt. It was murder, it had to hurt. A cry. A sharp, wailing call. Leaning down harder. The eyes, scorching me with their accusations, their slow-burn hatred. Eyes chocolate brown beneath bottle-blond hair, fanned out across the thin pillow, the one with the blood stain in the corner she'd never been able to wash out, not all the way, not completely. The doctor in black, like death, Gisela in her black slip, face pale and lined, the room dark, a darkness that never left us.

Leaning.

Leaning harder.

Stop her moving.

Stop the pain, damn it!

A scratching on my left wrist – Gisela's nails raking the soft skin in her agony.

'Let go, man!' Someone pulled at me, at my jacket collar. I opened my eyes. It was Brandt. She punched me and snapped my head back.

I released the girl, and she curled her legs into her belly and turned onto her side and vomited over the edge of the bed. The vomit spattered my shoes.

27.

Brandt took me down the stairs to a dark bathroom with a tiny, open window. She left me there with a command to clean myself up.

The reflection in the bathroom mirror told me I was crying. Had been for some time, from the redness and swelling around my pinhole eyes. I ran cold water into the sink until my fingers had gone numb.

Splashing my face brought on more tears. I lurched for the toilet and collapsed to my knees. Then I threw up too, and kept on throwing up until there was nothing left and I was hurling up thin strings of stomach acid, and kept on crying until I reared up and smashed my fist into the wall.

I thought of my darling Lilli, all alone in limbo – or was it purgatory? Or was I the one going to hell for it? I sat on the floor in the corner of the room beneath the sink and hung my head on my knees.

They burned them after. The foetuses, that is. After the procedure they were burned.

I flushed my puke away, then I took off my shoes and washed them in the sink.

The door opened as I was sitting on the toilet putting my shoes back on. Brandt stuck her head into the room. I tried to speak, my voice coming out scratched as I coughed hot acid streaks into my mouth. I stood and drank water from the cold tap, gargling and spitting to try and get rid of the taste.

'How is she?' I finally managed.

'Doing fine. She'll be up there for another hour, but the danger's passed.'

'And how's... what's his name?'

'Stefan. He's groggy, but otherwise okay. It's you I'm worried about.'

'Don't be.' I finished tying my shoelaces, got to my feet and pulled Brandt into the room with me. 'You helped out Emma Gross didn't you?'

'Yes, why?' She rubbed at her left eyelid to calm the twitch that had broken out there.

'When was this?'

'Last year. Why –'

I cut her off. 'When last year?'

'February.'

'Why did she come to you?'

She lowered the toilet seat, sat on it and crossed her arms. Her eyelid was still twitching. 'What is all this?' Surprise had unlocked her mouth for those first few questions but her brain had caught up to the idea that gabbing about her activities might not be clever. Especially not to a policeman.

Her twitching eyelid gaze me an idea. Here was an addict, tired after a tough few hours' work – hell, maybe it had taken all night. I bellowed Stefan's name and he clambered down the hallway from the direction of the shop. He tried to get a look inside the bathroom but I blocked his view with my bulk.

'Fetch some morphine, Stefan. Then go and look after the girl upstairs.' He stretched his neck in another effort to look past me. I showed him the Luger and flashed my teeth at him. 'You like being a pharmacist, Stefan? Like helping people?'

His eyes were rooted to the barrel of the pistol.

'You want to keep on being a pharmacist?'

'Are you okay in there, Frieda?' Stefan shouted.

'Not exactly, Stefan, no,' Brandt called back.

I wiggled the gun and Stefan skulked away. Then I shut the door and turned back to Brandt.

'You do know Emma Gross is dead?' I said. That didn't have the impact I'd expected. She squared her shoulders and faced me down.

'I do read the papers, yes. You don't want to bust me. Do you?'

'That's very astute of you. But it doesn't strike you as significant that she died in the same month she came to see you?'

'Pregnancy is an occupational hazard for *beinls*. Violence, too. Believe me, I've seen it enough times to know.' She shivered and scratched her left cheek so hard she left red marks on the skin.

'You don't care that the child's father might have been her killer?' I said.

'I thought you caught the killer last year? Johann Stausberg wasn't – ?'

Brandt clutched at her belly and doubled over. She stifled a groan. Stefan knocked on the door. I opened it, took a phial of morphine and a glass syringe fitted with a hypodermic needle and shut the door again. I flicked the bolt on the door and ignored Stefan's continued knocking while I arranged the items on the side of the sink.

Brandt had closed her eyes. When she opened them again they were threaded with swollen blood vessels.

'How long has it been since your last shot?' I said, tapping the morphine phial.

'What are you,' she broke off, grimacing, 'what are you jawing about?' She threw me a weak smile.

I reached over and pulled up her left sleeve, then her right, in the crook of which I got the tell-tale needle scars and scabs.

'I spoke to Dr Flensburger. He told me about your addiction, the reason you do all this.'

Brandt slid off the toilet and pawed at the seat. I stretched to help her and she jabbed an elbow at my groin, so I grabbed her hair, pulled her head back. She retched and I let go of her. She pitched forward onto her hands and knees and spilled her guts over the floor.

When she'd finished, a tremor shook through her and she raised herself up and into the bathtub away from the spreading pool of vomit.

'You got a cigarette?' she said.

'This is what you need,' I said, holding up the phial. 'Tell me about Emma and you can have some.'

The knocking on the door grew louder. Stefan's voice: 'Frieda?'

'She's sick,' I called back.

'What are you doing in there?'

'Helping. I told you, she's sick.'

'Are you okay, Frieda?' Stefan said.

Brandt laughed. 'Go away, Stefan,' she called out.

'Are you okay?'

'Go away Stefan, damn it!' The effort of shouting doubled her up again. She flopped her head over the side of the bathtub and heaved some more. Not much came out, but her body shook with the effort.

'Stausberg didn't kill her, Frieda,' I said. 'But I think the father of her child did. I need to find him. I need to know, so talk to me.'

'You're sure it wasn't Stausberg?'

'Uh-huh.'

'Well, that fits. He said he'd kill me if I talked. How do you like that?'

'Who did?'

'This... guy. This man. The father you're looking for. You want to know why she wanted my help? I'd say it was a bigger mystery why she'd agreed to bear his child in the first place.'

'Who?'

'He never told me his name, and neither did she. I just know she was scared of him. She wanted to keep the foetus afterwards to show him, so she could say it was a miscarriage, can you believe that?'

'What did he look like?' I said. 'Did he wear a green fedora?'

She shook her head.

'Did he have a jagged scar on his throat?'

She shook her head. 'He was slim and dark, and he had buck teeth.'

219

Christ, Ritter. She mimed the teeth, like that kid had done back when I'd been looking for Frau Stausberg's place a couple of days earlier.

'He was a cop?' I said.

'How should I know?' she said.

'Does the name Michael Ritter mean anything to you?'

She shook her head, vomit-slicked strands of her hair whipping about her face in time to the movement. I'd got as much from her as I was likely to. She looked too weak to inject herself, so I took off my belt and rolled her right sleeve so it would stay up. Then I tightened my belt around her upper arm.

'Raise a vein,' I told her.

I crossed to the sink and opened the phial, dipping the syringe needle into the liquid morphine. When I turned around she'd tightened the belt still further and a fat vein was popping in the crook of her arm. I waved the syringe in front of her face.

'Too much?' I asked.

'Huh?'

'Is this too much morphine? I want to bring you round, not kill you.'

She started laughing. More giggling, really. She was too far gone to be of any use. I jabbed in the needle and pressed the plunger once I was sure I'd pierced the skin. I pulled the plunger back until some of her blood clouded the clear syringe contents, then I shot half of the pinkening mixture into her vein and pulled out the needle.

She winced, then she groaned. The groan stretched and altered in tone from sharp complaint to languid pleasure, the sound of waking up on a Sunday morning. I dumped the syringe into the sink, then I cupped my hands and ran some water into them. I went back to the woman and splashed the water on her face. She gasped and opened her eyes wide.

'This man who threatened you,' I said. 'When did he come to see you?'

'I don't remember now,' she said. 'A week or so after I'd done the procedure on Emma.'

'And what did he say to you exactly?'

'He said to forget all about Emma Gross and what I'd done for her. Otherwise he'd kill me.'

'That didn't make you suspicious when she died?'

She latched onto the sides of the bathtub and clawed her way upright. 'Mister, I make my living by breaking the law so I can get my daily fix. If I don't come across something suspicious on an average day, I know I'm going to get the sweats all night. Now will you leave me alone?'

'Gladly.'

'Just promise me something will you?' Her voice sounded sleepy.

'What?'

She clasped my hand and squeezed. 'Promise me you'll get the bastard, okay?'

I squeezed back. I retrieved my belt and left the pharmacy. There was no point hanging around, and my mind was boiling with the idea that Ritter had killed Emma Gross because she'd aborted his baby. But why agree to have a baby with a streetwalker? It still didn't make sense.

Then a thought hit me. Those kids at the playground near Frau Stausberg's place, they'd spoken to Ritter when Ritter had asked them about Johann Stausberg. According to the file, Ritter had interviewed Frau Stausberg only at headquarters, not at her home. And Ritter had interrogated Johann Stausberg only at headquarters, not at his home. Once Ritter got the case he'd conducted it all from Mühlenstrasse.

So why had he been talking to some kids in the neighbourhood about Stausberg? When I'd talked to those kids, I'd just assumed Ritter's presence was connected to the complaint the kid's father had made. But what was a plainclothesman doing dealing with a *Schupo* matter? And even if that was the reason he'd been there, why had none of this made the Stausberg file?

I needed time. I needed space. I needed to think, and I needed to cleanse my head of the dark memories floating around within.

I wasn't going to get any of that though. More than all of it, I needed answers, and if I stopped now I might never get them.

28.

Frau Stausberg opened her door and looked at me with red-rimmed eyes, but I'd had enough of her crocodile tears. I pushed into her room, got a chill down the back of my neck from the draught coming through the window crack.

She closed the door, tightening the belt on her threadbare dressing gown as she walked past me and sank into one of her dog-eared easy chairs. There was a glass in her hand. She lifted it to her lips, drained the clear contents and blenched.

'I knew you'd come back,' she said, husky-voiced.

'Tell me about Ritter,' I said, husky-voiced to match. I hadn't moved since she'd taken her seat. 'He came to see you before Johann strangled those women, didn't he?'

The woman nodded.

'Tell me,' I said.

She plucked a bottle of schnapps from the floor under the chair, where I hadn't seen it, and refilled the glass.

'I went to see him yesterday, after you left here,' she said. She slurred her words, the effect akin to the way her son talked while sober.

'Who, Ritter?'

She shook her head, spilled some of her drink. 'My goddamned son. He's gone backwards, retreated inside his head. Thanks to you and that damned doctor and all your damned meddling.' She drank off her schnapps. Some of it dribbled out of the corner of her mouth and she caught the spill on the back of her hand.

I waited her out.

'He hasn't spoken since you went to see him,' she said.

'He won't talk. Not one word. And that... Michael Ritter... his promises were worthless.'

I went up to her and knelt at her feet.

'He came to you before Johann attacked those women in April. Didn't he?' She looked away. 'What did he promise you? Ritter. What did he promise you?'

'He promised that my Johann would be well cared for in the asylum. That he'd be happier there than he ever could be. Out here.'

She flung an arm in the direction of her cracked window, then she heaved herself out of the chair and stumbled to the window. She flipped the catch and swung the window open. The breeze ruffled her hair.

'What did you do, Frau Stausberg?'

'I just opened the window,' she said. She looked out and added, 'Oh, that man's there again.'

'What man?'

I crossed to the window. The grey net curtains flapped about my face. I batted them away as best I could, and ended up clutching them in my hand to stop them obscuring my view of the street.

'There.'

She was pointing at the corner where her street intersected with the main road. An auto drove past, followed by a truck.

'What man?' I said again.

'Oh you won't see him now, he's gone again. The one with the funny green hat and the scarf. Though he's not wearing his scarf today. Too warm, I suppose.'

I pulled her back from the window. She tumbled to the floorboards and took me down with her.

'You've seen that man before?' I asked her, the tip of my nose touching the tip of hers.

'Once or twice,' she said. Schnapps laced her breath.

'Who is he?'

'I don't know. We've never spoken. I've just seen him, is all.' She shoved at my chest. 'Get off, will you?'

Her gown had come open and my elbow rested on her

224

exposed right breast, what there was of it. I stood and patted down my clothes.

'Sorry.' I helped her to her feet and looked away while she rearranged her clothing.

She slunk back to her easy chair. I stayed at the window, standing back a little so I couldn't be seen too easily from down in the street. That damned green man again. What did he want with Frau Stausberg? Or with me?

Frau Stausberg retrieved her glass and poured herself another drink.

'Did you want some coffee?' she said, resting the full glass on the arm of her chair. She was quicker than I expected. Either the schnapps had oiled her joints or I was just too damn slow. Whatever it was, she got all the way to the door and had it halfway open before I got hold of her arm. I held it tight as she tried to pull away. There was iron in those thin muscles, even while she was full of drink and close to mental collapse.

'Tell me about Ritter,' I said.

She let go of the door. It swung to, though it didn't click shut. She leaned against me as I steered her back to her chair and pressed her glass into her hand.

'He even took to visiting me every month,' she said. 'Checking how my boy was getting on at the asylum, if everything was okay, if I needed help. Went so far as to lend me money once or twice, when the rent was getting tight.' She snorted. 'Blood money.' She took a drink.

'What for?' I returned to the window. There was still no sign of the green man – or any other kind of man – in the street below.

'I'm sorry?'

'Ritter was the one who fed Johann the information for his false confessions, wasn't he?'

Children's squeals drew my attention. A grubby gang of them sprinted along the pavement outside, trying to outrun a delivery van. The van honked its horn.

The street sounds somehow deepened the silence between us. I'd asked my question and now I waited for her to answer. I went through the rigmarole of lighting another cigar, though I knew my throat wouldn't be able to stand it. I'd got as far as touching a flaming match to the tip when she spoke again.

'He came to do a deal.'

'What sort of a deal?'

'We made it look like Johann killed those people and Ritter guaranteed Johann would get sent to Grafenberg.'

I blew out the match and perched the cigar on the window sill. I circled the chair. The woman was grinning, her glass hanging heavy in her fingers like she would drop it again at any moment. 'He told us what to say,' she licked her lips, 'and we said it. He told my Johann what to do and he did it. Ritter'd found out about Johann's fondness for rope, you see.'

'This was in March?'

She nodded.

This was the evidence I needed to start building up a case. 'You'll need to testify again,' I said. 'To give me a new statement.'

Her dry laughter stopped me dead as I went behind her chair. She beat at her chest with an open palm, and this time her glass did fall. It rolled towards the door, leaving a trail of spilled alcohol.

'*I* framed my son,' she said. 'How could I possibly testify against Ritter without risking jail for myself and risking that my boy be released? With no one out here to care for him? Just how long do you think he would last on his own? No.' She shook her head, stooped to retrieve her bottle. 'No, there's no way out of this for me.'

'We could prove coercion.' I reached over the chair to take the bottle from her. 'Say he tricked you into going along with it.'

'For a year?'

'His visits. They were his way of checking up on you, seeing that you kept on doing what he wanted.' I returned

226

the schnapps bottle to the floor and leaned both my arms on the back of the chair. God, I was tired.

She moved to the door and bent down, reaching for her glass. The door opened and clipped the glass, knocking it away.

The green man paused in the doorway, the sight of Frau Stausberg crouching so close seeming to put him off. But then he raised the claw hammer in his left hand and swung it at the prone woman's head.

I didn't have time to think. I picked up the chair I'd been leaning on and I hurled it at him.

Frau Stausberg's skull crunched and she gave a cry. The green man stumbled under the impact of the chair, but not for long. He gathered himself and ran at me, the woman's blood slicking his hammer head. I went for the pistol in my pocket, but I rushed it and the pocket twisted around my fist so that I couldn't shake loose. My knuckles had swollen from punching the bathroom wall in the pharmacy.

The green man raised his hammer, then surprised me by dropping it. Stupidly, I watched it fall as he drove his right fist into my stomach.

My body tried to double up and wasn't giving my brain any say in the matter, only I couldn't fold up like I wanted because the green man was in the way. I leaned on him like an exhausted boxer and dry-heaved.

He got me round the throat and pushed me back until I was hanging over the sill of the open window at my back. Shit, he was trying to push me out. A few seconds more of this and my cringing innards would be decorating the street below.

Parts of me were catching at the sill, stopping me from falling. I jabbed at his eyes, at his Adam's apple – anything vulnerable.

He stepped back, holding me in place one-handed while he scrabbled for his discarded hammer. Good Christ, was he going to hammer me off the sill? The thought jolted me. I latched onto his jacket lapels and pulled myself back into the room. He twisted to try and throw me off. Some part of my brain registered that now he was between me and the window. I kicked down at the floorboards and managed to get some purchase, then I pushed him as hard as I could.

He hit the sill and went over, his grunts turning to a cry as he disappeared from view. I hugged the floor and waited for my head to stop spinning.

29.

When my head started to clear I went over to Frau Stausberg, trembling as I did so. Blood dribbled down the side of her face and into her eyes from a tear at the top of her skull. The wound was swelling already. She rubbed at it with her fingers. I knelt and cradled her head, trying not to press too hard in case the bones were broken.

'Don't move,' I said.

She spoke, her words slurring beyond recognition, her blood soaking into her dressing gown. Oh, sweet Jesus, she couldn't die. Not now, not when I was so close to a solution. She was my only real evidence against Ritter and if she died the case against him died too. The door was still open though, and that gave me the chance to do something.

'Frau Wenders!' I shouted. I managed to pull the door with my foot. 'Frau Wenders!'

Footsteps echoed up the stairs. Frau Wenders entered the room, wearing an apron over her dress as she had been on my last visit. She stopped when she saw Frau Stausberg struggling in my arms.

'Get the police,' I said.

Wenders' mouth hung open.

'Go out and call for the police, woman! Quickly!'

'What happened?'

'Here, give me your apron.' I held out a hand.

Wide eyes drawn to the bleeding woman in my lap, Wenders complied, untying her apron strings without looking at what she was doing and then passing the apron to me.

'Damn it, will you fetch the *Schutzpolizei* or not? And an ambulance. Now!'

She jerked back into life and ran down the stairs. Her shouts rebounded through the open window as she went out into the street. Fine pair of lungs on her, that one.

Where was that damn schnapps bottle? It lay behind me in the middle of the room, untouched by the brawl and just out of reach. I dropped the apron and grabbed for the seat cushion of the chair I'd thrown at the green man. The chair lay close enough that I didn't have to move, or so I thought. I stretched for it, my fingertips pushing it further away. I shifted beneath Frau Stausberg, slid her head down my lap. Blood had saturated my trousers and it was beginning to get sticky.

I managed to hook the cushion and pull it close. I threaded my fingers and supported the back of Frau Stausberg's head with them, easing her onto the cushion. She mumbled.

Her head supported now, I backed away and got to my feet. My knees gave way and I fell onto all fours. I crawled like that to the schnapps bottle, picked it up and crawled back to Frau Stausberg. I opened the bottle and poured the contents over Wenders' apron, folding it into a kind of pad and pressing it to Frau Stausberg's head wound. She flinched, tried to speak once again.

I shushed her into silence. She lay still, though her eyes moved about the place like she was following the trajectory of a fly. I shushed her some more, kept on dabbing. *Come on Frau Wenders, where the hell are you.*

Something Frau Stausberg had said clamoured for my attention. Something about Ritter having told Johann Stausberg what to do with a rope?

Did that mean Ritter had planned for Johann to strangle those girls in April? It was possible. Ritter could have heard about Stausberg from the father of the kid I'd spoken to when the father had made his complaint. That would explain how Ritter had found out Stausberg liked playing with rope and had a temper. And if that was true, it meant that not just the murder charges, but the *whole case* against Johann Stausberg was a frame-up concocted by Michael Ritter.

But why? And what was the importance of the rope? The marks on Ohliger's neck had suggested strangulation by hand, not ligature. And had Scheer even been strangled at all?

Voices bounced about the stairwell, male and female. Stiff soles clomped up the steps. A *shako* came into view, followed by the head of its wearer, a fresh-faced *Schupo* whose waxed moustache looked like it had been grown to add some gravitas to the youthful features.

'Oh my,' the *Schupo* said. He took in the bleeding woman and the blood on my hands and he went for his baton.

I dropped the apron and went for my ID.

'Just hold it there, mister,' the *Schupo* said.

'Frau Wenders?' I shouted. There was no sign of her. But surely I'd heard her in the stairwell before this blue coat had come up? Where'd she got to now?

'What's your name?' I asked the officer. My tone threw him off. He paused and stroked his moustache, the baton hanging loosely in his hand.

'Who wants to know?'

I came up empty for my ID in the first pocket and tried another. He frowned and raised his baton.

'Wait!' I shouted. Again, he paused.

'Who are you?' he said.

No luck in that second pocket either. Damn it, please tell me I hadn't lost my ID now. That would just top it all off. I searched a hip pocket. My fingers closed around the Luger and without thinking I pulled out the gun.

The *Schupo* went for the bayonet hanging at his belt.

'Wait!' I tried again. 'I'm Thomas Klein. Detective Thomas Klein.' I dropped the Luger and dove into my other hip pocket. There it was, my ID. I pulled that out too and flashed it in the boy's face.

'Detective Klein?' he said. 'Well why didn't you say so?' Then, after the usual *Schupo* hesitation, he added, 'Sir.'

'We need medical assistance, urgently,' I said.

'That woman who found me, sir. She said something about fetching a doctor.'

'That's a start. Do you think you could arrange transportation to the nearest hospital?'

He scratched the back of his neck.

'A taxi, a passing civilian auto, a delivery truck,' I tried. 'Anything. Just go.'

'Sir.' He went for the stairs.

I called him back. 'Round up any other *Schupo* on the beat nearby, will you? We'll need to secure this room, and the street out front.'

He looked puzzled but he snapped off a salute and went down the stairs. His police whistle tore at the air outside the window. Then came the sound of more footsteps. Frau Wenders returned to the landing, along with a bearded overweight man in a grey flannel suit.

He popped a pince-nez on his nose, sized up the scene and then dropped to one knee with a click. 'Damned arthritis,' he said, to no one in particular. He opened his kit bag on the floor and started rooting through it.

He took away my hand and the folded apron.

'She was hit with a hammer,' I said.

'Well... possible fracture of the parietal...' He hummed and sat back on his heels. 'There's little I can do here. She needs to get to a hospital as soon as possible.'

'Will she live?'

He ignored me and crouched over Frau Stausberg. He pulled a small bottle and a cloth from his bag, wetting the cloth and dabbing it at the wound the way I had with the schnapps-soaked apron.

The *Schupo*man reappeared.

'Sir,' he said. 'Got a taxi downstairs. And another couple of men outside.'

'Good. Help the doctor get her into the taxi.'

'What do you want us to do after?'

'Secure the scene, like I said. Then inform the detectives at the precinct house.'

'What happened, sir?'

'She was attacked, man. Can't you see?'

'Yes sir, but begging your pardon, who attacked her?'

'The man on the pavement outside, of course, you imbecile.'

The *Schupo* swapped glances with Frau Wenders and the doctor.

'But there isn't any man outside, sir,' the *Schupo* said. He spoke as one would to a backwards child.

'What?'

I crossed back to the window and looked out into the street. A crowd had gathered, but I had no eyes for the vultures. To me the pavement was empty.

The green man had gone. And there was no sign of his hammer anywhere, not in the room and not down on the street.

A small pool of blood was all that remained to suggest he had ever been there at all.

30.

I stumbled down the basement stairs to Willi's. The double bass and kick drum on the stage pulsed through me, the trombone catching the tone of my caffeine rush. I parted the flag from the doorway and staggered in.

Bern came over as soon as he saw me lean on the bar. I had to lean on it. I was trembling too much not to.

Bern ran a hand over his head stubble and flexed his tattooed arms beneath a shirt so sweat-soaked his nipples and his chest hair were visible through the material.

'You're drunk,' he said, reading me all wrong. 'You here to cause trouble?'

'That depends. Where's Trudi?'

He checked the watch in his apron pocket, then frowned and touched his Kaiser Bill.

'What is it?' I said. 'Hasn't she turned up?'

I checked my watch: twelve-twenty a.m. Assuming she was working the same shift that night, she should have been out on the floor by then. I cast an eye over the tables and the naked girls bearing trays of drinks and snacks. Trudi wasn't among them.

I had no time for this. No time. I'd spent hours at the hospital answering questions about the attack and waiting for news about Frau Stausberg's condition. Detective Kaufmann had come along for the questioning and I'd had to answer the same questions two or three times over. He'd called out the lab boys to scrape the blood off the pavement and see if they could ID it as human. I'd got the feeling from the looks he gave me that he was humouring me, telling me that.

I asked him about witnesses and he sidestepped my question in such a way as to avoid saying what I hadn't wanted to hear: no witnesses. At least, not to my version of events. No one had come out yet and said I was talking shit, but really, when you looked at it, what were the chances of a man falling out of a third floor window and getting up again afterwards?

Frau Stausberg, no one could tell me about. I still didn't know if she was going to be all right.

In between all that, I'd dozed. Still hadn't got much in the way of what you'd call real sleep, though. My mind had raced ahead, putting together what Frau Stausberg had told me with the information I'd extorted from Frieda Brandt.

It was the question of the rope that had tugged at me, and a Karl Berg phrase from the Gross autopsy: *asphyxiation from forcible strangulation with a ligature of at least five mm in diameter.*

A ligature. Ritter had got Stausberg to attack those girls with a rope in April because Gross' killer had used a rope in February. Because Ritter had used a rope. He'd murdered Gross because she'd gone back on their agreement. Then he'd stabbed the body to make it match the murders of Ohliger and Scheer and make it look like part of a wider pattern.

Ritter had realised the need for a scapegoat he could control, someone who would confess to all three murders and make the heat go away. Someone mentally unstable, to cover the killing of so many random victims. Prone to playing with rope, to explain the ligature marks on Gross' corpse. So he'd brainwashed Stausberg and sent him out to attack those women to establish a similar pattern to the killings.

What with all that on my mind, it had taken me until after eleven to work out Trudi might be in danger too.

I rapped the bar. 'Hey, has she turned up or not?'

Bern's face told it all. Trudi wasn't there, and she should have been, and turning up late for the job was not something she made a habit of.

'Why don't you just clear off, bull?' Bern said. 'Christ, you look like you've been sleeping under a hedge.'

Not quite. I'd been existing on coffee, waiting for Trudi's shift to start. And now here I was at Willi's, and here she wasn't.

'Where does she live?'

Bern turned away without a word. I'd had it with this guy. Pure adrenaline propelled me over the bar. I got him in a choke hold with my left arm. I pulled the Luger, kept it below bar level as I dug the barrel into his spine.

'Give me her address or I'll paralyse you with a bullet, damn you.'

31.

Those top-floor apartments, they'll do it to you every time. I took the ill-lit stairwell at a jog to try and keep the adrenaline pumping around my system. I was getting that tell-tale sharp pain at the back of my knees that meant my legs were about ready to give out. When I got to the top and knocked on Trudi's door my breath was coming in short, painful bursts and those now-familiar white and purple fairy lights sparkled in my corneas. Or did I mean my retinas? Either way, I was going to have a hell of a time at my next medical. That's if I was still in the department by the time my next medical rolled around.

'Yeah?' Trudi called, once I was through knocking. I recognised her voice. Still alive then, though her voice had a tremor in it and she didn't open up. Maybe there was someone in there with her. Someone with a weapon.

I got out the Luger again and tried the door handle. Locked.

'Who is it?'

I kicked in the door and she came at me with a kitchen knife. My boxing instincts took over. I backed away from the knife and let Trudi's momentum carry her over my hip. She careered over me and landed face-up on the landing. The knife dropped. I kicked it away down the stairs and trained my gun on her.

'Are you alone?' I said.

She gurgled and shook her head, though whether that meant she couldn't answer me or no she wasn't alone, that was anyone's guess. She'd been wearing a cloche hat so tight-fitting it was still perched on her head, even after she'd practically somersaulted over me. That was some quality workmanship, right there. I pulled her inside the apartment and shut the door. Tried to, anyway. It wouldn't shut properly. Too much of the door frame had come away from the wall where I'd kicked it.

'Don't move,' I told her. I walked further into the room, pistol out in front of me. A studio apartment: bed – a stained mattress on the floor – wooden chair bearing an open and over-stuffed cardboard suitcase, a wardrobe that was too big for the room, a washstand. Three sky lights, all open and doing nothing to dissipate the stifling heat. It was like my room, only lighter for more of the day, no doubt. A bare light bulb dangled from a fraying cord near the door. There was no other door, there was no alcove, and there was nowhere for anyone to hide, save the wardrobe.

I crept to the wardrobe and pulled it open. Empty, not just of Ritters or green men, but of clothes too. Bare wire hangers swung on their pole. The shelf compartments were empty, clean patches edged with dust to show where the folded linen had been. I crossed to the open suitcase on the chair. It was full of dresses and underthings, and more clothes lay atop rumpled blankets on the mattress.

Among the clothes was a framed photograph that made me look twice. The print showed Trudi with an arm around a still-blond Gisela Ritter. I blinked the image away. No, not Gisela, but a younger and thinner version of her.

I pocketed my Luger, checking for knife tears in my jacket and not finding any. I took the framed picture over to Trudi, who was heavy-breathing where I'd left her. I bent over and showed her the photo.

'Who is this with you?'

'Emma,' she croaked.

'Emma Gross?'

She nodded. I looked again at the photo. *Gott in Himmel*, was this why Ritter had wanted to have a baby with Gross? Because she looked like his wife? It was the cheekbones and the way she held herself that made her look like Gisela. I'd seen cadavers aplenty in my time and I knew the distorting, diminishing effect of death on the human form, but still it was impossible to match this smiling young woman with the corpse I'd seen in Gross' crime scene photos. In this picture, she and Trudi were standing in front of a large beer barrel bearing a sign advertising the chance to bob for apples for half a pfennig. Gisela had a half-eaten apple in one hand and was offering it to Trudi. From Trudi's appearance, it looked like the picture had been taken some time within the previous couple of years.

'Why did you break my door?' Trudi croaked.

'I thought you might be in trouble.'

'Oh.' She choked and coughed and turned her head to spit phlegm at the floorboards, her gold earrings reflecting the light.

'Why did you attack me?' I asked.

She swallowed a couple of times and gasped, 'I thought you were him.'

'Who?'

'Emma's regular suitor.'

'Ritter?'

'Huh? The cop? What do you mean?' Her blue eyes clouded and she frowned. Upside-down, as I saw it, it was an odd effect. She hadn't known that Ritter was the guy.

'Michael Ritter was the regular suitor, the father of her child,' I said. 'The one Brandt aborted.'

'You found her then.' She gave me a grin.

'You could have saved me a lot of trouble if you'd told me, instead of sending me out on a blind treasure hunt.'

'I didn't know where she was, you dumb bull. Emma never told me. Didn't want me involved, she said.'

'And you never asked around?'

'I respected her wishes. Besides, when I told Ritter what I knew last year it didn't go anywhere. I thought you were going to be like him. Another bull who didn't care.'

239

'But he did care, Trudi. More than anyone.' I eased her into a sitting position. She took deep breaths. 'You all right?'

'I think so.'

I gestured to the suitcase. 'So was that why you were leaving? Because this man might come after you?'

'I knew with you blundering around asking questions, not knowing anything, there was a chance you'd bring him out of the shadows. I thought by giving you Brandt's name it would keep the heat off me long enough to get out of town.'

'I need to know what else you know,' I said. 'Have you seen a man wearing a green fedora or a green scarf? When he's not wearing the scarf he has a wide scar on his throat, like this.' I traced a line from my ear to my Adam's apple.

She shook her head.

'You sure?'

'I'm sure.'

'Okay then, forget about that. Let's go back to Emma and Ritter. Did you see them together the night she died? Did you see him leave in the morning? Anything like that?'

She rubbed the back of her head. 'No. I don't know what else I can tell you.'

'What did you tell Ritter? Back when he was investigating, I mean.'

'Nothing I haven't told you already. Like I said before, he didn't give a shit so what was the point of trying, you know?' She patted down her hair, her fingers catching the gold hoop in her left ear before stopping and caressing it for a moment. 'Wait.'

She went over to her suitcase and pulled out a box covered in split leather. She opened the box, palmed something from it and returned to me.

'When I found Emma's body that morning I noticed something glinting at me. Under the bed. I took it. Should have handed it in when the police came I suppose, but that Ritter was such an *arshloch*...'

Couldn't fault her on her character assessment. 'What was it?' I said.

I stretched out an upturned palm and she gave me what was in her hand. It was green, emerald green, cut in the shape of a tear and set in silver. Familiar as a piece of jewellery can be.

And that was it, bright and clear as a summer dawn. Ritter hadn't killed Emma Gross after all. But now I knew who had.

32.

I entered the Church of St. Rochus while the morning service was still going and I put out my hand so the door would close without slamming. The windows diffused the morning light. I breathed deep and got a hint of those sweet spices lingering on the air. And to think that all of six days ago when I'd entered the same church I hadn't had to make any effort to do that. The aroma had just been there, all around me, penetrating my unswollen sinuses without my needing to think about it.

Dear God, was it only six days since then? What day was it now? Wednesday? Thursday?

Whichever morning it was, there was a hell of a crowd in the pews – so many people that I couldn't make out Gisela anywhere. The white-bearded priest, or deacon, or whoever it was that did these things in Latin ceremonies, was speaking to the faithful. I hoped I hadn't got there too early. If my timing was good they'd have dispensed with the communion by then and they'd be drawing the mass to a close.

Frau Stausberg's blood covered my trousers, my jacket sleeves and some of my shirt. I hadn't made it home yet to change. Or to sleep, come to that. After the train station, I'd returned to the hospital. I still hadn't slept well and I still didn't know if Frau Stausberg was going to survive and, on top of all that, my neck ached.

I headed for the chapel where I'd found Kürten. I could wait there without attracting too much attention. Well, without attracting quite as much, at any rate. The priest made the sign of the cross and recited some Latin. The congregation responded, a deep chorus, again in Latin, and then the people rose to their feet with a loud rustle of clothing. They began to file out to the accompaniment of the organ. The white-bearded priest led the procession. Once he'd made it to the baptismal font the congregation began to talk, voices echoing and blending into one long serpentine hiss.

Five minutes went by before I spotted her. I took off my jacket and rolled it over my left arm to try and cover the blood stains. I left the chapel, went up to the line of worshippers and tapped Gisela on the shoulder.

'There you are, dear,' I said, forcing some jollity into my voice. Her face betrayed no surprise at my being there. Looking at those nearest to her in the queue, she didn't seem to be with any friends. I pulled her out of line, tugging on the sleeve of her high-necked, low-hemmed black dress.

She took the hospital stationery envelope I handed to her and she came with me to the chapel. I beckoned her further inside. That red fire bucket was still in the same place by the side of the altar.

'What do you want?' she said, looking around.

'Here.' I took the envelope back. Relieved of her burden, she crossed her arms to shut me out. I unrolled the jacket and slipped it back on, then I slid the envelope into an inside pocket. I went to the iron rack for the votive candles. I selected a fresh candle, lit it and put it on the rack, offering a silent prayer to Lilli as I took a deep breath.

'I named her, you know,' I said.

'What are you talking about?'

'Lilli. That's what I would have named her. Our daughter. If she'd lived.'

'You...' She didn't know how to end her thought. I didn't blame her. 'If she'd lived? *If she'd lived?* How dare you do this to me, now, here, in my church. You were the one who insisted. You were.' Gisela pointed at me and her plump lips were turned down at the ends, as they had been ever since the day our Lilli died.

I took her glare and I didn't flinch. She deserved that much from me.

'Did you know about your husband's arrangement with Emma Gross?' I said. 'Was that why you killed her?'

She came closer, close enough that I could see the open pores and small clumps of face powder on her cheeks, the plain studs in her lobes where the tear-shaped emerald earrings I'd bought had once hung. Red spots bloomed along her cheek bones.

'Did you kill her because she'd agreed to bear him the child you couldn't? Or because she had it killed the way...' I took another deep breath and tensed my belly '... the way you killed Lilli.'

She flung a fist at me. I caught it and twirled her around into my arms. I held her close. She tried to pull away but I wouldn't let her.

There were tears in those chocolate brown eyes, and if there was a point I would've let her walk away from it all, that was it.

'I found your missing earring,' I said. 'Someone at the hotel picked it up at the scene and gave it to me.'

'Liar. Michael got that earring back and I –'

She stopped herself, realising too late what she'd said.

'Yes, that's what he told you. But he lied to you, honey. Was that why he suggested you stop colouring your hair too? In case anyone had seen you that night?'

She looked down at the floor and then back up at me. We held each other in a tight embrace. She was tensed to break free, while my arms began to ache with the effort of restraining her.

'Why, Gisela?'

'Why did you make me kill our baby, Thomas? Why did you make me do that?'

She looked up at me, eyes shining. The feel of her in my arms made me shake, and it wasn't just from the effort of stopping her getting away. I told myself it was the adrenaline kicking in.

'What I really don't get is why you agreed to him

having a child with her,' I said. 'I mean, the woman was a prostitute.'

She looked puzzled. 'Why did I agree? It was my idea, Thomas.'

'What?'

'He told me about her. She'd turned up at headquarters one day. Vice brought her in for a VD screening. Michael caught sight of her in the courtyard and asked about her. He was so struck by the resemblance to me that he told me about it later that night. I had my idea straight away. To help make amends for you and me. He should cultivate a relationship with her, have the child with her that I couldn't give him. I thought if the baby came out looking like me, no one would ask questions, and everything would be okay.'

Damn, but those plump lips of hers were inviting. She parted them and a small animal sound escaped, her whole mouth quivering.

'But then she betrayed him,' Gisela said. 'She changed her mind. And it was like I'd betrayed him, so many times over. First with you, then by becoming barren, then by suggesting getting that harlot pregnant. And then... the final insult. Another crime against the Lord.'

She closed her eyes then and began to hum.

'You mind not upsetting my wife, partner?'

Gisela gasped and spun her head around. Ritter stood at the entrance to the chapel, his back to the stragglers still shuffling out of the church. He was aiming his Walther *polizei* pistol at me. His hand was steady despite the purple flush of his cheeks and the hard look he gave me. Even with all those danger signs, I couldn't take my eyes off his terrible moustache.

'You didn't forget our appointment to meet for breakfast did you, darling?' Ritter asked.

Gisela sniffed and shook her head.

'Let her go,' Ritter said to me.

I pulled my Luger and dug it into Gisela's ribs, flinching from the bruising on my knuckles. Stupid to forget

245

about the swelling on my right hand. Even if I wanted to pull the trigger, I doubted I'd be able to. I hoped Ritter wouldn't notice.

'Oh come on, Thomas!' Ritter laughed.

'I have to turn her in,' I said.

'Why? This whole sorry mess is your fault.'

'Shhhh!' Gisela said. 'Not so loud, Michael.'

I swallowed hard. *Ignore him*, I told myself. *He's just trying to weasel out of this. Don't listen. Don't admit that a part of you thinks he's right.*

'I have to turn her in,' I repeated.

'Fine, go ahead. But with what evidence?'

'With the envelope she handled a few minutes ago. The lab should be able to match one of the latents on it to the print found on the divan at the scene.'

He looked at his wife. Her hair brushed my chin as she nodded.

'The odds are a thousand to one against getting a match,' Ritter said. 'You know that.' But the doubt was there in his voice. I didn't move, though Ritter had circled around the edge of the chapel. He was creeping closer, keeping his pistol close to his body to obscure it from anyone who might look across from the nave. I dug the barrel of my gun in deeper and Gisela stiffened. Ritter caught the movement and stopped under one of the windows. It cast him in shades of green.

I talked, to avoid having to think. 'Well then, I guess I'll have to rely on Frau Stausberg's testimony detailing how you framed her son.' I fired off another quick, silent prayer, this one for Frau Stausberg's recovery, hoping my one votive candle would cover a second prayer.

'She won't talk,' Ritter sneered. 'She wouldn't risk her precious boy getting released.'

'We'll see.'

'Besides, who will prosecute? You think the state's going to expose its police force to more public ridicule by charging one of its own with murder?'

'Gisela isn't *Kripo*,' I said, though he was right again.

246

No one would want to listen to me. No one could afford to listen to me. Gennat had warned me about this, and I hadn't taken him seriously enough.

'Oh wake up, man,' Ritter said. 'As far as the public is concerned, there's no difference. No one is going to derail the case against Kürten by trying the wife of the head of his murder commission. It would leave *Kripo* in tatters.'

And there it was, Ritter's trump card. I'd found my murderer, but there was nothing I could do about it. It couldn't all come down to this, he and I and Gisela stuck together in silent complicity forever. Even if I did go ahead and file charges, Ritter would bring up the abortion, and that would mean my instant dismissal from *Kripo*, another blow to the credibility of the Ripper case given how many of the interviews I'd conducted.

I could take us all down together. But no, that was where Ritter's argument became stronger still. From bringing down one man connected to the Ripper prosecution, the department would have to bring down two. It was a simple equation. Convict the Ripper, the man responsible for so many brutal killings, and begin to repair the department's reputation, or convict the murderer of a single, unmourned prostitute and wreck the Ripper case.

Ritter's eyes flitted to the chapel entrance and his mouth dropped open.

The green man stood there, his fedora battered but still perched atop his head, his jagged scar red raw. His eyes were black holes glinting from swollen flesh and he clasped his bloodstained claw hammer in his left hand.

'Ritter,' the green man said.

'You know this man?' I asked Ritter. 'Who is he?'

'Who am I?' the green man said to me. He trembled as he spoke. From shock, at a guess, and blood loss. Dear God, he looked worse than Frau Stausberg had when the taxi had taken her to hospital.

Ritter's eyes widened. 'Albermann?' he said.

I got a vision of little Gertrude, the blood-soaked girl in

the green coat lying on her pile of bricks by the Papendell roadside. So this was her father, his rage more just than mine, and brighter, making my anger at her death seem fraudulent, tainted by my ambition.

The green man rushed me. I hesitated a second too long before bringing up the Luger. He pushed Gisela to the marble floor and smashed my hand aside with his hammer. My middle finger snapped. The pistol clattered off the side of the altar as I screamed. Gisela retreated behind me and knocked over the fire bucket, spilling sand across the marble. I grunted and fell to my knees.

Ritter pointed his Walther at the green man. 'Don't move!'

'You're all in on it,' the green man said, staring down at me. He kissed his hammer and muttered something I couldn't make out.

He raised the weapon over my head. I curled up around my broken right hand and closed my eyes.

A gunshot boomed. The green man growled and I opened my eyes. Albermann was running towards Ritter. Ritter pulled his trigger again, and missed. The green man plunged on and flailed at Ritter's face with the hammer. Ritter's pistol fell from his hand.

Albermann swung again and again until the crack of bone gave way to the slap of wet meat. Blood beaded the wall, shining black in the tinted light.

Albermann stopped his attack and now the cries of our audience in the nave penetrated the relative silence. The killer panted, his chest heaving. Blood dribbled down his face and there was no way of telling whose it was, his or Ritter's. I looked around for the Luger. Gisela huddled beside the altar, surrounded by sand. She was running her fingers through it, letting the grains slide off.

'Where's the damned gun?' I shouted. She looked at me blankly.

Albermann hurtled towards us, silent but for his deep breathing and the echo of his footfalls.

The Luger's black grip poked out of the sand. I crawled

towards it, my right arm throbbing with pain each time I put weight on it. I heard the man's grunts close behind me. I thrust my left hand into the sand, curled my fingers around the grip and turned to see the hammer swinging down at my skull.

I aimed upwards, squeezed off three wild left-handed shots. One bullet shattered a window. The other two took him in the torso and spun him around. He staggered back towards Ritter's body and sank to his knees, the light through the window turning his earlobes a translucent green.

I pulled the trigger twice more and sent two bullets through the back of his head, splattering his face across the broken glass.

33.

Gennat took my statement in that second-floor corner office at Mühlenstrasse he'd made his own. We were alone, me cradling a half-bottle of cognac the big man had given me while he smoked one of his damn cigars. My broken finger was bandaged to a splint. It throbbed, and the pain was the kind that made you want to throw up each time you moved.

We both sat at the pine table below the window, side by side. Gennat probably thinking it better that we didn't sit facing each other across a desk. Best to avoid the confrontational approach. Top marks that man. Couldn't fault him. Couldn't think all that clearly, either. Oh, dear Christ, what had happened?

Ritter was dead, goddamn it. And what the hell Gisela was going through I couldn't even begin to imagine. Okay, so she'd killed a woman and he'd covered it up and tried to pin it on someone else. And yet...

I filled my mouth with cognac straight from the bottle and gulped down the warm liquid. I had a couple of unhealed cuts on my inside lip that I'd picked up from somewhere. The drink made them sting, brought tears to my eyes.

The window was closed, the air stuffy. I sneezed twice and wiped my nose on my shirt sleeve. I got a kind of seasick feeling, my head spinning, and I sat up straight, trying to stay as still as I could.

Gennat reviewed his notes.

'You have no idea why Herr Albermann attacked you?' he said, shuffling in his chair, his spectacles perched on the end of his nose.

Oh yes, he'd asked me a question.

'Sorry Ernst, what did you say?'

'Never mind. What were you doing with this?'

He put Albermann's Luger on the table in front of me. I reached for it and he made no move to stop me. The dark powder that came off in my hands when I handled it told me why: they'd dusted for prints already.

'Albermann brought it with him,' I said.

'Yes.' Gennat flicked back through his notes. 'Yes, you said that, didn't you? Yet somehow, despite his breaking your finger, you managed to take it off him and shoot him in the back of the head.'

I drank more cognac and he flipped his notes back to the front page. The pencil-marked paper crackled under his fingers.

'What about Frau Stausberg?' I said. 'Is she going to be all right?'

The door opened and Vogel entered the room. He caught Gennat's eye and shook his head, then he approached me.

'Couldn't get any sense out of her, chief.' He was talking to Gennat but looking at me.

I held my bottle out to him. He batted it away as he knelt down to gaze into my eyes. I put the bottle down on the table and clasped my hands together in my lap.

'Except she keeps talking about someone named Lilli, about killing her. Over and over again. Just that. You wouldn't know anything about that now, would you, comrade?'

Gisela. He'd been getting Gisela's statement. I didn't envy him the task. I was going to shake my head, but I was fairly sure that was a move that would end with me decorating Vogel's shoes with my stomach contents. Okay, they were shitty shoes, but still.

'No,' I said.

The silence dragged and Vogel didn't move a millimetre, so I tried a bit more.

'I don't know what she's talking about. She's had a hell

of a shock though. And in her own church like that.' I slurred my words.

Vogel held my gaze for a long time.

'Yeah, what I thought too.' He turned to Gennat. 'Better get a doctor in to see her now, chief. That's about all we can do for her, I'd have thought.'

Gennat waved him off. 'Call Berg. He'll probably know the right person.'

Vogel left the room, closing the door behind him.

'Frau Stausberg is still in a critical condition, Thomas,' Gennat said. 'The doctor I spoke to an hour ago thinks she could live, but she could have sustained some brain damage. It's too early to tell.'

How many people had died or lost their loved ones because of me and my investigation? Because of Ritter's goddamned cover-up? The thought made me shudder.

Gennat took a deep drag on his compost-scented cigar.

'You were lucky,' he said.

'Lucky?' This was supposed to be some kind of bad joke, perhaps. Gennat's face, shrouded in smoke, was unreadable.

A scream rent the air, piercing the walls of the building. Sounded like Gisela's voice, but all ripped up and ragged, like her brain had just registered the loss of her husband, of the man she'd always loved that little bit more than she had me. Even while she'd been sleeping with me behind his back.

And to think I'd bought her those earrings.

'I think you found what you were looking for,' Gennat said. I must've looked blank or puzzled for a moment because he added, 'At lunch the other day? Come on, don't tell me you don't remember now, surely? I think you found out who it was, didn't you? Who killed that *beinl*.'

'No.'

He smiled and it wasn't a nice smile. He raised his notes and put them on the table, pushing them away. He held up his pencil and put it in his breast jacket pocket with a flourish.

'Come on,' he said, 'you can tell me.'

'When did you say you were leaving?'

He watched me holding myself still and then he clapped his hands and let loose a full, for-the-gallery laugh.

He checked the wall clock, then his watch, and then he got up out of his seat. 'Yes, you were lucky my friend. Lucky. I tell you, you were born to this life. And you don't even know it. You had any sense, you could get a promotion out of this.'

'Promotion?' My brain was too numb to take in what he was saying. He hadn't just said that, surely?

'Think about it, my boy.' He stabbed the air with his cigar as he crossed to the door. 'We can't have Albermann's ID leaked to the press. There must be a cover-up, and a hero to draw the flack. There's only one of you that survived.' He pointed at me. 'And you know everything. More than enough to cake the department in shit for months to come if they don't treat you right. Plus there's an inspector's post going free, I hear.'

He winked.

'Don't go anywhere,' he said. As if I could, feeling as sick as I did. 'I'll be right back to wrap this up.'

He left the room, closing the door on a hallway that buzzed with conversation, hurried footsteps, a couple of ringing telephones – the everyday sounds of a busy criminal investigations department. I stared out of the window. The view took in the cobbles of Mühlenstrasse.

A promotion. Could it happen? If Frau Stausberg came out of the hospital brain damaged and if Gisela's mind had crumbled then it could. I could come through this with some credit.

I'd solved my little murder case after all, and some kind of justice had prevailed, no one could deny that. Emma Gross had been avenged, and in the only way possible. A death for a death, on the QT. Just between us and our maker, so to speak.

Hell, who was I to deny opportunity if she came knocking?

I had a lot to learn from Gennat, even now. Especially now, as I tried not to think about having killed Gertrude Albermann's father.

Ten minutes or so went by and an open-topped armoured car pulled up to the main entrance. The car disgorged blue-coated *Schupo* bearing bullet hoses. The car's engine ticked over as the *Schupo*men vanished beneath my line of sight and into the building. Flashbulbs popped.

The *Schupo* returned, marching back to the car in tight formation. In their midst sauntered Peter Kürten, hands cuffed, a plainclothesman at either elbow. Gennat followed along behind the group, beside another dark-suited man who looked like the public prosecutor. More cameras flashed, but the press contingent was small, fewer than a half-dozen guys. For once Gennat was doing something low key.

He said a few words to the reporters then he slapped the PP on the back and pushed him forwards into the press pack. The *Schupo* phalanx steered its cargo into the back of the armoured car.

Kürten's plainclothes escort went with him and pushed him into a seat. From where I sat, his hair looked freshly barbered, neat and oiled. His face appeared clean-shaven and his suit had been pressed. He looked a damn sight better than I did.

As the car pulled away, I stood to watch its passage down the street. Kürten looked up, or I imagined he did. Did he see me looking out, watching his progress towards Düsseldorf Prison and his eventual trial? His inevitable execution?

There was the man who'd terrorised first a city then an entire country for a year and a half – no, more than that even. The man who'd changed me for the worse. And the better. Whose phoney confession to Emma Gross' murder had led me to discover that I was a detective after all.

A killer too.

He was smiling, I swear he was, as the car turned the corner and took him away.

I thought once more of Gertrude Albermann, her torn panties and blood-caked little face. Kürten would die and Ritter was dead, but so was her father, and I was responsible for all three. What kind of a result was that?

'I'm sorry,' I whispered.

For all the good it would do.

Historical note

Several of the characters in the story you just read were based (loosely) on real people, including Ernst Gennat, Karl Berg, Emma Gross and, of course, Peter Kürten himself. I should stress that the character of Gertrude Albermann's father was entirely my own creation.

Gennat was one of the most famous detectives in Germany. So much so that he inspired the Inspector Karl 'Fatty' Lohmann character in Fritz Lang's 1931 expressionist movie *M*, just as Kürten inspired that of Lang's child killer Hans Beckert in the same movie, however much Lang half-heartedly denied it at the time. Karl Lohmann in turn proved popular enough for Lang to bring him back for his next on-screen crime epic, 1933's *The Testament of Dr Mabuse*. Both of these films are well worth checking out by anyone interested in interwar Germany or film history.

Back in the real world, Gennat played a major role in reforming Berlin's criminal investigations department. In 1926 he was finally able to establish the permanent homicide department he'd been lobbying his superiors for since at least the end of the First World War. He ran the department at a clean-up rate of around ninety-seven per cent until well into the 1930s. He also really did coin the term '*Serienmörder*' for a magazine article off the back of his experience on the Kürten case. This was more than forty years before the equivalent phrase 'serial killer' entered the English language.

In his capacity as forensic pathologist, Karl Berg interviewed Kürten ahead of the latter's trial, going on to publish a book called *The Sadist* shortly after Kürten's execution. If this book remains the closest we have to a definitive version of the case, it's because of its exhaustive reproduction of Kürten's confessions to every single murder and attack carried out over the course of his life, as well as statements from as many of the surviving victims as the police were able to track down. Berg's memoirs of the autopsies he carried out during the case are also invaluable. The book is out of print but anyone who lives near a large public library should be able to get hold of a copy with a little determination, and a little patience.

All the English language accounts of Kürten's crimes published since the 1930s are best taken with a pinch of salt, especially those to be found on the internet. Most – if not all – are hack jobs involving no original research. Some of them mistakenly place the February murder of Rosa Ohliger in March, while others claim that the 3rd February attack on Frau Kühn took place on 8th February. The Ohliger mix up seems to be the result of a typo in Karl Berg's book which has been copied over and over ever since by those in too much of a hurry to check their facts.

Having read as many contemporary accounts as I could, I believe the timeline that follows is the most accurate version of events published in English since the first translation of *The Sadist* appeared in 1938. If any readers know differently I'd be happy to hear from them.

Incidentally, although Kürten is well known to true crime hounds today as the 'Vampire of Düsseldorf', none of the accounts dating from the time of the case mention this, suggesting that this touch of melodrama was added later.

Peter Kürten timeline

Sun 3 Feb 1929
Frau Kühn attacked at around nine p.m. on 'a lonely road' in the south-western Flingern district of Düsseldorf. According to Kühn's statement, her attacker passes by and says good evening before grabbing her coat lapels in one hand and demanding she keep quiet. He then stabs her repeatedly. Kühn does not see the weapon, nor can she describe her attacker; her memory of the attack is hazy. Medical exam reveals twenty-four flesh wounds to head, arms and torso.

Sat 9 Feb 1929
Construction gang discovers fully clothed corpse of young girl at nine a.m. Body lies under a fence surrounding the building they're working on in Kettwigerstrasse, Flingern district. Body is partially burned and smells of kerosene: underclothes still smoulder. There are bloodstains and stab marks in the clothing. Autopsy reveals up to thirteen stab wounds on the left torso and left temple and concludes that internal bleeding from these wounds caused the girl's death. Bloated and livid appearance of girl's face indicates congestion in the head; suggests the girl was also strangled before death. Burn patterns are limited to upper thighs, neck, chin and hair; lack of soot in lungs suggests the body was burned after death. Microscopic examination of girl's underwear and genitalia reveals semen stains not visible to the naked eye. Medical examiner concludes coitus was not the aim of the attacker, but that he probably ejaculated and then inserted a semen-smeared finger under the child's panties.

Stomach contents indicate a time of death between six p.m. and seven p.m. on Friday 8th February. Police soon ID the girl as eight-year-old Rosa Ohliger. Girl's mother confirms Rosa ate lunch at two p.m. on the 8th before visiting a friend. The friend confirms Rosa leaving for home at six p.m. Police find no witnesses to the crime.

Local press picks up on these crimes and starts name-checking Jack the Ripper in its reports, implying a link between the attacks.

Weds 13 Feb 1929

Corpse of forty-five-year-old, disabled mechanic Rudolf Scheer discovered eight a.m., again in the Flingern district. Autopsy finds twenty stab wounds to the neck and back. This, along with absence of defensive wounds, suggests Scheer was stabbed from behind. Examiner deduces time of death between eleven p.m. and midnight the night before.

At this point there have been three attacks in ten days. The press warms to its Jack the Ripper musings.

Forensic experts involved in the case agree similarities:

1) all three victims attacked in isolated areas of the Flingern district;

2) the use of a stabbing instrument, perhaps the same one in each case;

3) absence of common motive such as robbery or rape;

4) attacks came at dusk or later; numerous stabs of the same type executed rapidly and always including at least one stab to the temple.

Karl Berg MD is one such expert. He performed the Ohliger autopsy and writes later: 'All these factors, taken together, make inevitable the conclusion that the same criminal committed the crimes and, furthermore, the abnormal character of the criminal.'

Tues 2 April 1929

Sixteen-year-old Erna Penning attacked on way home. Attacker throws rope noose around her neck. Penning struggles to get away but attacker closes in and attempts to tighten the noose with one hand while throttling her with the other. According to her statement, Penning prevents the man from tightening his noose and pinches his nostrils together so he can't breathe. This causes him to step back and remove the noose. Penning takes her chance and flees.

Weds 3 April 1929

Frau Flake attacked on 'ill-lit' street after leaving her workplace in northern Düsseldorf. According to her statement, she hears and then sees a man walk quickly behind her. She slows down to let him past. Instead, he flings his noose around her neck, drags her into a field by the side of the road and tries to stuff a handkerchief into her mouth. Flake resists and the man tells her to open her mouth while tightening the noose. Witnesses stumble on the scene and observe the attacker fleeing.

April 1929

Police ID the would-be strangler as twenty-year-old Johann Stausberg, a man variously described as an 'imbecile' and a 'cretin', with either a 'cleft palate [and] hare lip' or a simple 'speech impediment', according to whose account you read. Police arrest and interrogate Stausberg who confesses to the noose attacks on Penning and Flake. According to Berg: 'Naturally, nothing was simpler than to accuse Stausberg of the three February attacks... He knew so many details that he could not have known from the newspapers, being an illiterate. So it came about that he was suspected of having committed these crimes, and this despite certain grave doubts.' In short, Stausberg confesses to the murders of Rudolf Scheer and Rosa Ohliger, and the attack on Frau Kühn. His confessions are convincing, albeit hazy on the details.

Stausberg suffers from epilepsy, so detectives explain away the inaccuracies by pointing to the fact that many epilepsy sufferers have poor memories, particularly after suffering an epileptic seizure. Also, Stausberg's mother tells police that her son told her he'd murdered Rosa Ohliger on 9th February, when the case first hit the press. Stausberg's prosecution is stopped under paragraph fifty-one of the German criminal code – which allows for diminished responsibility in cases of questionable sanity – and he is taken to an asylum.

Tues 30 July 1929
Emma Gross, thirty-five-year-old prostitute, found murdered in a hotel near Düsseldorf's central train station; her body has been strangled and left naked on a divan. She has not been stabbed and her body bears no wounds other than bruising around the neck. Police take a relaxed view towards tracing the killer and seem to regard such attacks as an occupational hazard. Although Kürten will confess to this murder shortly after capture, he later retracts the confession. No evidence ever links him to the crime and the real perpetrator is never caught. Berg: 'There was nothing about this case to incline me to the view that it was another committed by the same unknown as in the previous cases under investigation.'

Sun 11 Aug 1929
Domestic servant Maria Hahn disappears during an afternoon off work. Hahn having recently resigned, her employer assumes Hahn has left before working out her notice and doesn't think to notify police. Hahn's body would turn up in November.

Weds 21 Aug 1929
Frau Mantel accosted near church square in the western Lierenfeld suburb of Düsseldorf. A stranger asks Frau Mantel if he can accompany her to the country fair being held in the area; he then stabs her in the back. A little

later, in the same area, Anna Goldhausen is stabbed between her ribs by a stranger, the stab piercing liver and stomach. Within an hour, Heinrich Kornblum is stabbed in the back while sitting on a park bench. All three victims survive their attacks. The knife cuts through Kornblum's leather braces, from which medical examiners determine the dimensions of the blade. Investigators see no evidence to contradict their prosecution of Stausberg for the stabbings and stranglings earlier in the year. Berg: 'On these data I came to the conclusion that the knife used in this case was not that used in the case of the Ohliger child or that of the man Scheer. This seemed to be one more ground for suspecting someone other than Stausberg.'

The German press dusts off its Jack the Ripper cuttings. Panic begins to spread in Düsseldorf.

Sun 25 Aug 1929
Bodies of five-year-old Gertrude Hamacher and fourteen-year-old foster sister Louise Lenzen are found on allotments two hundred metres from their home in the Flehe district of Düsseldorf. The girls had gone missing the previous evening after attending a fair in the market place. Aware of Jack the Ripper reports in the press and fearing the worst, family and friends had been searching for the girls most of the night. Hamacher's body lies on a patch of runner beans. Lenzen's body lies seventeen metres away on a bare patch of earth. Locals report hearing children's cries in the area at nine-fifteen p.m. on the 24th, which detectives interpret as the time of death. Autopsy confirms this conclusion. Footprints at the scene and the wounds on the bodies are the only physical evidence of the crime. From these, detectives and medical examiners piece together the girls' last moments. The Hamacher girl is strangled until she loses consciousness. Lenzen probably calls out for help – the cries that the passers-by later reported. The killer strangles Lenzen, cuts her throat and stabs her in the back. Still alive but

weakened, Lenzen tries to flee but collapses due to blood loss. Footprints indicate the killer walks back from Lenzen's body, probably to cut Hamacher's throat.

Later that Sunday afternoon, in the village of Oberkassel near Düsseldorf, twenty-six-year-old domestic servant Gertrud Schulte accepts a stranger's offer to escort her to the nearby outdoor market at Neuss. The stranger introduces himself as Fritz Baumgart. According to Schulte's statement, when they come to a meadow near the market, Baumgart forces Schulte to the ground and attempts to remove her panties. Schulte tells him she'd rather die, to which he replies, 'Well die then,' and stabs her several times before fleeing. A group of youngsters hear Schulte's cries and take her to hospital. Medical exam reveals thirteen stab wounds and the point of the blade used in the attack lodged in Schulte's back. Schulte describes Baumgart to police, putting him in his mid-thirties.

End of Aug 1929

Based on the August attacks, Düsseldorf Kriminalpolizei (*Kripo*) conclude the following:

1) Fritz Baumgart is likely the same man who attacked Frau Mantel, Anna Goldhausen and Heinrich Goldblum on 21st August;

2) despite lack of semen or other evidence of sexual violation, the killings of Hamacher and Lenzen were likely lust murders, either for the thrill of the kill itself or with the unconsummated intention of sexual violation;

3) Baumgart was not the same man who killed Hamacher and Lenzen. They are looking for at least two criminals.

Writing later, Berg says: 'We had formed the opinion that a sadist who had satisfied his sexual appetite on Saturday by the murder of two children would not have troubled to tackle a victim capable of offering a stout resistance already by the following Sunday... strangulation, a characteristic common to all the other crimes, was here absent.'

The press goes big on the attacks and begins to criticise *Kripo* for lack of progress.

Mon 30 Sept 1929

Body of domestic servant Ida Reuter found at seven a.m. in meadows on Düsseldorf outskirts. The girl's underwear and handbag are missing and the body lies with bare legs parted and genitals exposed. The head bears a circle of bruises which Karl Berg in his initial exam of body believes to be the marks of hammer blows; this conclusion is confirmed via detailed examination of victim's skull during autopsy. Autopsy yields two cubic centimetres of sperm from Reuter's dissected vagina. From this, the digestive state of stomach contents and the body's complete rigor mortis on discovery, Berg assumes a time of death of before midnight on the 29th.

Due to use of new weapon, Düsseldorf *Kripo* now suspects a third killer has entered the scene.

Weds 2 Oct 1929

Düsseldorf *Kripo* requests consultation with the Berlin homicide department, at this time the only specialised homicide detective unit in Germany. Düsseldorf *Kripo* has been operating under the common system of assembling temporary murder commissions to solve specific murders. Since formation in 1926 under leadership of Chief Inspector Ernst Gennat, Berlin homicide has had an average annual clean up rate of around ninety-seven per cent. With Gennat's expert advice, Düsseldorf *Kripo* concludes that it is now looking for up to four different sex killers.

Sat 12 Oct 1929

Elisabeth Dorrier, unemployed servant girl, found wounded and unconscious in Flingern district at six-thirty a.m. Crime scene shows Dorrier was attacked and then dragged to the spot where she was found, similar to the Reuter crime scene. Dorrier also bears similar bruises to Reuter on the left temple. Her attacker has torn her vagina and left the imprint of his finger nails in the mucous membrane.

Sun 13 Oct 1929

Dorrier dies without recovering consciousness. Karl Berg performs autopsy: 'After comparison of the head wounds I came to the following conclusions: the wounds of Reuter and Dorrier conform to such an extent that it is necessary to presume the same criminal and the same instrument of murder in both cases.'

Fri 25 Oct 1929

Frau Meurer, thirty-four, attacked on way home. Stranger accosts her at eight p.m. while she walks along the Hellweg in Flingern. According to her statement the man asks, 'Aren't you afraid? Quite a lot of things have happened here already.' She ignores him and he attacks her. An hour later some passers-by bring her into hospital. She is unconscious and her forehead and right ear bear oval wounds two centimetres in diameter which are deep enough to expose her skull. She regains consciousness but with no memory of the attack itself. Two weeks later she is well enough to leave hospital. Berg later says her wounds could have come from hammer blows and points out: 'This episode was important because two weeks earlier in that same place Dorrier had been killed by similar wounds.'

Later that evening, prostitute Frau Wanders is approached in the Hofgarten by a stranger she takes for a potential client. They negotiate prices for sex before the man knocks her out with a blow to the head. Wanders regains consciousness soon after and, being a good citizen, goes to the police to give a statement before going to hospital in search of treatment. Doctors treating her find four head wounds. Later, Karl Berg examines her. He finds 'a square depression fracture' over the left ear and 'two smaller depression fractures' on the crown and the right temple: 'They were square hammer impressions.'

According to Margaret Seaton-Wagner, author of *The Monster of Düsseldorf: the Life and Trial of Peter Kürten* (1932), police try to avoid leaking too much information to the press about these last two attacks: 'Not only were the police at a dead end; they were the subject of embittered press attacks...' She mentions that local Communist newspaper *Freiheit* has been the most consistent critic of the police investigation so far. It is the only paper publicly to claim Johann Stausberg's innocence of the February murders.

Thurs 7 Nov 1929
Last sighting of five-year-old Gertrud Albermann, at six-forty-five p.m. in Flingern. Press goes big with the story, stoking what Seaton-Wagner calls 'mingled feelings of wrath, terror, and the sense of being fooled by a maniac of almost supernatural powers.'

Sat 9 Nov 1929
Gertrud Albermann's body found among brick rubble and nettles, lying against a wall surrounding the factory yard of a firm called Haniel and Lueg in the Düsseldorf outskirts. Body lies face down, legs parted. On removing the girl's coat, police find that her killer removed her clothes to expose her bottom, tearing her underwear in the process. Berg performs the autopsy and writes later: '[Albermann's] body... was discovered in so typical a position that she must have been killed and sexually violated where she was found. The position, with the knickers torn up behind, arouses the inevitable suspicion that the child had been put in this position in order to rape her from behind.' Autopsy reveals facial congestion and thumb marks indicative of strangulation, two stab wounds in the left of the head and thirty-four stab

266

wounds in the breast. From stomach contents and details of meals eaten at two p.m. and four p.m. on the 7th, Berg estimates a time of death of seven p.m. on the 7th, some fifteen minutes after Gertrud was last sighted. Rainfall on the 7th and 8th washed most blood from the crime scene; the girl's clothes absorbed the rest. Berg concludes that the killer strangled the girl at the place her body was found, until she passed out and fell to the ground. The killer then stabbed her through her coat. He removed the coat and arranged her so he could rape her, only to change his mind and replace the coat without following through.

A few hours after police discover Gertrud's body, the *Freiheit* newspaper receives a letter posted on the 8th purporting to be from the killer. The letter includes a sketch map showing the location of Gertrud's body which tallies with the crime scene. The outer edge of the map shows some forest and a cross, along with the words: 'Murder at Pappendelle. In the place marked with a cross a corpse lies buried.' Police headquarters receives a similar letter and is forced to go public with the murder, since *Freiheit* already has the information. Unfortunately the letter casts more bad light on the investigation. As Berg comments: 'Once already, on the 14th October 1929, the police had received a peculiar communication describing the interment of a body at the edge of the woods and containing a plan on which the burial place was marked.' According to Seaton-Wagner, the earlier letter mentions a 'big flat stone' which supposedly indicates the exact spot of the murder. Berg neglects to add why police did not follow up on the October letter, but Seaton-Wagner says that police treated such previous letters as 'hoaxes'.

Police investigation gets second wind. Besides the Haniel and Leug factory, the Pappendelle district comprises meadows, woods and ploughed fields. Not far from the factory is a café which receives little passing trade except on Sundays. Police think it likely that any missing person from the area went missing on a Sunday. The investigation:

1) sifts local missing persons cases;

2) begins to dig at and around the spot marked on the sketch map;

3) photographs a battered straw hat and set of keys a local farmer found on his land in the preceding weeks.

Tues 12 Nov 1929
Police publish photos of the keys and hat in local press.

Weds 13 Nov 1929
Local novelist recognises keys and contacts police; the woman's housekeeper, Maria Hahn, originally from Bremen, had left the house for a Sunday afternoon off in August and never returned. Police make enquiries and analyse records from Düsseldorf and Bremen. There is no record of anyone having seen Hahn alive since Sunday 11th August.

Ripper stories reappear in local and national press, which stresses that the London Ripper of 1888 also wrote to police to inform them of his work. Tone is critical of police, some articles claiming there could be hundreds more bodies buried in the fields around Düsseldorf. Press is indignant, as Seaton-Wagner puts it, 'that in these days of enlightenment, telephone and aeroplane, any old-time tale of mystery and terror could repeat itself.' Much like the tone of the London papers in 1888.

Two women come forward; they claim to have seen Hahn on 14th August with a man in his early thirties who wore horn-rimmed spectacles and a smart suit. They stress his apparent good manners. Police appeal for snap-shots taken that day, describing Hahn as pretty, fair-haired and wearing a pink silk dress on the day she disappeared. Dozens of letters arrive at police headquarters containing sketches and photos and hints of further murders.

Local police make two arrests, both of young men who are released without charge. Budapest police arrest a man for accosting a woman and implying he is the Düsseldorf murderer when she refuses to accompany him on a walk in the woods. In Düsseldorf, 'any man seen talking to a child ran the risk of being followed as a suspect' (Seaton-Wagner). Neighbours vent grudges by reporting each other's nightly prowlings to police. Women report hearing screams from the woods on the city's outskirts.

Prussian Justice Ministry intervenes and sends murder squad detectives from Berlin *Kripo* to Düsseldorf. Seaton-Wagner: '[This] aroused some local jealousy but it helped to restore the faith of the population in those responsible for public law and order.'

Fri 15 Nov 1929

Digging detectives – now under direction of Berlin *Kripo* – find flat stone mentioned in October letter. Further digging at that spot uncovers Maria Hahn's body. Body is unclothed and police deduce it is Hahn from her hair and build.

Berg conducts the autopsy: 'A comparison of the autopsies of the Albermann child and Maria Hahn show a considerable affinity. Evidence of throttling could not, of course, be proved in the latter case, but the stab wounds were alike in both cases. Each body had stabs in the temple. In the skull there were the same triangular forms showing a knife with a rather broad back. The largest stab, in the case of Hahn, was in the forehead.' Berg concludes that Hahn was killed close to where her body was buried.

Winter 1929-1930

With the discovery of Maria Hahn's body, the Düsseldorf killings come to an end. Police are no closer to finding a killer or killers.

Police refine theory of four perpetrators and believe they are looking for:

1) a strangler;

2) a stabber;

3) a hammer killer;

4) a 'homosexual maniac'.

However, during a press conference announcing his involvement, Berlin's Chief Inspector Gennat talks up the Jack the Ripper link, claiming that the original 'was a mere beginner compared with his Düsseldorf disciple' and that 'no such case is known in the whole history of criminology'. (Seaton-Wagner)

Berg summarises the case later: 'It is only necessary to consider the facts as I have related them to appreciate how few were the clues in the hands of the police to assist them in their search for the perpetrator. Indeed, two of the attacks were perpetrated by Stausberg; the murder of Gross was at the hand of an unknown criminal; and, these three crimes apart, there remained an insufficient number of common factors upon which a theory could be constructed pointing unequivocally to a single criminal.

'Where a series of crimes are committed, the same technique inevitably suggests the same criminal. That is an old aphorism of criminology. But just this very thing is missing in our cases. Certainly, there were points in common. In five murders the sexual motive was perfectly clear from the condition of the genitals. In the other cases, that of the murdered Scheer or the stabbed Kornblum, or again, in the case of Frau Meurer, it could not be definitely demonstrated.

'... Further, the multiplicity of stabs in the one series of victims and the absence of stabbing in the case of the other series, along with the hammer blows, all argued against one and the same criminal. And to these factors was added the view that Stausberg had been responsible for the February attacks, an opinion which held good until the November findings on Albermann. It was in particular for a criminal who dealt death with a hammer that we sought...'

The ensuing investigation instigates raids on underworld premises across Prussia, extending as far as Berlin. Düsseldorf *Kripo* offer large rewards for Elisabeth Dörrier's handbag, Ida Reuter's handbag or Gertrud Schulte's purse. Police dress a mannequin in Dörrier's nightclub clothes. Plainclothesmen enter Düsseldorf's cabarets and dance halls carrying a long black box containing the mannequin; they stop the music and then show the mannequin on stage: a combined appeal for witnesses and a public service reminder to remain vigilant.

Police release two positive statements to the public:

1) Berlin *Kripo* graphologist Dr Schneikert examines six hundred letters and sketch maps sent in after November, concluding that two were written by the same person as the November letter;

2) Gennat announces he and his men are searching for the mistake every criminal makes 'once in the course of his career, and which in the end is bound to lead to his capture. Hitherto, in his opinion, the Düsseldorf Ripper's one mistake was his yearning for publicity.' (Seaton-Wagner) Within six months, the killer will make his mistake.

Sun 23 Feb 1930

Hildegard Eid survives a rape and attempted strangulation in the Grafenberg woods. Her attacker takes her home and makes her promise not to tell anyone what happened. A week later on Sunday 2nd March he visits her at home and, weirdly, she goes out with him again, visiting several beer gardens before accompanying him back to his flat in Mettmannerstrasse. They go to bed but are interrupted by the man's wife returning home before coitus can take place. At the wife's insistence, Eid dresses and allows the wife to escort her back home. Eid fails to report anything untoward to the police.

March 1930

Two young women, Marianne del Sant and Irma Becker, survive rape and strangulation attempts in the Grafenberg woods on separate nights. On the 30th, Syvilla Wil is talked into having sex on a park bench with a man she's just met. According to the statement she gives later (after Kürten's arrest and confession), this man doesn't attempt to harm her.

April 1930

Five more women suffer sexual attacks involving attempted strangulation. All survive.

Wed 30 April 1930

Charlotte Ulrich goes to the Grafenberg woods with a man she meets that evening. Upon reaching the woods, Ulrich's companion hits her on the right temple with a hammer. Ulrich collapses, screaming, feels a second blow to the temple and loses consciousness, waking up alone in the woods to find her hands covered in blood and her bag missing. On staggering to the nearest railway station and asking for help, she rejects advice to go to the police. Ulrich is up and about again after two weeks' recuperation at the home of some kindly strangers. Later, it transpires she wouldn't go to the police because she was wanted for theft. She ends up serving a three-month jail term. While she's in jail, Berg examines her to find that the hammer attack had fractured her skull. 'This case proves a striking instance of the power of the will to accelerate recovery,' Berg later notes, somewhat dryly.

May 1930

Berg and Seaton-Wagner's accounts of events at this point match on essentials but differ on dates, and, oddly, the name of the killer's next victim. Berg has her name as Maria Butlies, Seaton-Wagner as Maria Büdlick. Generally, I prefer to give Berg the benefit of the doubt, but what follows is my attempt to reconcile the two.

Weds 14 May 1930

Maria Butlies travels from Cologne to Düsseldorf in search of work as a domestic servant. On the train she makes friends with a Frau Brucker, who promises to meet her at Düsseldorf's central train station to help find her accommodation. Butlies waits but Brucker does not show up. According to Butlies' statement, at eight p.m. a man approaches her and says he'll show her the way to a women's hostel. In fact, he leads her to the Volksgarten, at which point Butlies demurs. The man argues with her; a second man approaches the pair and demands to know the first man's intentions, scaring him off. This new stranger says he lives in a nice three-room flat in Mettmannerstrasse and would Butlies like to rest there for a while before going on to the hostel? Butlies agrees and they go. The flat turns out to be a poorly-furnished one-room attic flat. The man gives Butlies a cup of milk and a slice of bread and ham. This is around eleven p.m. After eating her food, Butlies insists on leaving. Stranger escorts her onto the tram, saying the hostel is a 'short tram-ride' away. Butlies notices the tram is heading out of town. They get off near some woods on the city's outskirts. The stranger leads Butlies deeper into the woods. Then he stops and says: 'You're alone with me in the middle of the woods. Now you scream as much as you like and nobody will hear you!' He kisses her, seizes her by the throat and throws her to the ground. Mindful of Düsseldorf Ripper stories, Butlies allows the man to rape her, hoping that compliance will save her life. When he's finished, the man asks if she remembers where he lives. Butlies lies and says no. The man leads her back to the tram line and leaves her there. This decision not to kill Butlies proves to be the mistake Gennat was waiting for.

Thurs 15 May 1930

Butlies finds refuge at a women's hostel run by nuns – the Gertrudishaus, or hostel of St. Gertrude. She tells them of the attack but makes no effort to contact police.

273

Fri 16 May 1930

A man calling himself Franz Weidlich gets talking with a young woman named Gertrud Bell. They have sex in her rented room and make a date to meet again on Saturday 24th May. 'Weidlich' doesn't attempt to harm Bell physically, though this could be because her prying landlady drives him out of the building soon after coitus. Fate will soon intervene to ensure that 'Weidlich' fails to make his appointment.

Sat 17 May 1930

Butlies writes a letter to Frau Brucker detailing her rape. Blind luck intervenes to help the police: Butlies misspells Frau Brucker's name and her letter is delivered to a Frau Brugman, who takes the letter to Düsseldorf *Kripo* at headquarters.

Weds 21 May 1930

Late morning: plainclothesmen track down Butlies at the Gertrudishaus and ask her to try and find her attacker's address. Earlier that morning, Butlies had already tramped up and down Mettmannerstrasse trying to find the right house. She had asked inhabitants of different houses along the street if a 'fair-haired' and 'rather sedate' man lived there. At number seventy-one, inhabitants recognised the description as matching Peter Kürten, a man who lodges in the attic flat with his wife. Around lunchtime Butlies leads the detectives to number seventy-one. Waiting in the lobby, Butlies asks a woman passing through with her daughters if a man answering Kürten's description lives there. The woman turns out to be Kürten's landlady who lives in the flat next door to his. She escorts Butlies to Kürten's flat and lets Butlies in. Kürten returns home and surprises Butlies. He leaves with hat pulled low over his eyes, eluding the two detectives.

Fri 23 May 1930

Morning: detectives take Frau Kürten from work to interview her about her husband. At this point police know only that they are tracking a violent rapist. There is nothing in the case to point to Kürten's being the Düsseldorf Ripper besides the circumstantial fact that he has attacked a woman.

Evening: Frau Kürten informs police that her husband has arranged to meet her at the Church of St. Rochus at three p.m. next day. She tells detectives her husband has confessed to her to being the Düsseldorf Ripper. She denies all prior knowledge and appears to be in shock at the news.

Sat 24 May 1930
Three p.m., police surround the church square and arrest Kürten who surrenders without a struggle. Kürten's personal appearance is smart, including:

1) make up;

2) hair pomades;

3) well-brushed suit, creased trousers;

4) polished shoes;

5) slim;

6) good-looking (Berg)/plain (Seaton-Wagner);

7) thick yellow hair carefully parted;

8) blue eyes (clever looking: Berg);

9) small scar on right cheek (apparently hard to spot) – from quarrel in 1904;

10) despite being in his mid-forties (born 1883), witnesses and surviving victims have all underestimated his age at between twenty-five and thirty-five.

That evening, theatres and cabarets in the city interrupt their performances to announce Kürten's capture; cinemas flash the news on-screen The public reacts sceptically, causing police to publish reports regularly during their interrogation of the suspect.

Sun 25 May 1930

Kürten's interrogation begins. The Chief of the Düsseldorf Murder Commission conducts the first interview in the presence of the Rhineland Police Chief, the Attorney General and the Public Prosecutor. Once first protocols are taken, the Chief of Police and Chief of the Murder Commission drive Kürten to the scenes of the crimes he has confessed to, to verify his statements on the spot.

Graphologist Dr Schneikert summoned from Berlin by telegram to study Kürten's handwriting.

Gertrud Schulte picks Kürten out of a line up. The missing tooth in Kürten's upper right jaw seems to be a key aid to Schulte's memory.

Murder Commission releases a statement confirming Kürten as the attacker of Maria Butlies and Gertrud Schulte. Statement adds that it is seeking to establish proof of Kürten's guilt in the Maria Hahn murder.

Tues 27 May 1930

Crowds wait outside police headquarters to watch Kürten taken from magistrate's room to police cell.

Murder Commission publicly confirms Kürten as Maria Hahn's killer based on Kürten's confession, particularly his description of the spade used to bury the body; police subsequently find the spade near the scene. Police add that Dr Schneiket has confirmed Kürten as writer of the 'murder letter', which proves he also killed Gertrud Albermann. Police announce discovery at Kürten's flat of two pairs of scissors which Kürten claims he used on several of his victims. Police add that this claim tallies with the medical evidence. Karl Berg later writes that he believes Kürten used these scissors in his attacks on Ohliger, Scheer and Kühn in February 1929. Kürten says he changed weapons after this because the scissors broke.

25-30 May 1930

During his extended interrogation, Kürten is watched at night by three men picked for the job. These men report

Kürten sleeps so soundly that he has to be woken in the mornings. Kürten also likes to talk to these men about the children he killed – assuring them that he never intended to hurt any of his child victims.

Detectives prove Kürten wrote his murder letters on the same thick white wrapping paper used at the shop where he bought groceries.

Kürten leads police to a bush in a park where he claims to have hidden two hammers used in the attacks. When they arrive, the hammers are gone. Police circulate their description and later two small boys hand them in.

Police find handbags of Ida Reuter and Elisabeth Dörrier in the front gardens where Kürten said he'd thrown them.

To police, Kürten claims his motive was compensatory justice: innocent blood of his victims to torment his tormentors and shock the society that imprisoned him for so many years. He claims this was why he wrote letters to police. Berg later claims Kürten specifically did not want to be known as a lust murderer. Therefore, accusations of this type in initial interviews are likely to anger and upset him.

Kürten's criminal record is extensive, totalling seventeen prison sentences for theft, desertion from the army, discharging firearms and molestation. His first prison sentence was in 1897: two years for theft. His last was the six years from 1915 to 1921. His longest stint in jail was seven years in Münster from 1905 to 1912 for desertion. During interrogation, Kürten claims that in prison he was treated 'worse than a dog': he uses this to back up his declared motive of murdering to avenge himself on society.

Fri 30 May 1930
Kürten officially handed over as remand prisoner to examining magistrate.

Through the week, *Freiheit* and other left wing papers have been pronouncing their outrage at Johann Stausberg's

April 1929 arrest and continued imprisonment. Police respond on 30th May with the following: 'All other cases are cleared up, but those of Ohliger and Scheer are still uncertain and wrapped in mystery.' In reality, it seems that Kürten has already confessed to the Ohliger and Scheer murders. Indeed, Kürten has also confessed to two murders in Altenburg, Thuringia, which Düsseldorf *Kripo* believes he couldn't possibly have committed. He also admits murdering Emma Gross, though, as Seaton-Wagner reports: 'here he had not the correct knowledge of time, place and position which he betrayed in all the other charges laid against him.' Police disregard this confession and Kürten later retracts it. Police never discover who killed Emma Gross.

Tues 24 June 1930
Under examination by the magistrate, Kürten changes tack and denies being the Düsseldorf murderer. He claims he got the details of the crimes from the newspapers and made up many of the details. After several weeks of cross-examination, Kürten reverts to his original statement. He is the Ripper after all.

June 1930 – April 1931
Kürten is a remand prisoner under observation by several psychiatric and psychological experts. Karl Berg, as forensic pathologist, plays a key role in psychological cross-examination and later publishes a book of the case based on his findings. Over several months, Kürten admits to seventy-nine cases of attacks, rape, murder and arson, stretching back to November 1899 (after he was released from his first jail term). He committed his first murder in 1913. Frau Kühn's case, which first alerted Düsseldorf police to the possibility of a serial murderer in their city, becomes case number forty-five on Berg's list.

To Berg, Kürten also gradually reveals the sexual nature of his crimes, involving ejaculation without orgasm from the intense pleasure he got at the sight of his victims' flowing blood. Experts assess Kürten's mental health under paragraph fifty-one of the German criminal code, which states that a criminal is absolved of responsibility if found to be experiencing 'a state of consciousness or a diseased disturbance of mental activity which impedes the operation of free will...' Berg argues that Kürten's lucid memory of his crimes is the first indication of his legal sanity.

Mon 13 April – Thurs 23 April 1931
Kürten's trial at a special session of the Düsseldorf Criminal Court held in a hall in police headquarters to protect Kürten from public attack. The court charges Kürten with ten murders and convicts him of nine of them. The court sentences Kürten to death by guillotine.

Thurs 18 June 1931
Frau Kürten writes to inform her husband that she has received four thousand Reichsmark in reward money for turning him in to the authorities.

June 1931
Kürten petitions Prussian Justice Minister for a reprieve.

Weds 1 July 1931
Petition declined.

Thurs 2 July 1931
Kürten taken to Klingelputz Prison in Cologne and executed by guillotine.